A PRETTY PICKLE

A MULBURY MYSTERY

JUNO HARVEY

mulshurang
press

First published by Mandurang Press 2022

Book cover by Melissa Williams Design

ISBN: 978-0-6452604-7-2 (ebook)

ISBN: 978-0-6452604-8-9 (paperback)

To Aaron

ONE

Rosemary Exeter pulled on her thick navy jacket and flicked her braid over her shoulder before opening her balcony door. Behind her, hunkered down in her bed near the fire, Sunny gave a short meow. 'I know,' her mistress said. 'It's freezing. I'm checking on my coriander.'

Winter had hit Mulbury with a frozen fury the town had not seen for more than a decade. Most nights were heavy with frost that lay mean and glittering under cloudless skies. The days were pale blue and magnificent, but the temperature stayed at rosy-cheeked chill levels. The weather reminded Rosemary of a previous birthday month as a child when it had been so cold it had snowed. Rain stayed away, leaving the ground hard and almost impenetrable. Rosemary had left her vegetable garden to fallow and made garden boxes to sit under the relative cover of her porch.

The coriander was fine, as she suspected it would be, as was the row of hardy lettuce mix despite the layer of silvery ice on them. Rosemary glanced across at the adjoining balcony to her right, spying a light in Mrs Lionel's kitchen.

A radio played softly, too. No doubt her friend was already preparing for another day of trading at The Green Mulbury. The faint fragrance of dried lavender seeped towards Rosemary, and she wondered what infusion Mrs Lionel was making.

Stretching away to Rosemary's left was Jasper Lu's balcony, which in turn attached to Patti and Gerry's. The four shops, with their built-on housing, straddled Goldmarket Road, linked together forever by a vast veranda at the front and balconies at the back. Both of Rosemary's neighbours' balconies were empty, but a thumping sound made Rosemary step to the edge of hers and look down into the long yards below. There, dressed in a black woollen coat and a beanie with an outrageous red pom pom, was Jasper. He had his long hair tucked into the neck of his coat and short puffs of mist escaped his mouth with every thrust of his shovel.

'Jasper,' she called. 'What are you planting?'

Jasper stopped, held the shovel handle away, and rubbed the back of one hand across his forehead. 'Rosemary.' He shook his head and dropped his gaze.

Rosemary leaned further over but she couldn't see a bare-rooted tree or anything that could be planted in winter without dying. She studied her neighbour. He didn't move. 'Are you alright?'

He shook his head again.

'Wait there.'

Rosemary threaded her way through her house and went into The Preserved Mulbury. She left the blinds down and the closed sign on display as she exited the shop's door. Ten strides and she was at The Read Mulbury. She pushed the door open, hearing its familiar heavy sigh, and hurried past the bookshelves laden with old titles. The connecting door to the house was open. She steamed through, pausing to pat Snowy as the old dog lay snoring on the couch, and out to Jasper's balcony. The steps down to the garden were in poor condition but she took them two at a time. She landed next to Jasper, who still stood with his head down, leaning heavily on the shovel.

'Right. I'm here. What's going on?'

Jasper looked up. His soft, brown eyes were watery, and Rosemary didn't think it was anything to do with the bitter weather. 'Rosemary,' he said.

'Is that all you can say?' She tugged the shovel away from him. 'Whatever you're doing, you aren't making much headway.'

Jasper stared down at the shallow hole at his feet. 'The ground is hard.'

'Yes. Obviously.'

'But I need to finish.'

'Finish what? Jasper Lu, you're being insanely annoying in your inability to answer me.'

A smile twitched at the corner of Jasper's mouth. 'Sorry. I hate annoying you.'

'Okay then.' Rosemary speared the shovel into the ground and waggled it. 'One more chance or I'm leaving you to freeze out here.'

'It's for Snowy.'

Rosemary frowned. 'Snowy is on the couch. I just saw him.'

'The vet says to be ready. He's very old.'

'Yes, he's old. So? Is he sick?'

'No.' Jasper dragged some dirt away from the hole with his toe. 'I took him for a vet check and he's perfectly well for an old dog. But the vet said that I should be aware that he won't be here forever.'

'So you're digging a hole for him.'

'Remember my family curse? I thought I should be ready.'

Rosemary gave him back the shovel handle. 'Your supposed curse is a whole lot of rubbish. You might have a hole in your backyard for a very long time.'

'I hope so.' He rocked the handle.

Rosemary put her hands into her pockets. They were standing in the shade. Ice glimmered on the grass around them. She tilted her head. 'It'll warm you up to dig, so you keep going.' She started back to the stairs.

'Where are *you* going?'

'I'm making tea so that when you finish, you'll have something hot to drink.' She paused with one foot on the bottom step. 'Has Snowy had breakfast?'

Jasper nodded. 'He ate the lot.'

'Have you had breakfast?'

'No.'

She shook her head. 'Right. Ten minutes and eggs are on the table.'

Rosemary climbed the rickety steps and went into Jasper's kitchen. Snowy was upside down on the couch. His tail hung over its arm, and he wagged it when she called to him. *Still alive then.*

Jasper's kitchen had a bottle-green benchtop with a multitude of nicks in its old surface. A red, cast-iron saucepan sat on the wood stove and she moved it to the hottest area in preparation for scrambled eggs. As she stirred, she picked up a book that was lying pages down on the little kitchen table. Jasper, it seemed, had reached the midpoint in a novel from his favourite genre, Regency romance. She started reading. '*Miss Middleton stepped back and put a hand to her pale throat. "Mr Agency," she said, head held high, "you are sadly mistaken if you think that your advances are welcome or indeed warranted-'*

Jasper's shout made her slam the book down. She pushed the pan from the heat and dashed down the steps again.

Jasper stood a little way from where he'd been digging. The shovel lay on the ground next to him. 'Rosemary, I think...I think...'

'What on earth, Jasper?' Rosemary put a hand on his arm.

'Look in there.'

The hole was now about two rulers deep. The dug-out soil beside it was a light brown, with a smattering of dark from the topsoil. Rosemary peered into the depths, catching sight of a layer of sticks curving out from the bottom. She squatted down for a better look. No, not sticks. 'Ribs,' she said.

'I've dug up someone else's dog?' asked Jasper, kneeling beside her.

Rosemary bent forward and carefully brushed away more dirt. The flat surface of a skull emerged. She kept going, more slowly, until it was obvious what was in front of them. 'This isn't a dog, Jasper,' she said, sitting back. 'It's human.'

THE POLICE CAME from Big Town, taking enough time for Rosemary to lead Jasper up the steps to his kitchen and feed him breakfast. Jasper ate obediently, a little to her surprise, and finished by mopping up his plate with a slab of homemade bread. She sat at the table next to him and sipped her tea. 'Good?' she said.

'Wonderful.' Jasper sat back with a sigh. 'I haven't had a decent breakfast like that in a long time.'

'I see. You seem to be taking your discovery in your stride.'

Jasper pushed his plate away. 'Well, it's typical, isn't it?'

'What is?'

'That *I* should be the one to discover a skeleton in my backyard.'

'Not on about that curse again, are you?'

'What else do you think it is?'

'Coincidence?' Rosemary shrugged. 'I might have a skeleton in my yard as well.'

'Hardly.' Jasper put his head in his hands and rubbed at his hair. 'I wish I hadn't disturbed it. I've disrupted its peace.'

'It might turn out for the best.'

'In what way?'

Rosemary shrugged. 'I'm not sure at the moment.' She sat up. 'You've got visitors.'

The rap at the door sounded again, businesslike and loud. Jasper hurried into his shop and to the front door. Men's voices, then a broad figure appeared in the doorway with a tall one a few steps behind. 'Hello, Rosemary.'

'Geoffrey. Welcome to Mulbury.'

The older police officer smiled grimly. 'One day I'll visit here without having to do any work.'

'That would be good.'

'How is my good friend, Mrs Lionel?'

'She's fine. Her usual busy self.'

Geoffrey smiled briefly. 'Of course. Now. What have we got here?'

'This way,' said Jasper, indicating the balcony. 'It's in the backyard.'

The police wound their way out and down the steps, leaving Rosemary and Jasper in the house. She watched her friend's face, noticing that it had lost its breakfast shine. 'You're pale,' she said.

Jasper touched a hand to his cheek. 'Oh. Am I? Well, it's quite a shock, isn't it? I mean, surely even you would be pale if you found *that* in your backyard.' When she said nothing, he shook his head. 'But I'm okay.' He smiled softly. 'I'm tougher than you think.'

Not tough in the same way I am, she thought, but said aloud, 'I'll go back to my shop. Call if you need me.'

Jasper clasped her hand briefly before dropping it. 'Thanks.'

Rosemary let herself out the bookshop door and shut it quietly behind her. Goldmarket Road was empty, which wasn't unusual at that time on a Monday morning. The presence of the police car, though, had made some shop owners in Goldmarket Square come out early. Kelly Flanagan and Rakisha stood under the mighty Exceptional Tree in the Square's centre. Rosemary nodded to them but didn't approach. She tried to speak to Kelly as little as she could, and she had to be in the right mood for Rakisha. Which Rosemary wasn't.

Back inside The Preserved Mulbury, Rosemary pulled up the blinds to fill the shop with light. The rows of preserves on the shelves around the walls caught it and spilled some summer into the wintery gloom. The last of the jumbleberry jam glowed like rubies above a row of golden apple jelly while thick tomato chutney sat on the shelf below waiting for the tourist trade.

Rosemary surveyed her stock. After the flurry of preserving during autumn, winter was a slow time. She had spent the day before straining flavoured vinegars, removing strands of oregano and rosemary. Today she would finish the last batch of olives in brine and move them into jars. Winter was a time for garden renewal and planning for spring, and usually she felt it was also a time for rest and recuperation. Perhaps the discovery of the skeleton had put an end to that. She lingered for a moment with her hand on a bottle of tomato sauce. Human bones in Jasper's yard. It seemed so unlikely.

The door jangled open. 'Are you in, dear?'

'Yes. Come in out of the cold.'

Mrs Lionel stepped inside, holding the door wide as if waiting for someone else to enter, before closing it firmly with a final clang of the bell. 'I saw the police car.'

'As did the whole of Mulbury, no doubt.'

'Everything alright, dear?'

'Jasper unearthed a skeleton.'

Mrs Lionel started. 'Literally or figuratively?'

'Literally. He was digging a hole to bury Snowy next to his vines and discovered it quite unexpectedly.'

Mrs Lionel's hand went to her throat, reminding Rosemary of the plight of Miss Middleton. 'Snowy's *dead*?'

'No. Snowy is perfectly well. Jasper has a bee in his bonnet about being ready when Snowy goes.'

Mrs Lionel's hand dropped. 'The loss of your pet dog is a huge affair.'

'But Snowy is well and truly alive.' Rosemary shook his head. 'Jasper is planning too far ahead.'

'The poor dear.'

Rosemary shrugged. 'He's very fond of that old dog. As you were of Percy.'

At that, Mrs Lionel glanced down at the floor. 'As I am still.'

Rosemary looked down as well but saw only the warm, tan floorboards of The Preserved Mulbury. 'Is Percy here?'

'No, dear. He stayed in the house.' Mrs Lionel tilted her head. 'You haven't changed your mind about me?'

'What do you mean?'

'Don't give me that, Rosemary Exeter. You are allowed to think I'm losing my marbles if I tell you my little dog is still with me.'

Rosemary studied her friend's kind face. 'You have all your marbles. If Percy wants to hang around, I can't blame him. Or you.'

Mrs Lionel smiled. 'Thank you, dear.'

'Anyway, Geoffrey's at Jasper's. Want to see?'

They walked through Rosemary's house and onto the chilly veranda where the activity in Jasper's backyard could be clearly seen. The young constable had cordoned off an area with police tape and Geoffrey was interrogating Jasper. The dirty white of a rib stood out from its surrounding earth. The women watched for a while until Mrs Lionel pointed at the hole. 'Those bones are old. There's a big story behind this one, dear.'

'Yes indeed. Do you know it?'

'No. I have no idea who that could be.'

'You've lived here the longest. Do you think anyone else would know?'

Mrs Lionel shook her head. 'I doubt it. Jules' family were old Mulburians but they're long gone. Jules and Roman moved back here fairly recently. But we could ask at dinner tonight.' She considered Rosemary. 'You didn't go to Monday dinner last week and you're usually a regular to our night gatherings. Are you coming tonight, dear?'

'Yes. It's at Patti and Gerry's.' Rosemary raised one

eyebrow. 'You know why I didn't go to Monday dinner last week.'

Mrs Lionel rubbed her arms to warm them and headed back into Rosemary's cosy quarters. 'You can't keep giving Kelly the cold shoulder forever. She'd done a lovely pork roast.'

'I don't like pork.'

'Rosemary...'

Rosemary smiled at her friend. 'I'll be there tonight. Will we walk together?'

'Of course.' Mrs Lionel headed for the shop door. 'Isn't it your birthday soon, dear? We could organise a special dinner.'

'A little premature to be doing that.'

Mrs Lionel chuckled. 'Not that premature, but I won't say anything tonight. Seems like there'll be plenty to talk about anyhow.'

Rosemary followed as Mrs Lionel went out and raised a hand in farewell. As the older woman walked away, Rosemary glimpsed an unfamiliar figure crossing the Square with an early-morning Mullings of Mulbury coffee in his hand. Not a tourist. He wore old jeans and a worn leather jacket. He strode across the ground as if he had somewhere to be, smoothing down neat, cinnamon-coloured hair. As Rosemary watched, he crossed the road leading to Big Town and entered Barry Holden's old mechanic shop which had been closed for the last three months. She waited but that was it. The man had shuttered himself inside.

Rosemary shook her head and went back to survey her vinegars. There would be plenty of talk around Patti's little dinner table tonight, but would it reveal anything useful?

TWO

At six twenty-five, Rosemary heard Mrs Lionel shut the door to The Green Mulbury firmly, sealing the noise of her electronic frog motion sensor inside. She stepped out of her own shop at the same moment as the older woman said, 'I wouldn't have to use that if you were still around.'

'I am still around.'

Mrs Lionel waved a finger at her. 'Not you, Rosemary.'

'Right,' Rosemary said, pulling shut the door of The Preserved Mulbury so the bell attached to it jangled furiously. 'I should change that to something quieter.'

Mrs Lionel shook her head. 'That bell is from the original sweet shop, dear. You are not changing it.'

Rosemary gave her friend a quick smile. 'You're correct. I'm not.' She pointed towards Patti and Gerry's. 'We're meeting Jasper.'

They walked another fifteen steps and there was Jasper Lu closing the heavy door of The Read Mulbury. 'Back to normal, dear?' asked Mrs Lionel, as Jasper turned his collar up against the cold evening.

'Sort of.' Jasper fell into step beside her. 'The crime

scene investigation team dug out the skeleton, took soil samples, did this and that, and went away. What they left me was a great hole and a long roll of police tape.'

'Well, they may have to come back once they've done some initial work.' Mrs Lionel fluffed her scarf around her neck. 'My, but it's chilly tonight. Another frost coming.'

'That will be five in a row.' Jasper stopped at the door of Patricia's. 'Everything's dead in my yard.'

Only Rosemary caught the irony of that. She waited until Jasper had opened the squealing door for Mrs Lionel before widening her eyes at him. He frowned, puzzled, then grimaced. 'Good grief,' he said. 'Did I really say that?'

'Yes, you did.' Rosemary stepped into Patricia's, giving Jasper a friendly elbow nudge as she did.

Patricia's was a fashionista's dream. It was also Patti and Gerry's reality. Patti's reputation for creating contemporary garments from discarded clothing, much of which she found by the roadside, was growing. The shop was crowded with racks and mannequins featuring unusual combinations of discarded denim jackets and silk. Patti even rescued shoes. A pair of sequinned sandals caught Rosemary's eye, not because she wanted them but because she imagined that their previously dilapidated state would have made the shoes much more comfortable to wear.

'Oh, you're here!' Patti waltzed into the shop, her floral swing dress bumping into various mannequins along the way. 'It's so lovely to see you!'

Rosemary opened her mouth to say that the shop owners along Goldmarket Road saw each other every day but Mrs Lionel had grabbed her arm. 'It's lovely seeing you, too, Patti,' she said instead.

Mrs Lionel's gentle double squeeze was a stamp of approval.

Patti's face coloured, giving her the appearance of a perfectly crafted porcelain vintage doll. She cupped the edges of her rolled, rose-gold hair and smiled. 'Gerry's set the table in the kitchen. It's a bit of a squeeze but won't that be fun!'

Once again, Rosemary felt Mrs Lionel's hand on her arm, but she hadn't been about to say anything. Gerry was the cook in this household, and the aroma of a rich lasagne obscured her thoughts. Despite being a slow Monday, Rosemary hadn't eaten much. She'd spent most of the day in her cellar counting stock and tallying the number of empty jars she had to fill. Honey had rung at lunchtime, and there'd been three or four customers, but otherwise nothing had disturbed her. Except for some errant thoughts about skeletons.

The lasagne was already in the centre of the little, round kitchen table. Crowded around it were Jules and Roman, and Kelly Flanagan. Rosemary let Mrs Lionel sit first and took the seat next to Roman. He smiled at her through his walrus moustaches, raising a glass. 'Ah, Rosemary. Another petty pickle in Mulbury.'

'*Pretty* pickle, Roman,' said Jules, rolling her eyes at her husband.

'He means the skeleton,' said Gerry, handing Rosemary a bulbous glass of primitivo.

'You know about that?' Jasper slid into the seat next to Rosemary.

'Everyone knows about it, Jasper,' said Kelly. 'There are no secrets in Mulbury.'

Rosemary took a large sip of her wine and said nothing.

'Tell us, Jasper.' Patti thumped a plate of salad on the table. 'Tell us everything while Gerry serves.'

'Shouldn't we wait for Robert Sparkling?'

'Oh, Gerry, sweetie. He only has to cross the road. He'll be here in two shakes.'

'And who is Robert Sparkling, dear?' asked Mrs Lionel, accepting a slice of bread from Gerry.

'Robert is our new mechanic, Mrs Lionel,' said Patti. 'He's bought the business now that Barry's gone.'

'How do you know that juicy bit of gossip?' asked Kelly. 'You aren't normally the first to know things around here.' She gave Rosemary a caustic glance.

'It was Gerry, actually.' Patti sat abruptly, sending a waft of sweet, floral perfume down the table. 'He saw someone in the garage and went to investigate.'

'He looks like a good fellow,' said Gerry, slicing the lasagne.

'So did Barry,' said Kelly. 'Look where that got us.'

Gerry shook his head. 'After only one meeting with this fellow, I can honestly say that he's about as far from Barry as a dugong is from a goldfish.'

The table occupants went quiet for a moment, contemplating the image, and then Jasper gave a rundown of his morning's activity.

'A skeleton!' Patti turned to Gerry. 'Do you think there's one in our backyard as well?'

'Not a human one.' Gerry finished serving and sat. 'Possibly lots of dogs and cats.'

Jasper gulped loudly and Rosemary put a hand briefly on his arm.

'This is fascinating,' said Kelly, a forkful of lasagne poised in front of her mouth. 'Any idea who it is?'

Jasper shook his head. 'It certainly wasn't mentioned when I bought the bookshop from Mr Arthur.'

Kelly grinned. 'It's not *Mrs* Arthur, is it?'

'There was no Mrs Arthur, dear,' said Mrs Lionel. 'Mr

Arthur was what one used to call a *confirmed bachelor*. Far too disagreeable to have a partner.'

'A mysterious skeleton.' Jules shook her head. 'Something to tell the children when they visit.'

'Will that be soon? I haven't seen Leif or Felicity for a long time.'

'Neither have we, Mrs Lionel.' Jules shrugged. 'Busy city lives. But, actually, Felicity and her lot will be visiting in the next couple of days. She says she needs a break, and the children are quite happy to come with her.'

'That will be lovely, dear.'

'That will be *noisy*.' Roman tipped his head at his wife, who watched him reproachfully. 'And lovely.'

The shop door squealed as someone opened it. A tentative voice called, 'Hello?'

'Down here, Robert,' said Gerry. 'Don't mind the dress racks. Push on through.'

Patti frowned. 'Not *push*, Gerry.'

'Mind the tulle!' said Gerry. 'And the second-hand denim and the old socks-'

'Gerry!'

'It's okay, I made it without mishap.'

Rosemary turned at the deep voice. A man stood in the doorway to the house, smiling at the dinner assembly. Although he had smart, new jeans on, his elegant black leather jacket was familiar. His hair seemed darker than it had as he'd crossed Goldmarket Square in the sunshine, and his eyes were almost black. He caught her looking and smiled more broadly. 'Hello,' he said again.

'Robert, so wonderful you could have dinner with us.' Gerry stood up and indicated the empty seat next to him. 'Sorry for the crush. You wouldn't realise that our little abode is the same size as the other shops next to us. We seem to need every available inch for Patti's work.'

'Well,' said Robert, easing into the chair and moving it back so that his legs fit under the table, 'I would prefer to see a house space that's properly used and not wasted like so many McMansions in the city.'

'Oh, yes, yes.' Gerry sat again and indicated the other occupants. 'I'll do a quick introduction, although not all the residents of Mulbury are here tonight. This is Jasper Lu who owns The Read Mulbury, Rosemary Exeter from The Preserved Mulbury, Roman Capriccio and Jules Capriccio who run The Leftover Restaurant, Kelly Flanagan from Mullings of Mulbury, Mrs Lionel from The Green Mulbury and, last but never least, my beautiful wife, Patricia Yale.'

'Patti,' said Patti. 'Only the shop gets called Patricia.'

Gerry nodded. 'Too true.' He smiled. 'Not here, but not far away, is Franco who is always busy in his patisseries, Rakisha who owns The Sweet Potato, and the sisters Hubbard, Hannah, Holly and Heather, who are magnificently in charge of their father Richard's Mulbury Feeds. You'll get to meet them in time, no doubt. Not Richard, as he is away.'

'That's a lot of names so I'm sorry if I forget most of them almost immediately.' Robert took the bowl of salad Patti offered. 'It's very nice of you to invite me here on my first day.'

'Tell us about *you*, Robert.' Kelly's singsong tone made Rosemary look at her sharply. 'What's *your* story?'

'Nothing much to tell. I had a business in the city and got sick of the traffic. Commuting to work takes hours.' He passed the salad along. 'I was born in the country, so it was easy to move back.' He glanced at Rosemary.

Kelly leaned forward. 'And does your family feel that way, too?'

Robert paused for a moment. 'My ex-wife was probably quite happy to be further away from me.'

Jasper coughed awkwardly. 'Oh, I know how that feels.'

Robert grimaced. 'Anyway. Onward and upward.'

'Yes, indeed.' Gerry pointed his knife at the lasagne. 'Help yourself, Robert. It's one of my best.'

'It is very good, Gerry,' said Mrs Lionel. 'Any secrets we should know?'

Gerry leaned forward. 'I used Rosemary's passata.'

'That'll be it, then.' Mrs Lionel smiled at her friend. 'Rosemary does the best passata in the nation.'

'Thank you,' said Rosemary, 'but that might be a stretch.'

'Not to us,' said Roman, waving his fork around. 'And I am an excellent judge.'

Rosemary shook her head slightly. 'I'm just following Aunt Lilibeth.'

Robert looked around. 'Is she another resident of Mulbury who isn't here?'

'She's dead,' said Rosemary.

Mrs Lionel shook her head. 'Excuse Rosemary, Robert. She *meant* she was using her Aunt Lilibeth's recipe book. Rosemary is as blunt as an axe.'

Robert laughed. 'Well, that's refreshing.'

Rosemary glanced in his direction, but he had turned back to his meal, eating heartily. *A single man,* thought Rosemary, *who doesn't cook regularly or he wouldn't be wolfing it down.*

There was no more conversation until the food had been polished off. Gerry put the empty dishes into the sink and sat down again with a sigh. 'I have tiramisu for dessert but maybe we should wait for a bit.'

'Yes, please.' Jules pushed her seat back with a sigh. 'That was delicious, Gerry. You'll be rivelling Roman in the kitchen.'

'You could come and help me, Gerry, my friend. We would be the dynamite duo.'

'*Dynamic* duo,' said Jules sleepily.

'Perhaps,' said Gerry. 'But perhaps I'll be busier than ever here.' He smiled at his wife.

'Has something happened?' asked Jasper.

Gerry put his arm around his wife. 'You tell them, Patti.'

'Oh,' said Patti, bright spots of colour appearing on both cheeks. 'You'll never guess!'

'What is it, dear?' asked Mrs Lionel.

'Do you remember the gown I constructed out of a neglected rugby top with the tulle skirt?'

'Yes,' said Jules, leaning forward and looking awake once more. 'You found that top in a gutter somewhere.'

'I find most of my garments in similar unhappy circumstances.' Patti put her palms to her cheeks. 'You might remember that a lady bought it for her film director daughter.' She bounced up and down in her seat. 'That same daughter is Adelia Lochard!'

The silence around the table made Gerry shake his head. 'I didn't know her, either.'

'I do,' said Robert suddenly. 'Didn't her short film about rubbish dumps win an award?'

'Yes, yes!' Patti put a hand on Robert's arm. 'That's right! She's a documentary maker and won a stack of prizes. Well, she wants me to design costumes for her next exposé. Me! Patti Yale of Mulbury! Ohhhhh.'

Patti's excitement caught the rest of the table. There

were exclamations of amazement and congratulatory noises. Only Rosemary said nothing, although she smiled. Patti was a clever designer, and it was no surprise to Rosemary that someone else had finally recognised it. What was more intriguing was why a mechanic knew who Adelia Lochard was when clearly no one else at the table had a clue.

Gerry served dessert as Patti told the story of the phone call from the city. The bold coffee tang of the tiramisu was sharp on Rosemary's tongue. She ate as much as she could but had to leave a portion for fear of exploding. Next to her, Jasper had no trouble eating all of his. She smiled to herself. Jasper's sickness earlier in the year seemed to have finally left him and he was functioning at full steam.

Jasper must have sensed her looking at his plate. He put his fork down and sighed. 'After that,' he said quietly to her, 'I'm glad we're walking tomorrow.'

'Perhaps we'd better go twice around town instead of our usual once?'

'Really, after eating all this, we should be jogging.'

Rosemary shook her head, making her long braid fall forward over her shoulder. 'You're on your own, Jasper Lu. Last time I jogged was when dinosaurs roamed the earth.'

He chuckled. 'Walking will have to do, then.' He hesitated. 'I look forward to it.'

'That's good,' said Rosemary. 'You could walk more often, you know. You don't have to stick to our routine.'

'Would you come with me?'

'No.'

'Oh.'

One of Jasper's charms was the way his blush travelled so quickly from his neck to his cheeks.

'I'll stick to twice a week,' he said, tucking hair behind his ear.

'See you at five, then.'

'We'll be walking in the dark if we do two laps.'

'Bring a torch.'

He smiled. 'I will.'

The tiramisu had tipped most people around the table over the edge of satiation. Everyone sat back with their hands resting lightly on their stomachs. After a minute or two of quiet, Mrs Lionel pushed her chair away from the table. 'Thank you, Gerry and Patti. That was a lovely dinner and now I must go to bed before I fall asleep right here.'

'That would be alright, Mrs Lionel,' said Patti. 'You would be most welcome to stay in our spare bedroom.'

'Once we'd cleared it of clothing,' added Gerry.

Mrs Lionel smiled as she stood. 'Thank you, dears, but I'll make it back to my bed.'

Rosemary and Jasper stood as well, with the others following suit. They filed through the clothing shop, avoiding the racks of repurposed T-shirts, and went outside. Patti and Gerry waved them goodbye, looking oddly animated among the frozen mannequins.

'Off we go, then,' said Kelly, in that strange high-pitched voice Rosemary had heard before.

'Goodnight,' said Jasper, bowing slightly to the others. 'Mrs Lionel?' He held out his arm for the older woman to take.

'Goodnight, all,' said Robert. 'Thank you for making me welcome in Mulbury.'

'Anytime,' said Kelly. 'Anytime.'

Rosemary shook her head and turned to follow Jasper and Mrs Lionel.

'Can you see?' Robert appeared beside her. 'The path is very dark.'

'I'm used to it,' said Rosemary. 'I can see quite well, thank you.'

'I'm having a little trouble,' said Kelly, stepping down onto the road and glancing back at Robert.

'Use the light in your phone,' said Rosemary. 'You do normally.'

'Thank you, Rosemary.' There was no gratitude in Kelly's voice. 'You are of *enormous* assistance.' She stalked over the road towards her shop and home.

Jules and Roman's car pulled away, shining its lights briefly on Robert as he continued to stand next to Rosemary. She saw something in his eyes, a flash that could have been recognition or maybe was the luminescence from the car's headlights. 'Goodnight,' she said, turning to go.

'Goodnight, Rosemary Exeter.'

His voice was soft, friendly—intimate—and almost made her stop, but they'd reached Mrs Lionel's door. She saw Mrs Lionel in, waved Jasper away when he wanted to stay until she'd opened her own jangling door, and entered her home with a sigh. Sunny stirred, stretching out a paw in Rosemary's direction. *Interesting evening?* the ginger cat seemed to say.

'In more ways than one.'

Sometime during the night, Rosemary woke with a new conviction. Robert Sparkling knew her.

THREE

Rosemary's phone rang just as she pulled up the blinds of The Preserved Mulbury. The winter sun slanted low to light up the outside world but inside the shop it came through a centre skylight. She stood underneath to answer the call. 'Honey.'

'Mum. I'm getting your opinion about what's going on in Mulbury.'

Behind her daughter's voice, Rosemary could hear the voices of excited children echoing around the hall where Honey took her Honey Blossom's Academy of Dramatic Experiences classes. 'We have a new mechanic.'

'No, that's not what I meant. Good for Mulbury, a new mechanic, but what about the *other*? The skeleton, Mum.'

'Jasper was digging a hole and found a skeleton.'

'That's it?'

'Yes.'

'No other secrets that you've found? No weapons?'

'Not that I know about.'

Honey's voice muffled. 'Hey, Taylor! Put the unicorn head down!' Her voice grew stronger again. 'Sorry. I got the costume box out and they've discovered it. Well, the good news is that Ronnie has the case.'

Rosemary nodded, then realised Honey couldn't see her. 'Geoffrey was here, so that makes sense.'

'Uncle Geoffrey said that Ronnie's previous investigation was well done so he had *no hesitation* handing more work to Ronnie.'

Rosemary had no trouble imagining the pleasure that would have mottled her son-in-law's face at those words. 'I'm pleased. Ronnie is very determined.'

'It's given him loads of confidence.' Honey went quiet.

'Are you okay, Honey? How is Tallulah?'

'I'm fine, Mum.' Her voice dropped. 'I'm really proud of Ronnie. His private investigator business is getting legs. We won't be so dependent on my income when Tallulah is born.'

Rosemary imagined Honey's hand on her expanding belly, rubbing gently. 'You'll be surprised how little money you need to live on.'

'What does that mean, Mum?'

'When you were born, your father was out of work and I took time off my job. No maternity leave payments back then. For a while there, we were living on government welfare.'

'Oh, yes, that's right. I'd forgotten that. Sorry, Mum. I didn't mean to whinge.'

'Honey Blossom, you are not the whingy sort.'

The noise of the children cascaded, and Honey shouted into the phone. 'Anyway, class is about to start. I'd better go. Love you.'

'Love you, too, Honey.'

'Mum, wait!'

'What is it?'

'I forgot to ask. What are you making today?'

Rosemary walked back into her home, patting Sunny who had positioned herself on the arm of the couch as she did. 'The Hubbard sisters have promised me their lemons, so I thought I'd start with some lemon butter.'

'Oh, that's great. I can smell it now.'

'Honey, don't be ridiculous. The lemons are still on the tree.'

'Doesn't matter. That zesty tang of lemon rind is filling your kitchen. It's like the cold zap of frost, sharp and delicious. Then you start whisking the ingredients over the stove and the sharp fades to a buttery richness.'

'Honey, you're mad.'

Honey laughed her deep chuckle. 'See you soon, Mum.'

Rosemary put her phone down and stroked Sunny's stripey head again. 'You can't half tell she's a drama teacher.'

Sunny folded her front paws under her chest and gave Rosemary a baleful look. *She's your daughter*, she seemed to say.

Talking about the lemons reminded Rosemary that they did need to be harvested, and today was as good a time as any to do it. She took a cane harvest basket and went outside, turning her sign to read *Back in 5 pickly minutes*, which was her signal for 'Back when I get back', and turned towards the animal produce store. She'd only gone as far as The Green Mulbury when Mrs Lionel thrust the door open, making the electronic frog croak frenetically.

'Rosemary!' said the older woman as she saw her friend. 'Did you get the same message?'

'About what?'

Mrs Lionel grabbed Rosemary's arm and steered her towards Goldmarket Square with a surprising amount of strength for an octogenarian. 'About *this*,' she said, pointing.

A council work truck parked quietly behind the ancient Exceptional Tree. As Mrs Lionel propelled Rosemary across the road and into the Square, two workmen appeared with a range of traffic cones and long, wooden planks painted lime green. They had just put their equipment down when Rakisha shot out of The Sweet Potato and raced towards the men, purple frock flapping around her knees.

'What are you doing, darlings?'

The taller man put his hands on his hips. 'We're setting up a barricade. This tree has been deemed dangerous to the public.'

'That's just it.' Rakisha pushed her grey curls out of her face. 'What are you *doing*? This Tree is the centre of Mulbury. You can't just block it off like a rabid dog, darling.'

The man paused and frowned at his colleague who shrugged. 'I'm sorry, but that's what we've been asked to do.'

Mrs Lionel and Rosemary reached Rakisha just as she went to fling herself onto the ground. 'No, dear,' said Mrs Lionel. 'That's not the way.'

'I don't understand,' said Rakisha. 'Why are they doing this?'

'Darren's arborist report,' said Rosemary. 'The council have finally made some decisions.'

'About what, darling?' Rakisha's long hair wafted about her face as she looked from Mrs Lionel to Rosemary. 'Darren wrote that report months ago and nothing about the Tree has changed.'

'Despite his...' Mrs Lionel glanced at Rosemary '...short-comings, Darren is a fine arborist. He studied the Tree very carefully, and I'm sure his recommendations were accurate.'

The three women gazed up at The Exceptional Tree. The red gum's trunk was patched with silver and tan, and branches stretched haphazardly over the Square. No one really knew its age, but Rosemary considered that it could be at least 700 years old if its size was compared to other trees on the National Register. Its status protected it, but age was catching up. Every year, two or three more branches dried into dark spears although none had come crashing down as yet.

'Can you move back, please?' asked the workman, a traffic cone in his hand. 'We have to get this done by lunchtime. Other things to do, you see.'

Rosemary and Mrs Lionel stepped backwards, dragging Rakisha with them, and the men started to work. The barricade was almost to the edge of the Tree's drip line, which meant it would take up a considerable amount of the free space in the Square.

'I'm not sure that it has to be that lurid colour,' said Mrs Lionel, eyeing the green posts.

'Not worth making a fuss,' said Rosemary. 'We'll repaint it when they've gone.'

'We'll pull it down when they've gone,' said Rakisha, using both hands to clear her face from hair. 'The Tree's spirit will be harmed if it's caught within a manmade barrier. It will howl into the night!'

Over Rakisha's curly hair, Rosemary lifted her eyebrows at Mrs Lionel. 'Do trees howl?'

'Oh, yes, Rosemary, darling.' Rakisha trembled. 'They feel the earth's pain at having posts hammered into it and raise their branches to the sky.' Rakisha put her hands up and tipped her head back, but Rosemary put an arm around her shoulders and steered her back towards The Sweet Potato before she could demonstrate a tree howl.

'How about we have tea at your place?' asked Rosemary into Rakisha's ear. 'Don't you bake brownies on a Tuesday?'

'Yes, darling. Carob brownies sprinkled with crushed Himalayan Sea salt.' Rakisha tossed her hair back over her shoulders. 'That's what we need. A tang to sharpen our senses.'

Not my senses, though Rosemary, but she followed Rakisha into the musty confines of the bohemian café and sat with Mrs Lionel at a small table by the window to wait for Rakisha's homemade delights. From their vantage point they watched the workmen construct the barricade, and by the time they'd each choked down a dry, salty, bitter brownie with a weak lavender tea, The Exceptional Tree was in confinement.

Mrs Lionel shook her head. 'I know it has to be done but I have to agree with Rakisha. That tree looks miserable now.'

Rosemary said nothing. A slight breeze stirred the leaves on the upper branches of the Tree. It looked like the Tree was nodding to Mrs Lionel's words.

'Well.' Mrs Lionel pushed her rattan chair back and stood. 'Business time.'

'Yes.' Rosemary shifted the table towards her so that Mrs Lionel could more easily get out. 'I'm going to get some lemons from the girls first.'

'Open your shop, dear. I'll keep an eye out for visitors.'

They left Rakisha muttering about lime green monstrosities from behind her coffee machine and walked across Goldmarket Square to their shops on the other side of the road. Rosemary continued to Mulbury Feeds where the Hubbard sisters stood in the laneway of their shed, pointing at a delivery of dried dog food.

'Here's Rosemary,' said the smallest of the golden-haired women. 'She'll know.'

'I hope you're not going to ask me about animal food,'

said Rosemary, coming to stand next to Heather, who clutched her arm for a second before going back to gazing at the bags in front of them.

'What?' asked Hannah. 'Oh, no way. What would you know about the protein content of dried dog food?'

'Hannah...,' said Holly.

'No offence, Rosemary. But you don't own a dog.'

'True.' Rosemary shrugged. 'I've never owned a dog. The only dogs I've really known were Percy and Snowy.'

'Snowy,' said Heather, clutching at Rosemary's arm again. 'Snow, Snow, Snowy. Is the doggie alright?'

'He's perfectly fine.'

'It would be hard to tell whether that dog is dead or alive,' said Hannah, tucking the tablet she was holding under her arm. 'I mean, all he does is lie on the couch.'

'Well, I'm glad he's fine and Jasper was digging that hole for nothing.' Holly pushed at Hannah, who gave her sister a cheeky smile. 'Have you come to get some lemons?'

'Yes.'

'Heather will help you pick them.' Holly linked her arm through her youngest sister's. 'Let's leave Hannah to count puppy kibble.'

'Gee, thanks.'

Rosemary followed the young women through the produce shed. It was piled high with hay bales, bags of livestock feed, and packets of supplements. The hay gave the shed the smell of summer, which mingled with the sharper fragrance of powdered milk and pelletised grains. Heather's hair tumbled down her back in a glorious display of unbrushed wilderness while Holly's, although matched in golden colour, was pulled back in a fierce ponytail. Rosemary caught hold of her own thick braid and put it over her shoulder, smiling to herself at the contrast between the fairness of the Hubbard women's hair and the darkness—albeit streaked with one thick stripe of silver running the length of the plait—of her own.

'There,' said Holly as they emerged into the sunshine again and walked towards a lone Meyer lemon tree standing guard against the fence. 'We've already started harvesting. See the basket?'

'Yes.' Rosemary watched Heather as the young woman swung into action, deftly tugging lemons from their branches and placing the fruit into the waiting basket. 'Is Heather going well?'

'Yeah, she's good.' Holly smoothed the hair on top of her head. 'We give her things to do each day and she does them, no problems. Then she'll disappear for a few hours and come back with a bird or two to stuff. She's happy. More than ever now.'

'Any reason?'

Holly sighed and crossed her arms. 'Dad's coming home.'

'He's been away a while.'

'Five months, one week, three days. That was the thing we were going to ask you. If he said he's leaving Far North Queensland today, how long will it take him to arrive here?'

'If he's driving, it'll take days. He's over three thousand kilometres away.'

Holly nodded. 'We thought that. Thing is, we don't know how he's getting home. He didn't take his car but he might have bought another one. He could be hitch-hiking or he might have a plane ticket. We've got no idea.'

'But he's definitely coming home.'

'Oh, yeah. You want to know why?'

Rosemary frowned. Richard Hubbard, some-time musician and all-time neglectful parent, usually only arrived back home when he was flat broke. 'Money?'

'That's the weird bit. Remember that Hannah and I said that we wanted to buy Mulbury Feeds from Dad, which would have left him with a stack of money to do whatever his muse wanted?'

'Sounded like a sensible plan to me.'

'*Sensible* is never how I'd describe our father.' Holly glanced across at Heather, who was humming to herself as she swiftly plucked lemons, then back at Rosemary, who was startled to see tears of fury in Holly's eyes. 'He's selling Mulbury Feeds to someone else, and he won't tell us who.'

FOUR

Marmalade was Rosemary Exeter's least favourite preserve to make. Aunt Lilibeth had insisted that the peel be shaved from the fruit with a razor blade, and no matter how many taste tests told Rosemary that it made no difference to the outcome of the jam if you cut the peel off with a knife, she felt obliged to do at least one batch according to Lilibeth's recipe. *At least it gives me time to think.*

Heather Hubbard not only picked the lemons for Rosemary but carried them to The Preserved Mulbury at regular intervals. Rosemary didn't ask her what she thought of Holly's news and Heather didn't say anything, only hummed her way in and out of Rosemary's shop. Six baskets of lemons stood in casual arrangement around Rosemary's kitchen and dining room. Sunny was disgusted. She refused to go anywhere near them and spent her day on the windowsill staring disdainfully at her mistress. *They are repugnant,* she seemed to say.

'Sorry, Sunny. They'll be gone in due course.'

Sunny folded her front paws under her and gazed out the window, nose wrinkled.

Rosemary washed each lemon carefully, particularly since one basket Heather delivered had been topped with three roadkill magpies that she was taking home to taxidermy. No one in Mulbury denied that Heather Hubbard had an unusual talent of creating art with dead birds, but Rosemary thought it better to keep the process well away from the lemons.

It was clear that Heather was the happiest of the sisters to have her father coming home. Heather hummed everywhere she went, and her eyes were bright. Contrasting that was the thunderous look on Hannah's face as Rosemary returned a basket, and the weary one on Holly's. Mulbury Feeds had prospered under the management of the sisters. It was typical of Richard not to consult with his family before making the major decision to sell. Rosemary squeezed a lemon too hard at the thought, squirting herself in the eye.

The door of The Preserved Mulbury jangled furiously as someone entered, and Rosemary took a tea towel to dab at her tears as she went through to the shop.

'Oh, Rosemary, are you alright?'

Rosemary blinked her eyes clear and came face to face with her son-in-law. 'Ronnie. I'm fine.'

'You're crying.' Ronnie fumbled for his phone. 'I need to phone Honey.'

'To tell her that I have lemon juice in my eye?'

Ronnie stopped; the phone held between both hands like an offering. 'Oh. I thought...'

Sometimes Rosemary wondered whether Ronnie thought at all. 'I expect this isn't a social call. Here on business?'

Ronnie straightened, sliding the offending phone into a pocket. 'Yes. I'm helping Uncle Geoffrey again.'

'So Honey mentioned. Geoffrey said you did a good job last time.'

Ronnie's pale face evolved into a jigsaw of crimson spots. 'Oh, he said that? Wow.'

'Ronnie, you know he did. You need to take more pride in your own successes and not be hanging off every word other people say.'

'I know.' Ronnie scratched his head, making his straw-berry blond hair stand on end. 'Honey says that too.'

'She's well?'

'Oh, yes, she's...' For a moment, Ronnie's happy face dipped. 'Restless.'

'What do you mean?'

'Oh, not from Tallulah. Honey's feeling really good and Tallulah's doing everything she should be at this stage.' Ronnie let his satchel drop to the floor. 'But Honey is thinking of down the track. After Tallulah is born. When Tallulah's a toddler. When she goes to pre-school.'

'Honey likes to plan things.'

'She does, doesn't she? But I've always thought that having a baby meant that your plans sort of went out the window and that you had to go with the flow.' Ronnie shook his head. 'Maybe I'm wrong.'

'You're mostly right, Ronnie. You can plan some parts of your life, though, even with a baby. What's Honey particu-larly worried about?'

'She's not worried. She's...'

'Restless, then. What is she being restless about?'

'Work, mainly. She loves her drama classes, but she would love to be more home-based.' Ronnie grinned. 'Like you.'

'Like me?'

'Oh, yes. You and your preserves.' Ronnie waved his

hand around at the shelves of jams and pickles and jelly. 'And Mrs Lionel and her natural cleaning products. And Jasper and his books. And...whatever Patti does.'

'Upcycle.'

'Yes. That. Honey would love to have a home business as well.'

Rosemary considered this, watching Ronnie closely to see what he thought of the idea. The mottling had gone from his face and he was back to looking like he usually did, slightly dishevelled but kindly. 'She'll work it out, Ronnie. Don't worry.'

Ronnie sighed.

'Come and have tea. I've got to keep going with my marmalade.'

'Thanks, Rosemary. I'd love a cup of tea.' His face brightened. 'I can tell you what I know about the skeleton.'

Rosemary boiled the kettle while Ronnie roamed the living room, stopping to pat Sunny, who refused to purr and kept her nose pointed away from the offending fruit. Ronnie wandered back to the dining table, pulling his laptop from his satchel just as Rosemary placed a pot for one and a Ronnie-sized teacup at his elbow. 'You aren't having one?'

'I'll keep slicing while the town is quiet.'

Ronnie nodded and settled his computer in front of him. 'Well, I don't think there's a mystery as to who the skeleton is.' He peered at his computer screen. 'The list of missing people in this region is small, as most of them are thought to be either connected to the 1983 Scarlet Tuesday fires or through accidental falls into mineshafts.'

'Bushfires are wicked events.'

Ronnie frowned. 'Yes, they are, aren't they? I hadn't realised Scarlet Tuesday's death toll was so bad until I saw the list. The skeleton, though, pre-dates the fire.' He tapped the screen. 'She is thought to be Agnes Connelly, wife of Albert Connelly, who disappeared in 1950.'

Rosemary paused with the razor blade suspended in her hand. '*Thought* to be... so the mystery is not solved?'

'No. The pathologist hasn't given the police the final report, but it seems very likely. Connelly owned the printery at the time and was the one to report his wife missing.'

'Is he alive?'

Ronnie shook his head. 'No. Mr Connelly died in 1977 from lung cancer. He was a war veteran.'

'Another serviceman to die of smoking-related causes.'

'Sad, isn't it? Anyway, the really interesting thing is that Agnes Connelly was thought to have committed suicide by jumping into an old mineshaft. She left a note and everything.'

'They looked for her?'

'There was a search but, you know, this bushland is riddled with old goldmine shafts. Back then they weren't even capped. Easy enough to fall into one, as they thought at least ten people around the district had done. Double-easy to throw yourself down one and never be seen again.'

'They closed the case.'

'They closed it within a week of her disappearance.'

Rosemary picked up another lemon and sliced thought-fully. 'She clearly didn't die by jumping into a shallow hole at the back of the old printery.'

'Nope.' Ronnie shut the laptop. 'Nothing much can happen until it's confirmed that the skeleton is hers, but I thought I'd ask Jasper if I can look around the backyard.'

'Do you have a copy of the suicide note?'

'Not yet.' Ronnie scraped back his chair, making Sunny's ears flatten. 'They'll send it to me if Agnes turns out to be Agnes.'

'Any remaining family?'

'A daughter. Geoffrey said they'll be talking to her.' Ronnie stood, bumping the table and making the teacup rattle in its saucer. 'Oops, sorry, all good. Thanks for the tea, Rosemary. I'll go and see Jasper.'

'See yourself out, Ronnie. Saves me from stopping.'

'Sure thing.' Ronnie waved at Rosemary and went into the shop. She heard his footsteps stop. 'What's happening in the Square?'

'Do you mean the barricade around The Exceptional Tree?'

'Yeah.'

'It's meant to stop people from being hurt if a branch drops.'

'You'd think they'd make it a better colour.'

Rosemary smiled to herself. 'Lime green is sharp on the eyes.'

'Green? Well, that would be better than pink, don't you think?'

Rosemary put down her blade, wiped her hands on a tea towel, and went to stand next to Ronnie. Rakisha was hunkered down over the barricade, a broad paintbrush in her hand. Where she'd been, the lime green had been transformed into a pastel pink, giving the fencing a jaunty party vibe. 'We did say we were going to paint it a different colour.'

'Pink?'

'I had a more earthy one in mind.'

Ronnie laughed. 'You've got to hand it to Rakisha. She does things her way.'

'Yes indeed.'

'I'll see you later, Rosemary.'

Ronnie jangled out the door and went along the foot-path towards The Read Mulbury. Rosemary watched Rakisha for a moment, noting how Rakisha's flyaway grey curls were sticking to the new paintwork before going back to the marmalade. She reached the end of her razoring and put the blade away thankfully.

Between stirring the new marmalade and serving three busloads of tourists, the rest of the day raced. The tourists had taken a shine to a batch of chilli tomato chutney, making Rosemary wonder how bland their diets were. She replenished the shelves with stock from the cellar and closed the door right on five o'clock. One minute later, Jasper heaved his door shut. 'I'm ready,' he said, pulling his beanie over his ears.

'It's cold.' Rosemary zipped her jacket as high as it would go. 'Still want to do two laps?'

'Yes.' He smiled shyly. 'I never feel cold when you're next to me.'

'Jasper...'

'Sorry.' He shrugged. 'Can't help myself.'

Their walk took them up the hill on the left-hand side of the Square, past Jules and Roman's Leftover Restaurant and several old buildings including the boarded up, but still magnificent, mayoral residence. The hill was steep. Rose-mary glanced at Jasper, but he managed the gradient easily, pom pom swinging to the rhythm of his stride. The fatigue that had plagued him since he'd caught pneumonia was gone, although he stopped as the path turned to run along the top of the hill bordering the cemetery and grasped the lookout rail with both hands.

'Okay, Jasper?'

'Yes.' He grinned at Rosemary. 'I am. Isn't it great?'

She smiled back, noting the way his face had lit up. His colour had returned as the fatigue had faded and he was no longer the pale and skinny owner of a second-hand book-shop. *He is*, she thought, *the tall and somewhat handsome bookshop owner.*

He put a hand briefly on her arm. 'I see you looking at me.'

Rosemary startled. 'You look different. Better.'

'Was I bad before?'

'Yes. Sickly is how I'd describe you.'

'Oh.' He straightened. 'I feel lucky I didn't end up there.' He waved his hand at the graves behind them. 'Although, the view is marvellous.'

'Not worth dying for.'

He chuckled, then fell quiet, gazing out over the town that was mainly distinguishable by bright windows. 'Winter darkness falls quickly.'

Rosemary tugged at his sleeve and they walked on. Jasper kept his head down, staring at the path, and she had to steer him away from a pile of twigs that had snapped off a tree above them. 'Jasper. What's up?'

He raised his head. In the dimness she could just see how his face had lost its shine from a few minutes ago. 'It's the skeleton, Rosemary. Why was it in my backyard? Why wasn't it in yours?'

'Because it's probably the printer's wife. So Ronnie said.'

'Oh. Well. But why did *I* have to find it? Why was I digging in exactly the same spot of the entire yard that happened to have a dead body in it?'

'Coincidence.'

Jasper shook his head. 'No. It's my curse.'

'Jasper.'

He stopped and turned to her. 'I know you think it's crazy, Rosemary, but I feel it.' He tapped his chest with a clenched fist. 'In here. I carry it with me. Always.'

She stared into his blanched face. It reminded her of when he was at his sickest, in hospital, struggling to breathe. That he recovered so well was evidence, to her anyway, that there was no curse, but she knew that wouldn't convince him. 'What would it take for you to let it go?'

'What?'

'The curse. You say you carry it with you. What would it take for you to put it down?'

He took so long to answer that the path and the silent cemetery behind them went black. Light still glowed from the town below, making one side of his face faintly orange. 'Finding my father.'

Rosemary nodded and linked her arm through his. They continued walking, careful not to trip on the bumps and bits strewn along the path until they could descend again into town with its soft street lighting. His arm felt warm against hers, and strong. Discovering that he had a different father to his siblings had knocked Jasper Lu, even at the age of fifty-five. She suspected that he thought it explained a lot about his family, the difference between himself and his older sister, the secret writing life of his mother, the feeling that he didn't fit in. It was another mystery, just like the skeleton in the hole.

They got to the bottom of the hill. She extracted her arm and gave his a pat. 'I'll help you,' she said. 'I'll help you find your father and you can say goodbye to this.' She put one hand flat on his chest. 'But we need to find a place to start.'

He gripped her hand briefly. 'I hoped you'd say that. I *need* you, Rosemary Exeter.'

Well, she thought as they headed up the hill to walk another lap, *it is nice to be needed.*

FIVE

By Thursday, the rush of senior citizen buses and midweek fishermen trips had abated. The first batch of lemon marmalade had sold in one morning. Rosemary abandoned the razor blade and used her food processor to chop more, keeping Aunt Lilibeth's recipe book face down on the table. 'I know,' she said to Sunny over the roar of the appliance, 'I'm being ridiculous.'

Sunny graced her mistress with a slight angling of her head before staring back out the window. *Just get rid of those things as quickly as you can,* her twitching tail seemed to say.

Rosemary added Seville oranges to her mix and pulsed the processor. The noise covered the sound of her phone, but she saw it flash, switched the machine off, and pressed speaker. 'Honey.'

'Mum. Busy?'

'Always.'

'Yep, yep.'

Rosemary settled her elbows on the kitchen counter. 'Everything okay, Honey?'

Honey gave her low chuckle. 'Of course, Mum. Tallulah and I are tracking along completely normally, so the midwife says. I sleep well, feel well, eat well. Ronnie does the housework, I cook. We have a natural harmony to this household.'

'I see. And yet...?'

There was a moment of quiet. Rosemary bent over the phone and thought she could hear Cuddles the Golden Retriever panting happily.

'I'm bored, Mum.'

'Ah. You cut down on work too soon?'

'I dropped the tot class early on, as you know. That was fine because I was tired. Then the hall bookings changed, and I had to condense the primary classes into one. It's big and noisy, but it's fine. The senior classes are going along the same. They're easy because everyone wants to be there.' Honey sighed. 'I find myself with too much empty time on my hands.'

Rosemary counted the number of classes Honey had. Even coupled with the amount of administration that businesses created, it still left hours in the week that a busy person like Honey had to fill. 'You need something else to do. Mrs Lionel could always use a helping hand.'

'Ronnie's happy to do that when she wants him. How about I help *you*?'

'You're welcome to come into the shop any time, as you know, but I don't need your help.'

'Gee, Mum, tell it like it is.'

'I always do.'

Honey sighed. 'I know. I also know you don't need help. You've got it worked out.'

'Yes.'

There was a tapping sound through the phone as if Honey was drumming her fingers on the table. 'Okay, well, I'll work this out, too. I need something to occupy me now but not something that's going to make me too busy in three months' time.' The tapping stopped. 'Anyway, enough thinking about that for now. Is Ronnie keeping you up to date with the skeleton?'

'As much as he can. He was waiting to get a copy of the suicide note.'

'He's expecting that today or tomorrow.' A sigh whispered down the line. 'I'd better go, Mum. Let you get on with your day.'

'Right.'

'Oh, but what are you making?'

'Marmalade. Orange and lemon.'

'Your kitchen smells like a citrus orchard, all tangy and tart.'

Rosemary smiled. 'Honey, you're daft.'

'And the fragrance will drift into the shop as you cook, leaving enticing tendrils of bittersweet sharpness to curl out the door and pull enthralled customers in.'

'Honey, you're daft and a nut.'

'Love you, Mum.'

'Love you, Honey Blossom.'

After the call ended, Rosemary smiled across to Sunny on the windowsill. 'Enticing tendrils, Sunny?'

The cat sniffed and refused to look back.

MORE MARMALADE WAS COOLING in its jars by the time Mrs Lionel jangled into the shop at lunchtime. 'Rosemary, dear?'

'In the kitchen.' Rosemary wiped the last of the jars and threw the cloth into the sink. 'Are you here for lunch?'

'What's on the menu?'

Rosemary tipped her head at the row of golden jars on the bench. 'Warm marmalade on toast?'

Mrs Lionel admired the jars then shook her head. 'I was thinking we could have lunch at Rakisha's.'

Rosemary couldn't stop the grimace before her friend saw it. 'Legume buns?'

'Some of her items are quite nice.'

'Not that nice. Not when I could easily rummage up an omelette.'

'Well, dear, that's not the point.'

'What is the point?'

'We need to check on Rakisha. She's been very upset by the barricade around The Exceptional Tree.'

'Even after redecorating it?'

'*Especially* after redecorating it. Kelly doesn't like the new colour and complained.'

'Complained to who?'

'Rakisha. Me. The other shop owners in The Square.'

'What does Franco think? His patisserie is just as close as the others.'

'It's hard to get anything out of Franco.'

'Yes. What about Roman and Jules?'

'Most of their business is the evening trade. They aren't that concerned.'

'The main complainant is Kelly.'

'We anticipated as much.'

Rosemary untied her apron. 'Right. Lunch at Rakisha's. We can keep our eyes on the shops from there.'

Outside, the day was cold but blue. Weak winter sun lit the Square, making the pink barricade shine. *It is a sight. As bad as lime green.* Even so, Rosemary tried not to empathise with Kelly Flanagan.

Rakisha stood behind her counter, serving coffee substitute to a group of unsuspecting older tourists. She chatted happily to them about the benefits of juiced kale, not noticing their slightly stunned expressions, until they left the shop clutching brown keep cups stamped with The Sweet Potato's logo of two crossed tubers. As the door shut, her expression changed. 'Rosemary. Mrs Lionel. That *woman* wants me to repaint that *disaster* out there!'

'By that woman, you mean Kelly?' asked Rosemary mildly.

'Who else would I mean, darling?' Rakisha came out from behind her counter, wiping at the wild strands of hair falling across her face. 'She said to me, and I cannot believe she said this, "Rakisha, that paint looks as if you've raided a preschool art room and made off with a years' supply of puking pink". Puking pink! She has no style, darlings. That colour...' Rakisha pointed with a shaking finger. 'That colour is the essence of strawberry, the core of watermelon, the inner chakra of pomegranate pulp.'

Rosemary's eyebrow shot up and Mrs Lionel nudged her.

'Well, dear,' said the older woman, 'it is a lovely colour but perhaps there's another that is more suitable to the ambience of Mulbury?'

Rakisha bunched her hair back and tied it off with a length of what Rosemary thought was brown string. 'Ambience of Mulbury? What would that be, darling?'

'Well...' Mrs Lionel glanced around the shop and its range of jars. 'What other colours can you produce from your collection of natural ingredients? For example, when I want to colour my soaps, I use zest or flowers. Surely you would have herbs and spices that would make more...'

'Earthy tones,' finished Rosemary.

'Tones that represent The Exceptional Tree, for example.'

Rakisha went to stand at the window, drawing the others forward to gaze at the ancient Tree that marked the centre of the Square. Its soft green leaves rattled slightly in the breeze, casting shadows on the silver trunk. 'I think I see what you mean, darlings. Oh, isn't that the new man, Robert?'

'In the Tree?' asked Rosemary.

'No, silly. Heading this way.' Rakisha gasped. 'And look! He has his keep cup, the one I gave him yesterday. Now that's something that I could never get Barry to do.'

'I suspect he's not a bit like Barry.'

'No, I hear he's changing the garage to be much more modern. Computers, darlings. All that sort of thing.'

Rosemary turned to Rakisha to explain that wasn't the main difference between the old mechanic and the new one, but once again Mrs Lionel's jab in the ribs stopped her. Besides, Robert was indeed striding for The Sweet Potato and Rosemary stepped out of the way of the door before it groaned open.

'Hello, Mr Sparky,' said Rakisha, scuttling back to her coffee machine. 'Refill for you?' She held out her hand for his cup.

'Oh.' Robert ducked his head to come through the door but stopped as he saw Mrs Lionel and Rosemary behind it. 'Sparkling. My name is Sparkling. But please. I'm Robert to all my friends.'

'Oh, darling.' Rakisha smiled, putting both hands to her cheeks and giggling in a way that made Rosemary cringe.

Perhaps Robert was regretting his loose use of the word *friends*. His face reddened. Not, thought Rosemary, in the way that Jasper Lu's deepened in colour when he was embarrassed. Robert Sparkling's cheeks got high spots of crimson that vanished almost immediately, leaving a blush that highlighted his night-black eyes. He came inside as Rakisha beckoned for the cup, but held it fast to his broad chest. 'Thanks, Rakisha, but I'm not here for a refill. I'm returning the cup you so generously loaned me yesterday.'

'That's quite all right, darling.' Rakisha waggled her fingers and Robert gave her the cup. 'It will only take me a jiffy to refill it.'

'No!' Robert held up a hand. 'I mean, no thank you, Rakisha. You see, I only drink legume coffee sparingly as I find the energy it gives me is so absolute that I have to space my drinks.'

That was a good try, thought Rosemary as Rakisha scowled.

Mrs Lionel came to his rescue. 'Robert, dear, we were just discussing the next colour that Rakisha will paint the barricade. Perhaps you have an opinion of which herb or spice Rakisha could base the colour on to more effectively blend in with the Tree itself?'

Robert studied Mrs Lionel for a moment, taking in her steady look and slightly widened eyes. 'Colour? Well.' He turned back to stare at the jars behind Rakisha's head. 'You might think it strange, but I do know a bit about colour. Ink colours, actually. Fountain pen ink. Pigments and inks are my thing.'

'Really, darling? How unusual.' Rakisha stepped out again and brushed her hand along a shelf of spices. 'Is there anything here you can see that would be more of what darling Mrs Lionel means?'

Robert went closer to the shelf. The shop went quiet as he tapped his fingers along each jar until he pulled one out. 'What about turmeric? I haven't tried it myself, but I have seen dye made from it. It's an egg yolk yellow.'

'Would it work on that dreadful barricade, darling?'

'I don't know but it's worth a try.'

Rakisha stared at Mrs Lionel, who nodded vigorously. 'Robert's right, dear. How about you try it?'

Rakisha brushed at her skirt. 'Well, I suppose I can, darlings. Anything to appease *that* woman.'

'Not me,' said Rosemary, as Robert glanced her way. 'Kelly Flanagan.'

'The small woman with the severe bob?'

'That's her. *Severe* is a good description.'

Robert smiled. 'A fan of hers?'

'Hardly.'

'Rosemary, Robert is new to Mulbury.' Mrs Lionel linked her arm through her friend's. 'Let him make his own mind up. And we must go.'

'I thought-'

'You promised me lunch, dear.' Mrs Lionel tugged at Rosemary's arm. 'At your place.'

'I should go as well.' Robert put the keep cup on the bench. 'Thank you, Rakisha.'

'Any time, darling. Remember where to come when your energy needs absolution again.'

'What? Oh, yes. Thank you.'

Rosemary pulled the groaning door open and held it for Mrs Lionel and Robert. He took an audibly deep breath as the door closed behind him. 'Thank you.'

'What for?'

He rubbed a hand through his hair, then finger-combed

it back. 'I actually meant Mrs Lionel. Thank you for getting me out of whatever I was getting in to.'

'Rakisha's a lovely woman,' said Mrs Lionel. 'But she is very passionate about her lifestyle. She would love others to embrace it.'

'Well, I don't mind a decent falafel, but the coffee really didn't suit me.'

'That's because it is as similar to coffee as Mount Everest is to a hill.' Rosemary pushed her braid back over her shoulder. 'Are you really into inks?'

'Oh, yes.' Robert shrugged. 'I have been since a little kid. Pen inks, mostly shades of blue. Although I recently discovered a gold that is very attractive. But I'm not telling you anything you don't know.'

'I know nothing about pen inks.'

There was a long silence in which Robert stared at Rosemary. She shifted uncomfortably, glancing at Mrs Lionel, who seemed just as puzzled, then back at Robert. 'Why are you looking at me like that?'

'Rosemary Exeter.' Robert tucked his hands into his jacket pocket and leaned back. 'You don't remember, do you?'

'Remember what?'

He shook his head sadly. 'We knew each other as children.'

Rosemary took a long look at the man's face. *I would have remembered those eyes,* she thought. *No one could forget depthless eyes like that.* 'Did we?'

'Yes.' He waited but Rosemary said nothing. 'A long time ago, back in school. Back when our families lived in a small town like this one and everyone knew each other's business.'

Rosemary tried, but her strongest memories of her

childhood were those of Aunt Lilibeth's kitchen with its homely smells of roast meats and apple pie, and she doubted Robert Sparkling had been part of that. 'Like you say, it was a long time ago.'

Robert's shoulders slumped momentarily, then he straightened and pulled his hands out of his pocket. Something glimmered in Rosemary's mind, a faint image of a tall, handsome man long gone which morphed into a young Alasdair, also long gone. She shook herself free of it just as Robert shrugged. 'It doesn't matter. I was at school with you. I can't have made much of an impact.' He gave a short smile. 'Not like the impact you made on me.'

Rosemary shook her head. 'I'm sorry, I really don't remember you.'

'Ah.' Robert Sparkling nodded. 'Perhaps it's for the best. We can start again.' He bobbed. 'I will see you ladies another time.'

'Well,' said Mrs Lionel as Robert walked back to his garage. 'That's not like you to forget anyone.'

Rosemary frowned. 'No. It's not.'

'You'll have to see what you can drag out of your memory banks.'

Rosemary's mind was already working on it.

SIX

The niggling feeling of not knowing something made the afternoon go very slowly for Rosemary Exeter. Mrs Lionel went back to her shop after lunch and the afternoon tourists were few. Rosemary didn't wait until closing time to shut the shop, but swung the sign around and pulled the blinds down half an hour before, feeding Sunny early and settling on her couch with boxes of photos retrieved from where they'd been stored in the coffee table drawer. 'Here it is,' she said to Sunny, who'd come back to her bed beside the fire now that the enticing tendrils of citrus had diminished.

When Alasdair had gone and Rosemary moved into The Preserved Mulbury, she organised furniture removalists to take what was in the old house and place it, undisturbed, into the next. She hadn't felt she could sort it at the time and, all these years later, she still wasn't in the mood, but curiosity won over and she opened a photo box.

Robert had been right on one thing. Rosemary had grown up with Alasdair in a town the size of Mulbury. That was where the comparison ended. Mulbury had been rescued from its goldmining slump to re-emerge as a historical tourist town, complete with period brick and sandstone buildings, retaining a sense of gold-rush opulence. On the other hand, March, Rosemary's hometown, was dead long before she'd been born, and its streets were full of derelict shops and rundown houses. Not that dereliction mattered much to its inhabitants, who still embraced families and hard work, but the only spark of joy to be found was with Aunt Lilibeth. After she'd died, Rosemary left for university and brighter fields with Alasdair, hope in their hearts.

'Ah, hope,' Rosemary said to Sunny who twitched her tail in response. 'It held us in good stead.'

With hope, they'd finished university, started various businesses, decided to have a baby, and ended up in Mulbury.

Rosemary tipped the photos from their box and let them spill over her lap. She hunted for ones from her days of primary school and studied each closely. A small town meant that the throng of children were the same from year level to year level, albeit with longer or shorter hair, braces there or gone, and various lengths of pants and skirts. Even within the three-teacher-sized school, children had fallen into natural groups. In March, it was based on where people lived. Rosemary and Alasdair had hung out with the children who lived at the centre of town in ramshackle houses, many of which were attached to vacant shops. She grunted. *That's probably why I like living where I do now.*

Sharp knocking on the shop door made her look up but she couldn't see who it was through the shuttered windows. *I'm clearly closed,* she thought and continued her scrutiny of the photographs. The knocking persisted, followed by a deep voice laced with concern. 'Rosemary? Are you in there?'

Jasper Lu.

Rosemary shuffled the photographs into their box and hurried to the front, pulling the door open so vigorously the bell nearly wrenched from its setting. Jasper had his black coat and beanie on. His brow was creased in worry. 'Did you forget our walk?'

Rosemary closed her eyes momentarily. 'Yes. I forgot.'

'Oh.' Jasper took a step back. 'That's okay. I can go by myself.'

'Yes, you could.' Rosemary sighed as Jasper's face dropped. 'Wait. I'll get my coat.'

Sunny tucked her nose further into her bed as Rosemary whipped in, grabbed her jacket, gave the cat a quick pat, and sped out the door. She closed it with a bang and turned to Jasper. 'Right. Let's go.'

'You really don't have to, Rosemary. I like your company, but I'm fit enough to walk without a chaperone.'

'I know you are, Jasper,' Rosemary said as they started along the footpath. 'I said I would come with you so I am.'

'Okay, but-'

Rosemary put her hand up abruptly and shook her head. Jasper grinned and fell quiet.

They'd reached the end of the path and were about to step onto the road to head up the hill when a creaking sedan shot out of Mulbury Feeds and nearly took them out. Behind it, hair flying behind them, came Holly and Hannah Hubbard, with Heather trailing behind. Hannah was first to reach Rosemary, who grabbed her arm before the young woman could take off down the road. Hannah struggled, growling, her eyes on the car now veering around the corner towards Big Town. 'Hannah! Enough.'

Hannah went still and dropped her head.

Rosemary dropped her grip. 'Your father is home, then.'

'Yep, he's home.'

Holly reached them, panting, and put her hand on her sister's arm. 'Let him go.'

Hannah stiffened, bringing her head up to stare at Holly. '*Let* him go? He's gone! He's always gone until he wants something. Then he comes back. And now, even when we promised him more money that he's ever had, he's gone again without talking to us.'

Rosemary looked from one sister to the other. 'Richard still won't tell you who he's selling the business to?'

'No!' Hannah reached out for Heather as the youngest sister joined them and brought her in close. 'The stupid man can't see a great thing like his daughters owning the business when it hits him in the nose.'

'You didn't, did you?' asked Jasper.

'What?'

'Hit him in the nose?'

'I felt like it.' Hannah hooked her short tufts of hair back behind her ear and scowled at Jasper.

'But she didn't.' Holly put her hands on her hips and stretched back, breathing deeply. 'I'm so unfit.'

'Why has Richard driven off like that?' asked Jasper.

'Oh, we were having a family discussion,' said Holly, letting her arms drop to her side. 'We presented our business case to him, hoping he'd change his mind.' She shook her head slowly. 'He wasn't in the mood. His muse was trying to speak to him and apparently we were interfering.'

'That's the point, isn't it?' Hannah smoothed Heather's hair away from the young woman's face distractedly. 'He could talk to the muse all day long if we ran the business. He could buy a million guitars and live on a tropical island and strum until his fingertips fell off. I don't know why he doesn't want to sell it to us.' She stared at Rosemary. 'Do you?'

'No idea,' said Rosemary. 'Perhaps that's where you'd better start.'

'What do you mean?'

'You need to find out why he doesn't want to sell *you* the business. Why he'd prefer to sell it to someone else.' She held up a finger as Hannah went to speak. 'Without yelling at him. You'll need to do some sleuthing.'

'Snooping, you mean.'

'Whatever works.'

'You think Dad has a genuine reason for not wanting to sell us Mulbury Feeds?' asked Holly, narrowing her eyes at Rosemary.

'It's a possibility.'

Holly tugged at Hannah's sleeve. 'Any thoughts on that?'

'No. I think he's just being stubborn and obstreperous.'

Holly grinned. 'Obstreperous? Do you mean obstinate?'

'Both!' Hannah spun around. 'I'm going to cook dinner.'

Holly watched as Hannah stomped home, dragging a humming Heather with her. 'Sorry. Hannah's pretty cut up about it all.'

'So I see.' Rosemary tucked her hands into her pockets. 'Will you be okay?'

'Yeah, we're fine.'

'I mean, if Richard sells it to someone else.'

Holly spent a long moment poking at a stone on the pavement with the tip of her boot. 'The new owners would be wise to let us carry on as normal,' she said finally. 'We know this business so well.' She put her feet together and glanced up at Rosemary. 'But I'm not staying. I've worked hard here, and the business is not going to grow unless Hannah and I get complete control over it. I'd take what I'd learned here and start somewhere else. Maybe not in animal produce, either.'

Rosemary nodded. 'Would Hannah go with you?'

For the first time, Holly's face crumpled. 'I don't know. I haven't asked her. But I'd take Heather with me. I wouldn't leave her with Dad.'

'You don't think your father would look after her?' asked Jasper.

'Oh, he'd try. He loves Heather. Loves all of us. But he follows his own pathway in life. Heather would have to go along with him, and I don't want her to be his extra luggage on his fits of musical passion.'

Jasper shot a look at Rosemary. 'Fathers, eh?'

'Yeah.' Holly wiped at her face. 'It would be different if Mum was still alive.' She shook her head. 'But she isn't. So we have to do what we have to do.'

'Whatever you decide will be the right decision,' said Rosemary.

Holly smiled. 'Thanks, Rosemary. That means a lot.' She shrugged. 'I'd better go help Hannah. In the mood she's in, she'll burn everything and make us eat it.'

'Wow,' said Jasper as Holly walked away, and he and Rosemary continued their walk up the hill. 'That's tough on them.'

'They'll be okay. Those three girls have got more going for them than their father ever will.'

'You don't have a lot of time for Richard, do you?'

'No.'

'Have you known him long?'

'Since we moved here.'

'So...' Jasper stuck his hands in his pockets and hitched his coat collar up around his ears. 'Not as long as you've known Robert?'

'What do you mean?'

'Oh, it's just the way he looks at you.'

Rosemary heard the bigger question in Jasper's voice and chose not to reply. They walked up the hill in silence. The encounter with the Hubbard sisters had made them even later than usual and the cemetery was dark as they made their way past. Below, the town hunkered down against the cold evening, smoke rising from chimneys and light glowing softly through windows.

A rustling in the fallen autumn leaves made Rosemary stop.

Jasper walked on for a few steps before noticing. He halted so suddenly he nearly tripped. 'What is it?''

Rosemary stepped to the stone fence around the cemetery and peered over. 'Patti?'

Even in the dim light, Patti glowed. She stood up from where she'd been squatting, her faux fur white coat catching the streetlights as they flickered on, giving her an apricot aura. 'Oh, Rosemary! Jasper! It's getting so late!'

'What are you doing in there, Patti?' Jasper stepped over the fence. 'It's dark.'

'Well, it is *now*. It wasn't when I came up. I'm treasure hunting! I left Gerry to close the shop. He's probably starting to get a bit worried.' Patti held up her phone which was clad in diamantes. 'It's flat.'

'Can I help you over the fence?'

'You are a sweetie, Jasper, but I'll go back along the path to the gate. I've left my bag here. I need to put this in it.' She held up a long piece of fabric that was splotched with dark patches.

'You're collecting discarded clothing,' said Rosemary as Patti stepped daintily around the headstones to the cemetery gate.

'Yes, that's right. You're so clever, Rosemary, with the way you work things out.' Patti swooped down and held up a garbage bag. 'I knew I'd seen some things behind this wall, so I said to Gerry that I'd nip up and get them but as I was climbing up the hill, I found a couple of old shirts in the gutter. That made me hunt around a bit more and I lost track of the time.' She peered into the bag. 'That makes six garments in one hunting trip! I am lucky.'

Rosemary tried not to grimace at the dirty objects Patti was so proudly surveying. They'd be transformed into bespoke fashion items before their life ended, but they wouldn't be the sort of clothes Rosemary was used to wearing. 'Are you actively looking for...' Rosemary waved her hand over the top of the bag.

'It's the film director, you see.' Patti closed the bag and twisted its top expertly. 'She wants three particular items for her next film: a dress for a male wrestler, a pair of stylish pants for a very short woman, and headgear for a vaudeville singer.' She laughed. 'Don't look at me that way, Jasper! I don't know why she wants them, but they are the orders I have.'

'Do you have any idea what to do? I mean, a pair of stylish pants for a very short woman?'

'Don't forget, Jasper sweetie, that every garment I make must be from someone else's discarded ones. She's very particular about that. I just love it!' Patti shivered in delight, making her neatly waved hair bounce around on her shoulders.

'How long have you got to make them, Patti?'

'Oh.' Patti paused and rolled the top of her bag up. 'A few days.'

'That's not long.'

'Maybe a bit longer. The director is coming to visit soon,

and I wanted her to at least see a design and perhaps one garment prepared.' Patti cupped one side of her hair and patted it into place. 'I've never had to work fast before. My creations have been allowed to bloom. This will test me.'

'They'll be magnificent, Patti,' Jasper said. 'Take your time with them. My bet is that the film director will come along and be inspired by you.'

'Or she'll be distracted.' Rosemary crossed her arms against the creeping cold of the evening. 'She'll be a creative person herself and probably has more than one project on the go. She'll give you time, Patti.'

'Thank you, both.' Patti held up the bag. 'Are you walking back down? It's too cold to do any more tonight.'

'Let me carry your bag.' Jasper held out his hand, but Patti pulled the bag closer to her body.

'Thanks, Jasper honey, but carrying it helps me think. I'm wondering whether I could turn this lovely cotton scarf into a turban for the vaudeville singer...'

As Patti wandered off, Jasper waggled his head at Rosemary, who waved him away to walk beside Patti. The seamstress was still talking and, although Jasper leaned towards her empathetically, Rosemary didn't think Patti was wanting Jasper's opinion. She was sorting her thoughts out aloud, a little like Alasdair had done when he designed shoes.

Rosemary shook her head clear of Alasdair. It was harder to remove Robert for, when they reached the bottom of the hill and Patti had disappeared inside Patricia's, it was clear that the mechanic was still at work. The garage door was closed but light glared from the row of windows set under the roofline.

'Should we go again?'

Rosemary had almost forgotten Jasper. She blinked at

him for a moment. 'Go where?'

Even in the soft darkness, Jasper's face could redden so rapidly it almost lit up the path. 'Another lap around town. We've only done one.'

'Yes. Sorry. No. Not tonight.' She saw disappointment make his body slump. 'You go. Take Snowy. If he's alright. Is he alright?'

'He's as good as gold, sleeping on the couch. You joke if you think I could get him to walk further than his food bowl.'

Rosemary opened her mouth to remind Jasper that she didn't joke when she realised that, perhaps, *he* was joking. 'Surely he goes outside?'

'Of course.' Jasper chuckled. 'Caught him yesterday digging at the hole I had been digging for him.' He stopped, putting his hand on his mouth. 'Do you think that meant something? Perhaps he knows what I was digging it for, and he'd decided that it *was* a good idea?'

More likely that the old dog smelled where the bones had been. 'Jasper,' she said, 'your imagination rivals Patti's. Perhaps you need to go into the garment business.'

'Treasure hunting, I could do. Garment making, I could not.' Jasper laughed again. 'Actually, I'm quite good at finding treasures. Old books and old bones come to mind.'

'I've got some treasure hunting of my own to do.' Rosemary reached out and squeezed Jasper's arm. 'I'll see you tomorrow.'

'Bye, Rosemary. I look forward to it.'

Rosemary caught his final, soft words as she opened the shop door and went into her warm house. Their meaning wasn't lost on her, but took second place when she saw the pile of photographs, all there, sans Robert Sparkling. Where amongst her childhood memories was he?

SEVEN

Mrs Lionel swept the pavement and Goldmarket Square every morning on sunrise. At this, the deepest time of the year, it was well past breakfast time before the sun managed to creep over the horizon. Even so, it was still cold, and she shivered as she swept. 'I should have worn gloves,' she said to Percy as she stopped for a rest and to rub her palms together.

The little dog, forever smiling, wagged his tail and panted happily.

Mulbury always had its share of tourists but winter was, of course, less busy. The good side of that was less rubbish left in the Square, but the downside was the amount of dirt and mud people tramped through on the way to coffee and cakes. Mrs Lionel made her careful way from Rakisha's and Kelly's towards Franco's patisserie, passing by The Exceptional Tree with its now dirty-yellow barricade. The turmeric paint had not covered the berry ink underneath it but at least the barricade blended better into the dirt of the Square. She leaned on the top rail for a moment and reached out one hand to try and touch the

Tree, but the branches were too far away. *It was sad,* she thought, *to not be able to lay hands on such an ancient artefact.*

The Tree sighed above her, rolling its leaves around as if in agreement.

Mrs Lionel had just finished the whole area when Ronnie Edwards pulled up outside The Preserved Mulbury. She could tell by the way he braked abruptly and his forceful pushing open of the door, which tried to retaliate by springing back on his foot, that he was in a hurry. 'He's not panicking, though,' she said quietly to Percy. 'He's waiting for us.'

Ronnie stood by the car as Mrs Lionel crossed the street. 'Hello,' he said, smiling brightly. 'Sweeping the Square?'

'Just finished. How are you, Ronnie, dear?'

'I'm good. Really good. I could help you sweep, you know.'

'You already help me enough with soap-making. No need to help me more.'

'I could keep you company. Then you wouldn't be by yourself.'

'Oh, I'm not by myself, dear.'

Ronnie frowned for a second but, before he could say more, the door of The Preserved Mulbury jangled open. 'You're here early, Ronnie,' said Rosemary.

'Yes. It's okay. Honey's fine.' Ronnie held up his satchel. 'I've got something to show you.'

'Come in, then. You'll want breakfast.'

'Breakfast? You don't have to feed me, Rosemary.'

Rosemary studied her son-in-law as Mrs Lionel chuckled. 'No, I don't. But I am. Fresh bread and jam. Would you like some, Mrs Lionel?'

'Yes, dear, I would indeed. Breakfast for me was some time ago.'

Rosemary held the door as Mrs Lionel propped her broom against the window frame and stepped into the shop. Ronnie smiled at her as he came in, holding the satchel up again. 'I got the suicide note.'

'Oh!' Mrs Lionel spun around. 'Suicide note? Whose note?'

'No one we know,' said Rosemary soothingly. 'Ronnie means the note that was meant to explain the skeleton's death.'

'Oh.' Mrs Lionel put her hand to her chest. 'Now I need two slices of bread and jam.' She sat down. 'That note could be part of the problem, Ronnie.'

'What do you mean, Mrs Lionel?'

'It was 1950 when the poor woman went missing, am I correct?'

'Yes.'

'Back then, suicide was a shameful matter for families. If it was suspected that the woman took her own life, the family would have wanted the matter hushed up as soon as it could be. Her death may not have been investigated very well.'

'I didn't know that.' Ronnie slumped. 'Things were so different back then.'

'Oh yes,' said Mrs Lionel. 'We are lucky that so many things have changed for the better.'

As Rosemary prepared second breakfast, Ronnie sat at the dining table with papers spread around him. 'The coroner has yet to relate her findings but my friend at the morgue is saying that they'll probably be unable to determine who it is beyond their sex and approximate age. The length of time the skeleton has been buried means it's an historical case and they won't find any DNA matches through their missing person's database.' Ronnie sighed. 'It's a sad fact but we'll only be guessing at who it is and what the cause of death was. *But.*' He held up a piece of paper. 'I have this.'

'The note, dear?'

'Yes, Mrs Lionel. It's from Mrs Agnes Connelly, the wife of Mr Albert Connelly the printer.' He waved the paper again.

Rosemary set two thick slices of fresh bread spread with summer's strawberry jam in front of Mrs Lionel. 'Read it, Ronnie.'

Ronnie cleared his throat. '"I am sorry, my dears, to do this to you but I must go. Life is deep and hurtful. You won't find me but know that I am in your heart forever."'

Rosemary took out her phone. 'Mind if I take a photo?'

Ronnie's face crinkled in puzzlement but he nodded as Rosemary took several close-ups. 'It's a sad note.'

'It doesn't say much about her intentions.'

'No.' Ronnie put the paper down. 'The official account recorded that she had been very unwell but didn't state why. Had a lot of pain, apparently, but doctors put that down to the fact she'd miscarried a baby. Hysteria, they said, causing bodily manifestations such as...' he closed his eyes, trying to remember '...hallucinations, hair loss, vomiting and tremors.'

Mrs Lionel took a loud sip of her tea. 'Poor dear. The way they dismissed women's suffering back then, she could have had any number of painful conditions and they wouldn't have bothered looking into it. I am glad that we have science on our side these days.'

Rosemary sat at the table and Ronnie handed the paper over to her. It was a coloured copy of the original handwritten note, and the writing was a flamboyant copperplate. The ink lines were steady, too, as if Mrs Agnes Connelly had thought hard about what she'd write and then penned it with the confidence of someone who'd made up their mind. 'This is definitely Agnes Connelly's handwriting?'

'As far as they can determine by comparing it to writing in an old parish book—she took care of the church buildings.' Ronnie took back the note. 'Uncle Geoffrey is waiting for the formal coroner's finding but he said it could take years. He's also waiting for what I can find out, but I don't think this case is a priority for him.' He pulled a laptop from his satchel and opened it. 'Even though he can't be sure of the skeleton's identity, he's contacted Mrs Connelly's nearest of kin who is a daughter. Dr Tabitha Connelly.' He swivelled the computer around. 'She was only three when her mother went missing.'

The computer screen showed an image of a frowning woman with short, silver hair. She was dressed in an academic gown and bonnet and stared into the camera lens with defiance. 'She worked in a university?' asked Rosemary.

Ronnie shook his head. 'No. But she completed her PhD recently on the topic of "Fragrant Memories", whatever that means. This is her graduation photo. It made the local paper where she lived but I'm not sure why.'

'Probably, dear, because she was simply an older woman who completed her PhD.' Mrs Lionel shook her head as she mopped up crumbs of bread with one finger. 'People still think it's a spectacle when an older woman achieves anything.'

'Oh, I didn't think of that.' Ronnie's face mottled. 'I mean, I didn't think that when I saw her photo. The picture was what came up when I searched for her name.'

'Geoffrey has contacted her?'

'Yes, he has. He thought it only right.'

'Where does she live, dear?'

Ronnie pulled the computer back and tapped at its keyboard. 'Sydney.'

'Quite a way from here.'

'Yeah.' Ronnie watched Rosemary. 'Do you think she would know anything useful to the case?'

'She was very young when her mother went missing.' Rosemary tapped a finger on the table thoughtfully. 'Children are often more perceptive than adults think, particularly in those days when children were seen but not heard. She probably wasn't questioned about her mother.'

'Would it be useful to ask her now?'

'You can't contact her, Ronnie.'

Ronnie's face glowed brightly. 'I know that. But if she happened to turn up.'

'Gentle inquiry could be useful.'

He closed the computer screen. 'Yeah, otherwise, I don't have anything else to go on. There was nothing of value in Jasper's backyard. Apparently when Mr Connelly closed his business, the new printer wasn't very interested in newspaper production. He produced flyers and the occasional book but the business didn't last. The printery was empty for ten years before Mr Arthur came along.'

'Mr Arthur didn't do any printing,' said Mrs Lionel. 'He started a bookshop.'

'What happened to the printing equipment?'

'I believe he got rid of it.' Mrs Lionel folded her hands together on the table. 'I was still on the farm then, but I heard he bundled it all in his van one day, drove to the city, and sold it for scrap metal.'

'That's a crime in itself,' said Rosemary. 'Printing presses were magnificent pieces of machinery.'

'He didn't think so. Mr Arthur had no time for *old things*, as he put it. His bookshop was only for the new. He did all right in his shop for a while but eventually business teetered out. As did Mr Arthur.'

'Where is he now?' asked Ronnie. 'Maybe he knows something.'

'Oh, the poor old fellow is dead.' Mrs Lionel didn't look sad. 'He went interstate after he sold to Jasper, and I heard that he had a heart attack while having a drink in a bar. Nasty way to go, but quick.'

'So, we really have nothing to go on.' Ronnie slipped his computer and paperwork back in his satchel.

Rosemary stood and filled the kettle again. 'Have you investigated events around the year that she died?'

Ronnie shook his head. 'Should I?'

'Sometimes it helps. It's easy to forget that 1950 was a long time ago and things were very different, as Mrs Lionel said.'

'Are you thinking of anything in particular?'

'No. I'll leave that up to you.'

Ronnie looked solemn. 'Thanks, Rosemary. I'll do that. At least it will be something to work on and put in a report. I hate handing a blank sheet to Uncle Geoffrey.' He stood to leave.

'How is Honey, dear?' asked Mrs Lionel. 'I haven't seen her for a little while.'

'Oh, the cakes are keeping her busy.'

Rosemary stopped putting tea leaves in the pot. 'Cakes?'

'Yeah, decorative cakes.' Ronnie glanced from one woman to the other as they waited. 'Didn't you know?'

'Know what, dear?'

Ronnie sat down again and fished out his phone. 'Well, when I got home last night, Honey was in the kitchen, baking, which is not unusual for Honey. But I wasn't allowed to eat anything. She'd made a massive, towering block of madeira cakes and then she did this to it.' He held out his phone.

Rosemary came out from behind the kitchen bench and stooped down next to Mrs Lionel. The picture on the phone showed a crooked, purple top hat complete with band. 'She put a hat on top of the cakes?'

Ronnie laughed. 'No! The hat is the cake! She turned it into something from the Mad Hatter's wardrobe.'

Rosemary straightened. 'This is her new venture.'

'On top of all her other ventures.' Ronnie put the phone back into his pocket. 'She says this one will be easier to do than drama classes when Tallulah comes along. And I've noticed she's not so...'

Mrs Lionel leaned towards Ronnie. 'Not so...?'

'Restless. She's been really restless.' Ronnie shrugged.

'Yes,' said Rosemary. 'You said.'

'She's not any more. Half of the dining table is covered with cake designs. The other half is my working spot.'

'Well, good for Honey.' Mrs Lionel pushed back her chair. 'No more tea for me, dear. I need to get sorted for the morning. It was good to see you, Ronnie.'

'I'll see you for soap making when you want me.'

'You are a good man to help me out. I do appreciate it.'

Ronnie flung his satchel on to his shoulder. 'Do you know what, Mrs Lionel? I like it. There's something really satisfying in making your own soap.' He paused. 'Is that crazy?'

'No,' said Rosemary. 'You're discovering some simple pleasures.'

'Aren't I too young for that sort of thing?'

Rosemary gave him a withering stare.

'Oh. Okay. Not too young.' He bolted for the door. 'See you both later.'

Mrs Lionel chuckled as Ronnie jangled away. 'He's not bad, is he? A harmless sort of man.'

'Yes.'

'What do you think of all this, dear?'

'All *what*, specifically?'

'Jasper's skeleton.' Mrs Lionel straightened her dress and walked towards the shop area. 'If it is that poor woman, she either didn't make it to the mine shaft and did herself in some other way, or...'

'Someone else did her in.'

'That's what I was thinking. I just hope she hadn't lived her whole life in fear.' Mrs Lionel turned to Rosemary. 'On a brighter note, Honey's cakes sound like a great venture.'

'Yes. She's an entrepreneur.'

'Like her mother. Like her father, to some extent.'

'I wouldn't call Alasdair an entrepreneur.'

'He tried, dear.' Mrs Lionel pulled the door open and stepped outside. 'He didn't have your tenacity.'

'No. He did not.'

Rosemary watched as her friend walked down the path towards The Green Mulbury. The older woman had a slight limp these days but her back was straight. She turned to open her shop door and disappeared from Rosemary's view, but not before Rosemary caught her talking to someone behind her. Or some*thing*, more likely. She hoped no one else was noticing her friend's attachment to the little ghost dog. And definitely not Richard, strolling up to Franco's patisserie for a pie, leaving his girls to run his business. Rosemary bristled. *What I'd really like to do,* she thought, striding to the shop counter to fire up its computer, *is to give Richard Hubbard a decent talking to.*

'I feel like a 1970s headmistress,' she said to Sunny who had appeared in the doorway.

The cat sat and watched her. *That role would suit you,* she seemed to say.

'Thanks, cat. You're meant to be on my side.'

Sunny stood, arched her back and rubbed it on the door-frame. *I don't take sides.*

Rosemary chuckled and went back to her computer. Instead of checking her stock as she normally would, she found herself thinking about the skeleton. Whatever had happened to it in the past, it had been wrenched rudely out of the ground, its peace disturbed as Jasper had said. *And stirring up the past,* thought Rosemary, *hardly ever turns out for the best.*

EIGHT

Saturday dawned mild and bright. The frost stayed away, leaving an unexpected balminess to the air. A tourist bus arrived right on opening time, spilling forth a crowd of happy people who were escaping the city. They dispersed like ants from an ant hill, entering each open premise with gusto. Rosemary found herself chatting to an animated group of women about preserving olives, and each one left the shop with at least three jars of various condiments. There was barely time for Rosemary to get herself a cup of tea when a raucous van pulled up in Goldmarket Road and a large, shouty family mounted the footpath to scan the shops. She braced herself for requests of chocolate spread, which she usually got when young people came shopping.

The crowd, though, by-passed The Preserved Mulbury. In fact, they gazed through every shop window under the veranda but didn't go into a single building. After a thorough checking-out, they gathered again on the pavement, then crossed the road as one large entity to pound on the door of The Leftover Restaurant. When it didn't open,

Rosemary crossed the Square to see them. 'Can I help you?' she called across the noise.

A dark-haired young woman with a cheery face smiled. 'Hello, hello! Yes, well, maybe you can. I thought I'd know where they were, but they obviously aren't here. Great day, though, isn't it? Terrific day.'

Rosemary nodded. 'A lovely day indeed. By "them", did you mean Jules and Roman?'

'Grum and Pops, that's who I meant. That's what we call them, don't we, tribe?'

Four children, varying in age from teen to just-school-aged, turned as one and gathered around the woman. 'Grum and Pops,' said the youngest sagely.

Rosemary studied the group in front of her. The two youngest children had wavy, fair hair that tumbled well past their shoulders. The older ones were almost as dark-haired as their mother. All four children, and their mother, had Roman's chocolate-brown eyes. 'You're Felicity.'

'Yes!' The young woman grinned broadly. 'How did you know? We haven't visited Mulbury since...I don't know. When was it, kids?'

'I wasn't born,' said the youngest.

'No, really?' The woman's face fell. 'You've never seen Grum and Pops in their home environment?'

'She has,' said the oldest, a tall boy with a narrow face. 'She just can't remember. We came here when I was ten. Four years ago. I remember because Grum gave me a watch for my birthday.'

'Still, four years is a long time.' Felicity shrugged and tilted her head at Rosemary. 'You must think me a terrible daughter.'

'I have no idea what sort of daughter you are,' said Rosemary.

Felicity's mouth fell open then she gave a little shake of her head. 'Well, anyway, here we are! But they aren't in the restaurant?'

'Jules will be at home. Roman might be sourcing produce for the evening.'

'Righto! Righto!' Felicity spread her arms to shoo her children like a flock of birds towards the van. 'Leif! Calvin! We're going to Grum's house.'

A man and an older teenage boy stopped trying to peer inside the restaurant's windows and walked briskly to Felicity. The man stuck out his hand. 'Leif Anderson. This is my nephew, Calvin, who lives with us. Pleased to meet you. Or, if we've met again, pleased to re-meet you.' He smiled. 'I have a shocking memory for faces.'

'We haven't met.' Rosemary took the man's hand and shook it briefly. 'I'm Rosemary Exeter. I've seen photos of your family.'

'Oh, yes.' Felicity smiled. 'Grum has lots of those around her house. I mean, there are a lot of us so it's no surprise that she has lots of photos of us.' She smiled wider as she contemplated the children in front of her. 'And they are so photogenic.'

Rosemary said nothing as she watched the oldest boy struggle to get in the van first as the younger ones held him around the waist, giggling. The smile on Felicity's face was full of love even as she called out, 'Hey! Cut that out and get in or you'll be walking!'

Leif gave Rosemary a conspiratorial wink as he put his arm around the teenager's shoulders and steered him away. 'She wouldn't make us walk, would she, Cal?'

'Only if we'd run out of petrol.'

Felicity ruffled the boy's hair as she strode past to the car. 'Lovely to meet you, Rosalie. No doubt we'll see each other again as we're hanging around for a week or two. We're going to find the Hand of Hela!'

Rosemary watched as the van kangaroo-jumped a few metres before taking off and turning up the hill to go the long way around to Jules and Roman's old Victorian house at the edge of town. As she crossed the road, Mrs Lionel came out of The Green Mulbury. 'Did I recognise Felicity Capriccio?'

'You did.' Rosemary stepped onto the footpath. 'The family have come to find the Hand of Hela.'

'That gold nugget is only an unsubstantiated rumour.' Mrs Lionel shrugged. 'It's lovely for Jules, though. Roman, too. I know they don't see them as much as they would like. It must be very busy with four children.'

'Five, by the look of it. They have a nephew with them.'

'That'll be Calvin, Leif's brother's son. He goes to school in the city so stays with them. I remember Jules saying how Calvin loves having the other children at home.'

Rosemary studied her friend. 'You've never believed that Jules' grandfather found that gold nugget?'

Mrs Lionel tapped her fingers on her lips. 'Oh, I hate being a spoilsport, particularly as Jules really believes the story, but I've been in this district for a very long time and the Hand of Hela was a whisper that I'm sure was started by Mr Montgomery who ran what was the general store back during the gold rush. He wanted people to think gold nuggets were lying around in the dirt so they'd come to these goldfields.' Mrs Lionel dropped her hand and frowned. 'It was an awful trick to play on people. Most gold miners found nothing and almost starved to death. Unfortunately, Mr Montgomery was not the sort of person who would sell his products for reduced prices to someone who could barely afford tea leaves.'

'Why is Jules so keen on the story?'

'Wouldn't you be, if you thought your grandfather had found something so amazing?'

'She's never seen it.'

'No one has seen it. That's the problem.' Mrs Lionel brushed down her skirt. 'Never mind. Felicity's family should have fun looking. Cup of tea?'

'Why not?'

Rosemary followed Mrs Lionel to the door of The Green Mulbury, pausing as shouting came from the shed of Mulbury Feeds. It stopped just as abruptly as it began. Mrs Lionel appeared not to have heard, but pushed the door open, making the entrance frog croak happily, and held it for Rosemary.

The Green Mulbury was, thanks to Ronnie's volunteer work, fully stocked with its range of green cleaning products. Rows of fragrant soap stood near the counter while tubs of self-serve dishwashing and laundry liquid sat against the wall adjoining The Preserved Mulbury. The other wall had more miscellaneous products, including wash cloths and aprons that Patti Yale had made from neglected tea towels and cotton skirts. The shop smelled fresh, like clothes drying on a summer line. Mrs Lionel led the way through the door into her home where soap sat drying on a table near the window.

Rosemary took a seat at the small dining table as Mrs Lionel filled the kettle. 'Have you seen the girls lately?'

Mrs Lionel took a moment to answer. When she turned to Rosemary, her face was grave. 'Not for a few days. Heather usually comes in to show me her latest taxidermy project, but I haven't seen her.'

'She may not have anything to work on.'

'Oh, she has. I saw her go past with a poor little

mudlark. She seemed happy, all smiles and hums, as she is when Richard is home.'

'That's not how the others are.'

Mrs Lionel opened a tin of gingerbread and placed it in front of Rosemary. 'Holly will be alright. She's the logical one. I do worry about Hannah. Far too fiery, that girl.'

'She has reason.'

Mrs Lionel set a teacup near Rosemary's elbow. 'I know you don't think much of Richard, but he's been through a lot. He suffered greatly when Louisa died. He's never recovered.'

'He had three daughters to look after.'

'He did look after them, in his own way. You must admit, they've turned out alright. Holly and Hannah do a marvellous job with that business, and they keep Heather close.'

Rosemary shook her head slightly, taking a biscuit and ramming most of it in her mouth to stop her saying more.

Mrs Lionel gave her a knowing smile and filled the teacup. 'Don't choke now, dear.'

Rosemary swallowed. 'Sorry. I can't help wanting to wring Richard's neck.'

'Ah.' Mrs Lionel lowered herself into her seat. 'I think you see a bit of Alasdair in him.'

'I don't.'

'You *do*. Richard goes away, just like Alasdair did.'

Rosemary tried not to let the little stab of pain she felt in her gut show on her face, but Mrs Lionel patted her hand and changed the subject to the Mulbury Gala to be held in spring. Rosemary hardly heard her friend's description of a new recycled fashion competition to be sponsored by Patricia's. She ate another two biscuits, savouring the sharpness of the ginger, before allowing herself to speak. 'Patti's a very generous woman.'

'She wants you to judge it.'

Rosemary narrowed her eyes at Mrs Lionel. 'No, she doesn't.'

The older woman grinned. 'No, she doesn't. You're right. There is no competition. I was checking that you were listening.'

'Very funny.'

'Seriously, Rosemary. Be careful with Richard and his girls. Their relationship is delicate. They don't need to lose their father as well as their mother.'

There were no more biscuits left in the tin. Rosemary sighed and leaned back. 'Okay, I'll be good. I won't wring his neck or even yell at him. I will try to be more understanding.'

'That's the way.'

Rosemary stood. 'Now that I've eaten all your biscuits and consumed a pot of tea, I'd better go back and see what's happening in my shop.'

'Yes, it's getting on, isn't it? The day flies by.'

It was Rosemary's intention to go back and check her shelves in order to move the remaining bottles forward to save her fetching new ones from the cellar but, as she went onto the footpath, she saw Jasper Lu outside his shop. 'Jasper,' she said.

'Rosemary.' Jasper stared out into the Square, his arms crossed.

'Are you alright?'

'I am.'

'And Snowy?'

Jasper shook his head. 'Oh, he's as fit as a Mallee bull. Can't you hear him snoring?'

'No.'

'Well, everyone in the shop can. I'm not sure what the vet did to him, but he's been better ever since.'

'It was your threat of a large hole in the backyard.'

'Yes, probably.'

Rosemary studied Jasper's solemn profile.

'Why are you on the footpath?'

'Didn't you hear it?' He pointed.

A branch had fallen from The Exceptional Tree. It was a medium-sized branch, heavy and silver, and had fallen directly onto the barricade that Rakisha had so carefully painted. The top rail was split in two and smothered in leaves.

'It made such a noise,' said Jasper. 'I came rushing out of my shop to see what was going on. But you didn't hear it?'

'We were having tea in Mrs Lionel's kitchen,' said Rosemary. 'The kettle must have been too loud.'

They stared at the Tree. The missing branch made no difference to the Tree's glorious canopy. In fact, it was difficult to notice where it had come from. Rosemary looked harder and could just see where the branch had departed from the trunk. The splintered end poked through the dense covering of leaves like the end of a weapon.

Jasper laughed. 'It seems the Tree doesn't like the barricade, either.'

'No.' Rosemary crossed the road and went over to where the barricade was almost hidden by the fallen limb. It was a wonder that no one else had heard it. She glanced towards The Sweet Potato and heard loud Gregorian chanting coming from within. Rakisha was no doubt grinding legumes and hadn't heard a thing. Kelly Flanagan had a crowd of tourists in her café and, even if she'd heard the crash, she couldn't have come out. In

Franco's patisserie, Rosemary could see Franco furiously putting pies into paper bags. He saw her looking and gave her a one-handed wave before continuing with his task. The only person besides Jasper who'd responded to the crash was Robert Sparkling. He stood outside his garage, hands in his grease-covered overall pockets. He nodded at her, but before she could react, Jasper Lu was back by her side.

'Big, isn't it?'

'The Exceptional Tree doesn't do anything by halves.'

'If someone had been standing underneath that, they would have been killed.'

'Yes.'

'Doesn't that worry you?'

'It's a risk we take to have the Tree in our Square.'

'Which is why they put that barricade up in the first place.'

'Yes.'

Jasper glanced at Rosemary. 'Why do I get the feeling that you're on the side of the Tree?'

'Because I am.'

'But you're not on the side of the barricade.'

'No.'

'Okay, glad I've got that straight.'

They continued to stare at the branch. A group of people came out of Kelly's café and went to stand at the branch as well. There were mutterings. Rosemary heard someone say, 'That is one dangerous tree. They need to cut it down.' She glared at the person speaking, but they were too busy eating a custard tart to notice.

A sudden screech echoed across the Square as Rakisha came out of The Sweet Potato, hands in the air and purple skirts flapping as she ran. 'What happened?'

'The Tree dropped a branch.' Rosemary tipped her head at Rakisha.

'I can see that, darlings,' said Rakisha, a scarf pressed over her mouth. 'But, darlings, the barricade! It's squashed.' She started to laugh, dropped her hands to her thighs, and leaned forward, her grey curls flipping upside down.

Jasper stepped forward in concern. 'Are you alright, Rakisha?'

Rakisha stood up momentarily, grinned at Jasper, then burst into laughter again. She pointed at the fallen branch, waving her finger at the V-shaped top rail of the barricade, and shook her head. 'It won!'

'She's gone mad,' said Jasper quietly to Rosemary.

'No. She's right.' Rosemary gave Rakisha a firm pat on the shoulder. 'Score one to The Exceptional Tree.'

Jasper shook his head. 'You're both mad.'

The rest of the crowd oozed out of Mullings of Mulbury, tailed by Kelly Flanagan, who shut the café door behind her. She rolled her eyes at the branch. 'Darren was right. Branches can drop spontaneously from these old trees.'

'Oh, darling,' Rakisha said, standing straight again and wiping at her eyes. 'That wasn't a spontaneous drop. The Tree *meant* it.'

'Right.' Kelly couldn't keep the disdainful look from her face. 'The Tree did this in a calculated way?'

'Oh, yes, darling. Of course.' Rakisha waggled her finger at the mess and laughed again.

Kelly stared across the branch to Rosemary. 'What do you think?'

'What I think has no bearing on the matter.' Rosemary pulled herself straight. 'Darren's an expert arborist and he had reported that old trees do drop branches. He is right, of course.'

Kelly gave a curt nod. 'You haven't lost your logic, Rosemary Exeter, even if it was my brother who wrote the report.'

'What I think about your brother personally and what his expertise is are two quite different things.'

'Well,' said Jasper, stepping forward and blocking Rosemary's view of Kelly like a boxing umpire signals a break. 'We'd better let the council know so the branch can be cleared away.'

'And the barricade fixed.' Kelly turned back to her shop. 'I'll ring them. At least then I'll know it's been done.'

Jasper and Rosemary helped the hysterical Rakisha back to The Sweet Potato, declining cups of complementary elderberry cordial that she offered as a celebratory drink. They left her with an unsuspecting customer who had to hear the tale of The Exceptional Tree's defiance before she could buy a brownie and went back over the road. Rosemary nodded to Robert, who still stood outside his garage.

'Perhaps he hasn't got much work on,' said Jasper sharply as he noticed her acknowledgement.

'He's new to town so perhaps he hasn't.'

They stopped outside The Read Mulbury. Rosemary noticed Jasper's rakish window display of books about recycling, placed there to benefit Patricia's as well as his own shop.

'Rosemary?'

'Yes?'

But whatever Jasper was going to say was silenced by the sight of Hannah Hubbard storming up the footpath towards Rosemary.

NINE

'That's it!' Hannah came right up to Rosemary and put one hand on her shoulder, giving it a little push. 'I can't stand it any longer. Sorry, Rosemary, I'm coming to stay with you.'

'Right.'

'What's the matter?' asked Jasper. 'You look really flustered.'

'Flustered?' Hannah took her hand off Rosemary's shoulder. '*Flustered* is not the word that I'd use to describe me at the moment. Anyway, is it okay?'

Jasper frowned. 'Is what okay?'

'Rosemary, is it okay if I come to stay with you? I don't take up much room. I'll go straight to work in the morning and then straight to bed when I come home at night. I'll even eat at Kelly's or Franco's. If I have to, I could go to Rakisha's.' Hannah shook her head. 'Whatever it takes. As long as I don't have to be in the house with that man.'

'Your father, you mean?'

'Yes, my father, *that* man.' Her shoulders slumped. 'I don't mean to sound terrible, but I just can't stand him at the minute. He comes home after months away, waltzes in, sits at the kitchen table, plays with Heather's birds, and expects Holly and I to continue with this business that feeds us all. What am I meant to make of that? When he doesn't want to sell it to us?'

'He might have his own reasons for not selling you the business,' said Jasper.

'Well, he's not telling us about it.' A tear gathered in Hannah's eye. 'I don't know what to do.' She coughed, wiped at her eye, and clapped her hands against her side. 'Yes, I do. I'm coming to stay with Rosemary for a while. Once I can talk to Dad without shouting, I'll ask him again. I'll ask him, why can't you sell *us* the business? Don't you think Holly and I run it well enough? Don't you need the money? Can't you go off and find your muse somewhere in Far North Queensland and leave us alone?'

Rosemary glanced at Jasper, who was biting his lower lip. 'I can see you're really angry, Hannah,' she said. 'You can stay with me as long as you want but sooner or later you will have to confront Richard and try to understand any reasons why he won't sell you the business. You don't have to eat at Kelly's, or Franco's or even Rakisha's. Sunny and I have early dinners. You're always welcome to join us.'

Hannah's face brightened, and she pushed her hair behind her ears. 'Thanks, Rosemary, you're wonderful. I'll get my things.'

Hannah turned and ran back down to Mulbury Feeds where Rosemary could just make out Holly's head sticking out around the shed door. As Hannah came up to her sister, Holly grabbed her arms with both hands and spoke sternly up into her face. Rosemary couldn't hear what they were saying, but she got the gist. It was a big sister telling a middle sister off.

'Well,' said Jasper. 'It's certainly been an eventful day. Do you think you'll cope with her?'

'There's nothing to cope with, Jasper,' said Rosemary. 'Hannah's usually a very easy-going person. She'll be a good guest.'

'I'll leave you to it, then,' said Jasper, as he spied a group of three older men pushing their way into The Read Mulbury.

Rosemary jangled back into her shop. There was little to do this late on a Saturday afternoon. She tallied the month's takings and noted them down on the paper in front of her. For the middle of winter, it hadn't been so bad. Of course, finding a skeleton in someone's backyard certainly helped business. The news of the skeleton had reached Big Town. It was in the paper, Honey had said, and once it got into the paper in Big Town, it made it to the city papers as well. Sightseers flocked to Mulbury for a day or two after the news. Now there were only trickles of people who seemed to expect the skeleton displayed at the front of Jasper's bookshop. While they were disappointed that it wasn't, they were quite happy to buy books and jams instead.

Rosemary had no further customers for the rest of the afternoon and Hannah hadn't returned as quickly as she'd surmised. At five minutes to five o'clock, Rosemary left the shop counter and went to close the door and pull down the blinds. Just as she clicked the lock shut on the door, a person appeared behind it waving frantically. 'Just a moment, Hannah,' said Rosemary. 'I'll let you in.'

But it wasn't Hannah. The person standing on the foot-path was a small woman, older than Rosemary by a good ten years. She was quivering.

Rosemary stared. 'Are you alright?' she said.

'Oh yes,' said the woman. 'I'm just a bit nervous.'

'Nervous about what?'

'About being in Mulbury.'

'Why would you be nervous being in Mulberry?'

'Because I haven't been here since I was a girl.'

Rosemary tipped her head and studied the woman closely. She bore a resemblance to someone, but Rosemary couldn't think who. 'Would you like to come in?'

'If you don't mind.'

The woman stepped through the door, pulling her jacket closely around her. She gazed at the shelves full of pickles and jams but didn't seem to take any of it in. 'This used to be a different shop,' she said.

'Yes,' said Rosemary. 'A sweets shop.'

'Yes, that's right.' The woman turned a complete circle. 'I remember the skylight,' she said. 'Or do I? Was the skylight always here?'

'No,' said Rosemary. 'I put it in. The shop was dark, which is good for preserves, but makes it hard to work in all day. I had this special skylight made.'

'Well, there you go.' The woman stopped spinning and smiled at Rosemary. 'How your mind tricks you when you're young. It's like noticing how everything is really quite small which is the opposite of how you think when you've only seen things as a child.'

'You lived here?'

'Yes, I did. It was just my father and me.'

'You lived with your father?'

'I did. After my mother died.'

'Where did you live?'

'We lived in the printery.' The woman looked Rosemary squarely in the eye. 'I'm Tabitha Connelly.'

Now Rosemary could see the resemblance of the

Tabitha Connelly in front of her to the picture of Dr Tabitha Connelly that Jasper had found. The Tabitha in front of her was a small, round woman with shoulder-length silver hair. The Tabitha in the photograph that Jasper had found was thin and frowning, with her hair in a short bob. But they had the same eyes, a heavy, blue gaze that was locked on Rosemary at that moment. 'Tabitha,' said Rosemary. 'You've heard the news.'

'It wasn't news to me.' Tabitha put her hands on her hips and gazed at the ceiling, not, Rosemary suspected, to study the skylight. 'My mother hadn't committed suicide. I knew she would be found somewhere other than a mineshaft.'

'What made you think that?'

Tabitha sighed. 'I don't really know exactly,' she said. 'As a child, I felt deep in my heart that my mother wouldn't do that to me. She was a lovely woman, as much as I can remember, anyway.'

'We remember things quite differently as children,' said Rosemary.

'But she wouldn't have left me with just my father. Surely not.'

'Was your father awful to you?'

'No,' Tabitha said. 'My father was perfectly wonderful to me. I don't ever remember him raising his voice. Especially after my mother died, he was particularly nice to me.'

'You think your mother didn't commit suicide?'

'I know that for sure. There were no deep mineshafts in the backyard.'

'Obviously,' said Rosemary. 'But her body could have been shifted.'

Tabitha shook her head. 'That wouldn't make sense.

Why move her when she'd been reported missing? No, she was murdered.'

'Murdered by whom?'

'If I knew that, I wouldn't be standing here in your shop.'

'Why *are* you standing here in my shop?'

'I went to the bookshop but there are people in there. I'm not really into fashion so I wouldn't go to that shop on the end. I came in here because you were the next shop.'

'Is that right?'

'Not entirely.' The woman let the bag slip from her shoulders to the floor with a bang. She folded her arms and looked at Rosemary again. There was something deeply sad in those blue eyes, Rosemary could see it now. 'I came in here because I don't know what else to do.'

'How about a cup of tea for starters?'

'Why not? Tea solves everything, doesn't it?'

'No. It's just an excuse to stop for a moment.'

Rosemary led the way through the doorway from the shop into her house. Sunny eyed the stranger balefully from her spot on the windowsill. She stretched and jumped gracefully to the floor once Rosemary had placed chopped chicken pieces into her bowl.

'What a beautiful cat,' said Tabitha. 'Such a glorious summery colour.' Sunny twitched her tail in response.

'Yes. Beautiful and intelligent.'

'The best kind of cat, then.'

'Please, take a seat.'

Tabitha slid into a kitchen chair and put her clasped hands on the table. She nodded in acknowledgement as Rosemary put a hearty mug of tea in front of her.

'I thought that a cup wouldn't do.'

'Thank you.' Tabitha extended her left hand to take the mug. 'I'm sorry, but I don't even know your name.'

'Rosemary Exeter. You haven't had the advantage of a photograph of me in the newspaper after a doctorate conferral.'

Tabitha nearly choked on her tea. 'You saw that? Why? Are you thinking of doing one as well?'

'No. I have no interest and no point. Ronnie found your photograph. He's a private investigator on your mother's case. He's also my son-in-law.'

'Oh, that's useful.'

'That he's my son-in-law?'

Tabitha laughed. *The first relaxed noise she's made,* thought Rosemary. 'I was thinking more that it's useful for me that he's working on my mother's case.'

'It may take some time to prove the skeleton is your mother,' said Rosemary.

Tabitha shook her head. 'They'll get there eventually when they match my DNA with that of the bones. I'm already convinced.'

'Apart from thinking that your mother was lovely, do you know anything else that makes you think it's impossible that your mother died at her own hand?'

Tabitha gazed at the steam coming from her mug. 'I know what you're thinking. Most people find it impossible to imagine that a loved and loving parent could take their own life, which is ridiculous. There are many reasons why people feel low enough to do it. But in my mother's case, it was impossible. It must be.' She glanced at Rosemary. 'I can see on your face that you feel sorry for me. Don't. I'm not mad or sad. Well, I am sad. Very sad. Not a bad sort of sad, just sad like anyone would be if they had been presented with bones instead of a live mother.' She gasped. 'Oh, that sounded terrible.'

'I get it,' said Rosemary.

'Thanks.' Tabitha sighed, a long wobbling noise that made Sunny turn her head.

'What now, then?'

'Yes, well, what now?' Tabitha drank heartily. 'Now that I'm here, and I see Mulbury as a strange land, I don't know what to do. I *do* know that I would like to see where my mother has spent the last seventy years. Maybe it would make me feel better?'

Rosemary leaned over to see out the glass doors to the sky above Mulbury. It was already dark, and the strong twinkling of the Milky Way indicated that the night would be cold. 'Visit Jasper tomorrow.'

'Jasper?'

'Jasper Lu. He owns The Read Mulbury. The bookshop. He found the skeleton.'

'He's the gorgeous one with the long hair?'

Rosemary thought about that for a moment. Jasper had an appeal that she wouldn't call *gorgeous,* more of a gentle look that was borne of his empathy and kindness. But he certainly had long hair. It hung in dark lengths over his shoulder blades. 'Yes. That's him.'

'Alright then, I'll see him tomorrow. You think he will show me the site?'

'Without doubt.'

Tabitha stood. 'It looks like I'm here for the night. Where would you recommend I stay?'

'There are a number of bed and breakfast places you could try, although some close for the winter. There are motels in Big Town.'

'Thank you for the tea.' Tabitha shrugged her bag up on

her shoulder. 'I'm sorry you had to see me like this. I'm not usually so...flimsy. It's the reminder of Mum. I still miss her.'

'I can see that.' Rosemary stood up as well. 'Dr Connelly, why don't you stay here for the night? It's quite late to go searching for a place to stay. I have a spare bedroom that I thought was going to be full tonight but apparently not. It's already made up.'

'Oh, well, that's very kind of you.' Tabitha smiled. 'If you're sure you wouldn't be put out? Perhaps I could shout dinner in exchange? I hear there's a very good restaurant in Mulbury.'

'The Leftover is a credit to the town.' Rosemary indicated the room coming off the back of the living area. 'Please, put your things in there.'

'If you're sure it's alright, I'll go and get my bag from the car. It's so very kind of you, really. I didn't expect it.'

Rosemary smiled. 'I'll let you out.'

They walked to the front door of the shop. Tabitha let Rosemary go first so she could work the lock and set the bell jangling. As she pulled the door open, she frightened Hannah Hubbard who stood with her fist raised ready to knock. 'Hannah!'

'Sorry, I'm later than I thought. Had to do some stacking and then the books and then I left a list of instructions for Holly in case something goes wrong even though I'm only next door.'

'You're staying tonight?'

'Yes, is that okay?' Hannah peered around Rosemary and spotted Tabitha. 'You've already got company?'

'The couch is yours if you want it.'

'Yeah, I do. I don't want to be in the house when Dad comes in.'

'Perhaps I should find somewhere else to stay?' asked Tabitha.

'No, we'll be fine.' Rosemary didn't dare look through the shop to where Sunny would be sitting, tail lashing at the unexpected visitors. 'We'll be dining at The Leftover Restaurant.'

'Really? Oh, how awesome is that! I'll just dump my stuff in there.' Hannah made her way past Rosemary, introduced herself hastily to Tabitha, and then ran into the house to put her bag on the couch. She was back just as Tabitha retrieved her own bag and placed it inside. 'Let's go.'

They crossed the road and walked to the old building that housed Jules and Roman's restaurant.

'Uh oh,' said Hannah, coming to a halt. 'Perhaps we shouldn't be eating here tonight.'

From inside came the sounds of shouting.

TEN

The door of The Leftover Restaurant was open, leading to a long, tastefully lit corridor which ended in a dazzle of light. The old building had once been a bank but the next generation to own it had closed in the tellers' area, creating an intimate series of rooms left and right. For some reason, the contemporary builders had left the long, wooden counter as it had been, making it look cramped in the remaining space. Roman and Jules used it as a dinner table, but one that had high-backed stools as seats. As Rosemary made her way down the corridor, she could see Felicity's family seated around the counter like a raucous bridal party at a medieval wedding. The noise so clearly heard outside was like Wall Street before the bells inside.

Hannah came up behind Rosemary. 'Who are they? Are they happy?'

Rosemary checked each person in front of them. Felicity was yelling at Leif who sat at the opposite end of the table. Calvin was trying to command the band of cousins who shouted past him to siblings seated away from them. Standing at the head, grinning broadly through his thick moustaches, was Roman. He held a large plate of sliced roasted meat from which rose a rich, beefy fragrance. He was speaking as well, but no one turned his way. 'They're Roman and Jules' family,' said Rosemary. 'Yes, they are happy.'

Roman caught sight of the small group standing in bewilderment at the entrance and waved them over. He set the plate of meat down. It was immediately attacked by seven hungry people who piled their plates, shouting appreciatively to the chef who bowed his head and left them to it. 'Hello, Rosemary, Hannah. You have a guest for dinner this evening?' He turned his smile to Tabitha, bobbing down a little so she could look up at him more easily. 'Welcome to the Leftover Restaurant.'

'Thank you,' said Tabitha, brushing her hair back from her reddened face. 'Why do you call it the *Leftover*? I mean, it's charming, but left over from what, exactly?'

'Oh.' Roman grinned. 'It's because we use what our local farmers and gardeners have left over. Rosemary's excess tomatoes, for example. Mrs Lionel's excellent oregano. And I grow my own happy beef kettle.'

Tabitha looked surprised.

'He means cattle,' said Hannah. 'Don't you, Roman?'

'Ah, my little Hannah, you know exactly what I mean.' Roman held his hand out. 'This way.'

He led the group to a table at the edge of the room and pulled Tabitha's chair out for her. The noise from the counter had settled, mainly, Rosemary suspected, because the family had their mouths full. Roman glanced at them, smiling fondly, then turned back to his other guests.

'Thank you for fitting us in, Roman,' said Rosemary, picking up a menu.

'It is always a pleasure to have you dine with us.' Roman

shook his head at Rosemary. 'You could do so more often to give us more pleasure.'

Rosemary thought of her quiet living room, Sunny on the couch beside her, a winter fire glowing softly, and a homemade pasty waiting on a plate on the coffee table. 'I like my solitude.'

'Yes, Rosemary my friend, I know you do. But you can have solitude and peace at The Leftover Restaurant.' Roman smiled as Leif guffawed loudly. 'Perhaps not tonight. I will ask Jules to tend to you.' He bowed again and walked swiftly back to his kitchen.

'He seems a lovely man,' said Tabitha, looking around at the room's splendour. 'Is everyone pleasant in Mulbury?'

'No,' said Rosemary and Hannah together.

Tabitha laughed. With that, something stiff fell away from her face. Rosemary watched as the frown lines softened on Tabitha's forehead, and her eyes brightened.

They studied the menu in silence for a while until Hannah closed hers with a sigh and leaned back in her chair. 'I haven't been out for dinner in years! Is this what it's like to relax?'

'It sounds like you work very hard then,' said Tabitha. 'What is it that you do?'

'My sisters and I run the animal produce store.' Hannah glared at Rosemary. 'With our father, apparently.'

'That does sound busy.'

'It's a thriving business,' said Rosemary, closing the menu as well. 'Holly, Hannah and Heather work very hard.'

'Well, not Heather. I mean, she works, but not hard.'

'She works hard at her taxidermy.'

'Oh, yes. She works hard at that. She's a bird taxidermist,' Hannah said to Tabitha.

'Goodness, that's an interesting hobby for a young girl.'

'Is it?' Hannah looked genuinely puzzled. 'What's being a girl got to do with it?'

Tabitha blushed. 'Oh, I'm sorry, Hannah. I didn't mean to imply... I just don't know anyone who does taxidermy and, when I think about it, I'm taken back to creepy museums full of scary stuffed animals that I went to as a child.'

'Heather would like nothing more than a creepy museum full of stuffed birds. Can you imagine, Rosemary? We'd never get her out of there.'

'True,' said Rosemary. 'Heather's taxidermy is an obsession, not a hobby.'

'Oh dear,' said Tabitha. 'Now I've offended both of you.'

'No,' said Rosemary. 'But you will find Mulbury very protective of Heather.'

'She sounds very special.'

'*Special* is only one word I've heard to describe my younger sister.' Hannah rolled her eyes and yawned.

The door to the kitchen flung open, and Jules stepped out. Her elegance was apparent even in plain white shirt and black trousers with a slim apron tied neatly at her waist. 'Roman said it was you,' she said as she arrived at the table. 'We are honoured to have you here, Rosemary. And, of course, Hannah and... my apologies, I don't know you.'

'Tabitha Connelly.' Tabitha reached out to shake Jules' hand.

'Oh. Connelly?' Jules glanced at Rosemary.

'Yes,' said Rosemary. 'Tabitha's father owned the printery that is now Jasper's bookshop.'

Jules nodded slowly. 'I see. Then I must extend my condolences to you on the finding of your mother's remains.'

'Those remains haven't been confirmed as Agnes Connelly's,' said Rosemary.

'I'm afraid we've all reached our own conclusion.' Jules put a soft hand on Tabitha's shoulder.

'Thank you for your thoughts.' Tabitha dabbed at the corner of her eye with her serviette. 'Does the whole of Mulbury think the same?'

'Those who care.' Jules gave Tabitha a squeeze before taking her hand away. 'We are very close-knit. Some more than others.'

The family at the counter increased their noise level. Leif had his glass raised, toasting something someone had said. Jules smiled affectionately.

'I didn't know you had so many grandchildren,' said Hannah, staring across the room.

'Four,' said Jules. 'Calvin is an extra. Lovely boy. Lovely family.' She smiled. 'Noisy, though. Our house will be ringing by the time they leave.'

'How long are they staying?' asked Tabitha.

'They haven't said but they have a couple of weeks' digging planned.' Jules widened her eyes at Rosemary. 'They're digging for the Hand of Hela.'

'I thought the Hand had already been dug up.'

'My grandfather found it when he was ploughing a paddock, but the family story goes that he re-buried it.'

'Why would he do that?' asked Hannah. 'I would have sold it in a heartbeat. Imagine how much it was worth!'

'Well now, that was the problem. Having sudden wealth—or the thought of sudden wealth—doesn't always bring out the best in people. Grandpa's brothers came around and demanded their share. The fighting could be heard for miles around. In the morning, Grandpa came into town, battered and bruised, and left on the train for the city. He never recontacted his family and the Hand of Hela wasn't seen again. He left a note that read "back from whence it came and can't cause any further woe".'

'What happened then?'

'The brothers tried looking for it but all they got for their trouble was a beating from Grandma's broom. She had two children to raise alone after that, and she never stopped blaming the brothers. And the gold. She became quite wealthy herself but not from finding a gold nugget. She bred cattle, the descendants of which we use for the restaurant. But you would not know that Grandma was rich. She lived a plain and simple life and left most of her money in a trust for single mothers.'

'That's a great story,' said Tabitha.

'It's a family legend.' Jules held her notebook up. 'Now, what would you like for dinner?'

As they ordered, Rosemary saw Felicity look across at her mother and, for the first time that evening, notice Rosemary and her comrades. She raised a hand in recognition, slid from her seat, and almost ran over to the little table. Although she didn't move quite as elegantly as her mother, Rosemary saw similarity in the shape of her face. 'Mum! This is the lady who told me where you were this afternoon.'

'Rosemary, you've met Felicity? And this is Hannah and Tabitha.'

'So pleased to meet you. Again.' Felicity shook each person's hand in turn. 'What I mean is, I'm sure I've met you all at some stage when I've been visiting Grum and Pops, but I had a terrible head for faces, if you get what I mean.'

'I've never met you,' said Hannah. 'I'd remember.'

'Always a first time, then!'

'I'm afraid I haven't met you, either. I don't live in Mulbury,' said Tabitha.

'Oh, either do we. We are city folk, really, caught up in that world too much.' Felicity looped her arm through her mother's and hugged it close. 'I am disgusted with myself that we don't visit often.'

'You're here now.' Jules gave her daughter's arm a squeeze, then pulled her own out of the grip and turned toward Rosemary's table. 'I'll deliver your order to Roman or you'll never eat.'

'Well,' said Felicity, 'I hope I see all of you around this week as we go about the business of finding the Hand of Hela!' She put one arm up dramatically, laughed, and ran back to her family.

'Such energy,' said Tabitha.

'She'd need it with that lot,' said Hannah. 'Can you pass me a bread roll, Rosemary? I'm starving.'

It didn't take long for their meals to be served. As they ate, Hannah told Tabitha about the world of animal produce: the amount of hay they bought, the special bags of feed for orphaned animals, and the tins of molasses that the older farmers bought as treats for their ancient horses. Tabitha nodded enthusiastically and kept her eyes on Hannah, leaving Rosemary to study them both. There were lines of dirt on Hannah's face, possibly where she'd wiped a hand to get the hair out of her eyes while unloading chaff bags. She had dark shadows under her bright eyes as well. Rosemary had seen her come back from early-morning bike rides when it was still dark, meaning that despite working hard all day, Hannah rose very early to keep her kilometres up. Burning the candles at both ends, as Aunt Lilibeth would have said.

Tabitha, though, had a different type of tiredness to her

pallor. Even though, after a glass of fine wine and halfway through a meal of crab apple and chilli glazed beef, Tabitha seemed relaxed and happy, Rosemary still saw the shadow of troubles on the woman's face. It was like an imprint of unhappiness which, she supposed, was related to the early and sudden loss of her mother. While Hannah and her sisters had experienced much the same, at least the Hubbard sisters had been given time to say goodbye to their precious mother. Rosemary found it hard to imagine what it must have been like for a three-year-old to wake up to a motherless life.

'Don't you reckon, Rosemary?' Hannah had her fork poised as she stared.

'Didn't hear you, Hannah. What were you saying?'

'That the Mulbury Gala will be a big hit this year.'

'It's always a big hit.'

'This year, it will be a bigger hit.'

'Why?'

'Every year it gets better and better. The committee will plan something amazing.'

Rosemary said nothing. She was on that committee and it was yet to meet.

A whoop of thunderous noise came from the tellers' counter as Roman emerged from the kitchen holding aloft a three-tiered cake blazing with candles. He placed it near the youngest child and bowed. 'Happy birthday, Eliza!'

The girl shook her head. 'But, Pops, it isn't my birthday!'

'Oh dear.' Roman lifted the cake and put it down in front of the other fair-haired child. 'Happy birthday, Antonio!'

'Pops, it's not my birthday, either!'

Roman moved the cake to the other side of the table. 'Then it must be Penelope's.'

'No,' said the tween, face bright red. 'Not mine.'

Roman shook his head, shifted the cake with its dripping candles along the table, and said, 'So, Marco, happy birthday!'

'I know what you're doing here, Pops.' The dark-haired boy slid the cake carefully along to Calvin. 'Happy birthday, Calvin! And happy birthday, everyone.'

'Yes,' said Roman, hands on hips and head to the side. 'I have missed making cake for my gemstone grandchildren and so we share this one together, even though no one has their birthday this month. Happy birthdays!'

'I think he meant *precious* grandchildren,' said Hannah to Tabitha.

'Ah,' said Tabitha, watching as Roman pulled a large knife from a scabbard lying against his leg and offered it to Calvin, who snuffed out the remaining burning candles with his fingers before pushing the knife deep into the cake.

Before the family had eaten the entire thing, Leif brought slices to the little table, setting the plate down in the middle. 'There you are,' he said, wiping his hand across his mouth. 'I have no idea what it is except that it is one of the most delicious things I have ever tasted. What a shame there's not an actual birthday this month to celebrate.'

Rosemary put her head down so he couldn't see her face.

'That's very generous of you,' said Tabitha, helping herself to a slab.

'Rum baba with caramelised oranges,' said Rosemary. 'I've never seen it tiered.'

'Roman doesn't just cook, does he?' Hannah's voice was muffled by cake. 'He creates. He sort of reminds me of Heather.'

Rosemary pursed her lips at that comparison, but

Hannah had her head down, eating. In a way, the creative process was probably the same no matter what art developed. It required imagination and courage. Roman and Heather had both.

They staggered out of the restaurant before the family's combined birthday parties had finished. Hannah went straight for the couch, sweeping a disgruntled Sunny into her arms before collapsing back on the pillows.

'Thank you for a lovely evening,' said Tabitha, smiling at the half-asleep young woman. 'I think I'll go to bed now, if you don't mind.'

'Not at all,' said Rosemary.

Tabitha made her way to the spare bedroom before turning back to the others. 'I hope that family finds what they're looking for.'

'I hope they don't,' said Hannah, eyes closed. 'I believe what Jules said.'

'Oh?'

Hannah opened her eyes and stared not at Tabitha but at Rosemary. 'Sudden wealth. It could change someone and not for the better.'

'You think it will affect your father?'

'Maybe. What do you think?'

Obviously, Rosemary took too long to answer. Hannah slid back on the couch, her hands falling away from the cat who took the opportunity to jump down and stalk back to her place near the fire. Rosemary covered the sleeping young woman with a blanket.

It wasn't until Rosemary was in her own bed, Sunny curled up on the duvet next to her, that she thought about the yearning in Tabitha's last sentence. 'Finding out family secrets is not always what it's cracked up to be,' she said softly to Sunny, who purred in agreement.

ELEVEN

Tabitha was not an early riser. Hannah and Rosemary had breakfast together as the sun rose, keeping their conversation quiet for the sake of their guest. Sunny was not so considerate. She yowled at her empty plate, startling Rosemary. 'You never do that,' said the cat's mistress, tipping kibble into the vessel. Sunny's tailed twitched. *Ah, but I can when I want to.*

'I've always loved Sunny,' said Hannah, chewing on muesli. 'I love the way she sits on the windowsill and looks out into the world as if she's seen it all before. Do you think she has? Seen it all before?'

'I don't believe in reincarnation.'

'Either do I normally, but animals like Sunny make me wonder.' Hannah finished her cereal and reached for a slice of toast. 'Percy was like that as well. He was, I don't know, *joyous* all the time. I used to think that he knew life was short and to make the most of it.' For a split second, Hannah's shoulders slumped. 'As if the rest of us hadn't figured that out yet.'

'You're thinking of Louisa.'

Hannah sighed. 'I've been thinking about Mum more than usual. I don't know why.'

'Is it because of the skeleton? Tabitha's mother?'

'I'm not sure. Maybe that discovery has made it worse, but I was thinking of her more even before Jasper dug his hole.'

'It's to do with your father.'

Hannah crunched her toast for a moment before answering. 'Yeah, I reckon. I can't help wondering what our lives—what Dad's life—would have been like if Mum had lived. Would we have kept the produce store? Would we have even stayed in Mulbury?'

'I'll tell you what I think.' Rosemary pushed her plate aside and gave Hannah a long look. 'Wondering whether our lives would be different if our paths had gone in another direction is a complete waste of time. We have no other path than the one we're on. The future might allow us to change but we have no control over the past.'

Hannah nodded slowly. 'I hear you, Rosemary. I do. I'm just not at the stage that I can take it on.'

'That's okay. You'll get there.'

Hannah rubbed a hand across her face and leaned back in the chair. 'It must be good being old. You can leave so much mess behind.'

Before Rosemary could think of a response, the door to the spare bedroom opened and Tabitha stepped out wrapped in an old dressing gown of Rosemary's which trailed behind her like a battered wedding dress.

'Hello,' said Hannah. 'I hope we didn't wake you.'

Tabitha waved vaguely in their direction and staggered off to the bathroom with the towel Rosemary had left on the bed under her arm.

'Some people are not good morning people,' said Rosemary as she rose to refill the kettle.

By the time Tabitha had showered, dressed and presented herself to the kitchen, Hannah had gone to work. Rosemary was utilising the time waiting for her guest by grating lemon rind for more lemon butter. Tabitha sat down heavily at the table, her head in her hands. She looked up after a minute. 'Sorry, I'm not a morning-'

'I understand.' Rosemary held up a cup and Tabitha smiled briefly. 'You don't have to talk until you've had tea.'

Tabitha raised her hand gratefully before letting it drop to the tabletop.

It took two cups of tea before the words started to flow.

'I must visit the bookshop before it gets busy.'

'No hurry,' said Rosemary, stirring her condiment. 'Sundays in winter are slow starters for Mulbury, especially on a day like this one when the sun is hidden.'

'Should I hurry up before it rains?'

'It won't rain. It's too cold.'

Tabitha laughed quietly and reached for a bowl. 'I've never understood that saying,' she said as she poured cereal.

'It's more evident in the country than the city.'

'And more evident down here in the south.' Tabitha spooned breakfast into her mouth and chewed thoughtfully. 'I suppose I should ask Jarrod if it's okay to visit today.'

'I've already asked him. It's *Jasper*.'

'Oh, sorry. I'm really not awake yet.'

Rosemary was genuinely surprised at how long it took one person, who'd slept all night, to wake up fully. The shop was open, and the freshly made lemon butter had sold out by the time Tabitha appeared in the doorway looking bright. She'd pinned her hair back girlishly. Rosemary had a glimpse of what a three-year-old Tabitha may have been like. 'I'll come with you to Jasper's,' she said.

'You don't need to if you're busy.'

Rosemary indicated the tourist bus pulling away from the otherwise empty curb. 'The town is empty for the moment. It happens like that. Bus in, people out. People in, bus gone.'

'Well, if you have the time...'

Rosemary pulled the jangling door closed behind them, flipping the card that said *Back in 5 pickly minutes*. She walked slowly beside Tabitha, matching her usual gait to the shorter legs of her companion. Patti waved at them from the racks outside her shop where she was showing a particularly well-dressed woman her merchandise, and Rosemary nodded back. The heavy door of The Read Mulbury sighed as she swung it open for Tabitha, who stepped in eagerly and stopped.

'Oh.'

Rosemary squeezed past Tabitha's frozen form so she could shut the door. 'Everything alright?'

Tabitha didn't answer. She stood with her eyes closed, breathing deeply. Jasper came striding through the shop to greet them, and Rosemary held her hand up so that he stopped a few metres away. 'What is it?' he whispered.

Rosemary shrugged and pointed to Tabitha, who now had a hand on her chest and was breathing like a weightlifter about to break a world record.

Jasper hooked his hair behind his ears, looking wildly around him until he saw a chair angled on to a bookshelf. He reached over and pulled it across to Tabitha, putting one hand on her shoulder. 'How about you sit down?'

Tabitha's eyes shot open. 'Oh. No. I'm fine. Who are you?'

'I'm Jasper Lu. I'm the one who found...who was digging the hole...' Jasper glanced across to Rosemary for help.

'Jasper owns the shop.'

'Yes, yes, of course.' Tabitha put one hand on her cheek. 'Do you know I haven't been in this building since we left when I was twelve years old. That's almost sixty-two years ago. But...' Her voice softened as she looked around. 'There's something about the smell that took me right back.'

'I have a lot of old books,' said Jasper, indicating the rows of leather-bound treasures on the wall. 'Perhaps their smell is a bit like a printery?'

'That might be it. Sense memory is an odd thing. The look of something, the feel, the smell...those things add up to recreate memories.' Tabitha walked slowly through the shop, running her hand along books that caught her interest. 'I'm really glad that you aren't a vegan coffee shop or something.'

'No, I leave that up to Rakisha across the road.'

Tabitha turned, a smile relaxing her features. 'Really? There *is* a vegan coffee shop in Mulbury? Dad would be turning in his grave.'

'Talking about...' Jasper's face warmed. 'Would you like to see outside?'

'Thank you.'

Jasper led them through the shop into the cosy darkness of his living area and towards the kitchen. As Tabitha reached the couch, Snowy gave a woofy snore, making her jump. 'Oh, a dog!'

Snowy woke enough to wag his tail at the acknowledgement, no small feat as he was in his customary position on his back with his head hanging slightly over the couch edge.

'That's Snowy. He's the one...well, I was digging the hole because of him.'

'Oh, dear, he was that sick?'

'No,' said Rosemary. 'He's not sick at all. He's old and likes to sleep a lot, something that I think he's allowed to do.'

'He was a bit sick,' said Jasper defensively. 'He coughed.'

'Once.' Rosemary shook her head. 'That's what you said.'

'Anyway,' said Jasper. 'The vet was concerned, and I was preparing for the worst.'

'I'm very glad you were,' said Tabitha. 'Or you would never have found what you found.'

Rosemary was sure, if Tabitha hadn't been looking directly at Jasper, that he would have stuck his tongue out at Rosemary. Instead, he led them out of the kitchen and down the back steps to where the hole lay still exposed but without its police tape.

Tabitha stood at its edge for a moment before sinking to her knees. Rosemary and Jasper knelt on either side of her, lacing their arms around her back in support. Tabitha nodded gratefully. 'Sorry, it's just so...raw.'

They stayed there for quite some time as Tabitha cried quietly. Rosemary felt Jasper's arm cross over hers, holding strongly. She watched him, and saw a tear roll down his face as well. Unable to do anything else in case Tabitha tipped over, she put her cheek momentarily on his sleeve. He gave her a quick smile, rubbing his face on his free arm and staring out over the backyard where magpies were scrutinising the ground for worms.

At last, Tabitha straightened. Rosemary and Jasper let their arms fall away and eased themselves up. Tabitha took Jasper's extended hand and stood unsteadily. The movement caused some dirt to fall into the hole. She sniffed. 'Could we fill it in now?'

Jasper checked with Rosemary, who shrugged. 'Yes. We haven't been told we can't.'

'I'd like to do that.'

Jasper went to his tool shed and brought back two shovels and a rake. The hole had been widely excavated by the forensic science team. Tabitha took a shovel but quickly ran out of steam, leaving the filling to Jasper and Rosemary. They worked steadily until Tabitha could finish the business off by raking the soil flat. 'Well,' she said. 'I guess that's that.'

Rosemary said nothing.

Jasper took the tools to the shed and steered Tabitha back into the warm kitchen where they washed their hands. Rosemary put on the kettle with the expectation that Tabitha would need tea heavily laced with sugar, while Jasper went to check the shop.

As Tabitha sat quietly at the table, Rosemary waited impatiently for the kettle to finish. Over its rumbling, she could hear Jasper's customer talking, not in the slightly reverent way people normally talked when they entered the bookshop, but in a firm, expectant tone that usually heralded a request. She made tea as quickly as she could, placing it in front of Tabitha and checking that the woman was alright before stepping into the shop to see what was happening.

Patti Yale stood halfway down the shelves, her face bright and her hair brighter. She swung a little as she stood, making the rockabilly dress she was wearing twist back and forth. She waved at Rosemary, then clapped her hands quietly once or twice, wobbling her head towards the shop counter where Jasper stood listening to the smartly dressed woman who Rosemary recognised had been studying Patti's frocks.

'Your mother, you say?' asked the woman, pointing a deep red nail at a row of books behind the counter.

'T. G. G. Duncan was my mother, yes.'

'You found this out when?'

'A few months ago.'

'So, what, for...' The woman studied Jasper closely '... fifty years you didn't know your mother was a famous writer of speculative fiction?'

'Fifty-five years, actually. And Space Westerns, specifically.'

The woman tapped her fingertip on her lips, making Rosemary curious to see whether she would stab herself. After a long minute's silence, Patti bounced forward. 'Rosemary, this is Adelia. She bought my rugby tulle garment.'

'My mother bought it.' Adelia raised a perfectly arched eyebrow. 'It is magnificent.'

'Oh, sweetie,' said Patti, flushing violently and seeming to have no awareness that *sweetie* was the last endearment Rosemary would have thought to bestow on a person that looked like Adelia Lochard.

Adelia moved her finger to point directly at Patti. '*You* are a genius. It's why I'm here.'

'Ah,' said Jasper. 'The film clip.'

'I label my works as cinematic creations. *Film clip* sounds so '80s, don't you think?'

From the startled look on Jasper's face, Rosemary suspected that Jasper hadn't thought much about film clips ever. 'You are Adelia Lochard,' she said.

'Yes.' Adelia shifted her gaze to Rosemary. 'You are aware of my work?'

'No.'

'Shame.' Adelia used her sharp nail to move a strand of hair carefully away from her face. 'You should watch my last few years. I have developed enormously.' She took a moment to survey the rest of The Read Mulbury.

Rosemary felt movement behind her and turned to see a pale Tabitha standing in the doorway, looking lost. 'Would you like more tea?' Rosemary asked, moving to the woman's side. 'Perhaps a biscuit? If Jasper has any left.' She gave Jasper a meaningful stare.

'Oh, yes. Franco's Florentines are in the tin next to the bread. I'm sure there are a couple left.'

Rosemary steered Tabitha back to the kitchen chair and settled her in before finding the tin. She could hear a new conversation starting, this time around holes in backyards. She rattled the tin to cover the noise, but Tabitha was looking out the window lost in thought and didn't seem to hear.

Fresh tea made, Rosemary slid into the chair next to Tabitha and helped herself to a biscuit. 'How are you now?'

Tabitha rolled her shoulders and took up her cup. 'Sorry, Rosemary. I didn't expect to feel quite as *affected* as this. It's not like I'm a young, emotional thing.' She laughed quietly. 'Quite the contrary. I forgot how the senses invoke memory, which is naughty of me, seeing as my doctoral thesis was on just that.'

'Fragrant memories.' Rosemary shrugged as Tabitha gave her a quick look. 'That was its title. It was in the paper.'

'Oh. It was about using the senses as an aide-memoir.'

'Interesting.'

'I thought so. It's like Marcel Proust said. "The smell and taste of things remain poised a long time, ready to remind us."' She shrugged. 'I didn't think it would ever apply to me.'

'I imagine that's a common thought researchers make.'

'Hmm.'

Rosemary heard the heavy sigh of the shop door and then Jasper was back in the house, stooping to pat Snowy before going straight for the teapot. 'Well, there you go.'

'There you go *what*?' asked Rosemary.

'That woman. Adelia. She's here to see Patti's designs.'

'Yes. We caught Patti treasure hunting.'

'We did, we did.' Jasper took a long swig of tea. 'She also wants to make me the subject of a film. A documentary.'

'That's good,' said Tabitha. 'Isn't it? Something about the shop?'

Jasper shook her head. 'I don't think she cares too much for the shop, to tell you the truth. What she said was, "You have all the angles of a great story."'

'What does that mean, do you think?'

'I'm really not sure.' Jasper leaned back on the bench. 'What do you think, Rosemary?'

Rosemary thought of Adelia's unsmiling face. 'I'd make sure that you benefit as well, Jasper Lu.'

He nodded slowly, but there was a smile on his face only partly hidden by his travelling teacup. 'You know, maybe she can unearth my father? A bit like they do on that TV show where they trace famous people's genealogy.'

'It may turn out to be the place to start but don't get your hopes up, Jasper.'

'No, no, of course not.' Jasper sipped his tea, but Rosemary caught the smile he tried to hide.

Tabitha put her biscuit down carefully. 'Can you remember how he smells?'

'Pardon?'

'Your father.' Tabitha waved her hand around. 'Can you remember how he smells?'

'I didn't ever know him. I don't even know what he looked like, let alone how he smelled.'

'Oh,' said Tabitha, taking up the Florentine again. 'That's a shame. Smell memory is the strongest of all.'

Rosemary saw Jasper's face droop and knew he was thinking about his total lack of memories associated with his biological father. *Memory is a very tricky residue indeed.*

TWELVE

Despite not really recovering from her backyard-induced pallor, Tabitha had declined Rosemary's invitation to stay another day and left that afternoon after saying that she would return on Saturday to explore more of her childhood town. This meant Hannah could sleep in a real bed after she finished at Mulbury Feeds, which she did the minute she made it back to Rosemary's house. Sunny stalked to the open door of the spare bedroom and stood with her tail twitching from side to side until Rosemary said, 'Leave her, Sunny. I'll shut the door so you won't be offended by her presence.'

The cat stared at her but went back to the windowsill where she lay with her tail settled beside her.

Hannah was up before Rosemary the next morning. She'd made buckwheat pancakes and didn't seem upset by Rosemary's insistence that she eat them all. 'Thanks again for letting me stay.' Hannah smothered the top pancake on the stack with a layer of jumbleberry jam before ladling yoghurt on.

'You'll have to sort it out sooner or later with your father.'

'Do I, though?' Hannah paused in her chewing. 'Isn't he the father figure who's meant to be setting some sort of example?'

'You're an adult, too. It doesn't all fall in Richard's lap.'

Hannah grunted. 'Maybe not. But most of it does.'

She left soon after, stacking the dishwasher before she went and taking time out to stroke Sunny's ginger head. 'Dinner is at Franco's tonight,' called Rosemary. 'Six-thirty.'

'I'll be there,' Hannah called from the doorway.

It was one of the best things about Mondays: the Mulbury residents' dinners. If divided evenly, Rosemary only had to cook for the crowd every eight weeks or so, and in the meantime got to enjoy pot roasts from Mrs Lionel, pasta magnificence from Roman, and vegan surprise from Rakisha. *Perhaps* enjoy *is too strong a word for Rakisha's cooking,* but surprise *is pretty apt.*

Halfway through the morning, the phone rang. 'Honey,' said Rosemary.

'Mum, I hear you have a boarder?'

'You've been talking to Hannah?'

'No, Holly. She's very upset about the whole situation.'

'She needs to talk to Hannah.'

'I think she's tried.' Honey sighed. 'And she tried talking to Richard. Hannah and her father are equally stubborn.'

'They have some things to work out.'

'You think Richard is wrong not to sell the business to his daughters.'

'Yes, I do.'

Honey was quiet for a moment. 'It would make good business sense, but I guess he has his reasons.'

'Do you know what they are?'

'No idea. If anyone did, I thought it would be you.'

'No.'

'Well, anyway, I just rang to invite you to dinner tonight.'

'We have dinner at Franco's.'

'Didn't you hear?'

'Hear what?'

'Franco's got a special order from Big Town on his bee sting cakes. He cancelled.'

'How do you know that?'

'And you don't?' Honey's deep chuckle made Rosemary smile. 'Holly told me. Mrs Lionel told her, and I imagine that at any moment, Mrs Lionel will tell you.'

On cue, the door jangled open and Mrs Lionel stepped inside the shop. She started to speak but put her hand over her mouth once she saw Rosemary on the phone. 'It's Honey,' said Rosemary.

'That's Mrs Lionel's voice, isn't it?'

'I'm putting you on speaker phone.' Rosemary held the phone out so they could all talk.

'Hello, Honey Blossom, dear. How are you?'

'I'm great, Mrs Lionel. Did Mum tell you what I'm doing?'

Mrs Lionel eyed Rosemary, who nodded. 'Your cakes, dear? The decorated ones?'

'I've had five orders this week! One Kewpie doll, two unicorns, another hat and a chicken.'

'A chicken?'

'I'll send you photos.'

'And how is the baby, Honey?'

'Tallulah's good. Doing all the things she should.'

Mrs Lionel shook her head and smiled. 'Lovely, dear. I

won't interrupt you, but I was coming in to tell your mother about dinner tonight.'

Honey laughed. 'Franco's too busy?'

'Oh, you know?'

'I've been talking to Holly.'

'Oh, yes, poor dear, she's very worried about Hannah.'

'Hannah's fine,' said Rosemary.

'I'm sure she is but that's not what she worries about. Holly has been the steady one in that family since Louisa died and I'm quite concerned about her.'

'I think she'll be okay, Mrs Lionel,' said Honey. 'Holly's a very strong person.'

Mrs Lionel looked steadily at Rosemary. 'Even the strongest of us need support sometimes.'

'I'll make sure I keep in contact with her.'

'Will you, dear? That would be great.'

There was a clank through the phone line as Honey moved something. 'I'd better go. I've got class this afternoon and the first of my cakes to deliver. Will you come to dinner tonight?'

Mrs Lionel shook her head, pointing along the road and miming using a knife and fork.

'How about tomorrow night? Dinner here appears to still be on, just not at Franco's.'

'Tomorrow then. I can show you my latest cake. Good-bye, Mrs Lionel.'

'Take care, dear.'

'Oh, Mum?'

'Honey?'

'What are you making now?'

Rosemary glanced back through the door towards the kitchen. 'Nothing right at this very moment.'

'But you've still got lemons, haven't you?'

'Yes.'

'Can you make me some Moroccan lemons?'

'Yes.'

'Oh, you've already started? I can smell the tang of cut lemons now.'

'Honey, you know I haven't started yet. You've just asked me.'

'Doesn't matter. The kitchen has that sharpness it doesn't have when you make jam. It's the salt. You've opened the big jar of Lake Tyrell salt. I can taste it.'

'Honey...'

'It tastes of hot summers and pink salt plains.'

Rosemary smiled at Mrs Lionel and rolled her eyes. 'I have a mad daughter.'

Honey laughed. 'Love you, Mum.'

'Love you, too.'

'I don't think she's mad,' said Mrs Lionel as Rosemary finished the call. 'She's delightful.'

'Yes.'

'But also wrong this time.' Mrs Lionel shook her head at Rosemary's sharp look. 'Only about dinner tonight. It hasn't been cancelled but there's a change of venue. Robert Sparkling is our new host.'

'Robert Sparkling.'

'The mechanic, dear.' Mrs Lionel patted her friend's arm. 'You know him.'

'So he says. Apparently, we're friends from childhood but I don't remember him at all.'

'He could be wrong. Mixing you up with someone else.'

'He knew Alasdair as well.'

Mrs Lionel nodded slowly. 'I see. Does it matter, dear?'

'That he knows Alasdair or that I can't remember him?'

'Both. Either.'

'Yes. I don't like not knowing why he's here in Mulbury, claiming he knows me.'

'Coincidence? The garage was for sale.'

'I don't like coincidence, either.'

'So I've noticed.' Mrs Lionel turned to leave. 'See you tonight, if not before.'

'Where exactly is Robert hosting dinner? He doesn't live in Mulbury and I am certain the garage doesn't have a kitchen.'

'Ah, well, that's the other surprise. Robert Sparkling *does* now live in Mulbury. He bought the mayoral residence.'

Rosemary put her hands on her hips. 'You are kidding me.'

Mrs Lionel grinned. 'Now, would I ever do that, dear?' She walked to the door, pausing to pick up a jar of tomato chutney. 'Jasper said he'd make his own way there, but pick me up at six twenty-five and I'll pay you for this then.'

'Swap you some soap.'

Mrs Lionel raised the jar and jangled outside.

Rosemary went straight to the kitchen where Aunt Lilibeth's recipe book was already open on the bench. As she started the process for Moroccan lemons, she knew that it wasn't Honey's request that made her work so furiously. Robert Sparkling was on her mind. She thought back on the box of childhood photos and still couldn't see where a little Robert might have appeared in her younger life. Alasdair was the socialite, even back then, and had been always surrounded by other children trying to vie for his attention. Perhaps Robert had been one of those who hung around him?

Rosemary put down her knife and went to the living area where the photo box sat on the coffee table. She lifted the lid and upended the box again so photographs spilled everywhere. There was one she needed, the class photo in the year she turned eight. She sat front and centre in a row of sitting girls wearing little blue and white checked school dresses. Behind them were two more rows, another of girls and one of boys. School photo occasions were really the only time the class mixed randomly, otherwise they stuck to their already-formed groups. They'd stood the boys together and their uneven heights made the back row look like a badly put together picket fence. Rosemary squinted as she stared, trying to remember their names. Dean, Craig and...

Robert.

The boy stood in between his friends, unsmiling. He had a mop of auburn hair that cascaded over his bright face. He was so little that there was nothing in his pale face or scrawny shoulders that resembled the mechanic Robert of today.

Rosemary put the photo down and frowned. It was coming back to her, little snippets of the other children in her class who weren't in their group. Margie and Jenny, who lived across the river and consequently stuck together. Jeremy, Craig and Glen, who lived in the communal residence built for hospital staff. And Dean and Robert. They were the only ones in class who lived at the edge of town in houses so splendid no other student had ever been inside one.

She sighed. *Got it,* she thought. *Robert Sparkling was a rich kid. No wonder I didn't recognise him. He was so out of reach I hardly even knew he was there.*

The thought pleased her more than she thought it should. It spurred her on to push the photographs aside and get back to the kitchen. It wasn't memory loss that had made her not recognise Robert Sparkling. It was pure childhood ignorance.

The Moroccan lemons took no time to finish. Even after marmalade, lemon butter and preserved lemons, there was still half a basket of Meyer citrus left over. Rosemary juiced them and poured the juice into an ice block tray to freeze. 'There,' she said to Sunny once she'd finished. 'No more lemons.'

Sunny stood up on her windowsill and stretched, pointing one forepaw daintily. She jumped down, sniffed the empty basket, and wrapped herself around Rosemary's leg.

'I thought you'd be pleased.'

The basket belonged to Heather Hubbard, but Rosemary felt disinclined to take it back that afternoon. There was still Richard to deal with, and she wasn't sure that, in the slightly irritated mood she was in, dealing with Richard was a good use of a Monday afternoon. Instead, she did another inventory, planned the rest of the season's preserving, and waited for the time to go to Robert's mayoral residence.

At six-twenty-three, just as she stepped out of the door, Ronnie rang. 'I haven't long spoken to Honey,' said Rosemary. 'Has something happened?'

'Yes,' said Ronnie, his voice wispy. 'No.'

'Yes or no, Ronnie? About Honey.'

'Honey's fine, Rosemary.' Ronnie hesitated. 'Isn't she? I mean, she'd tell me if something was wrong.'

We're all paranoid in our own way, thought Rosemary, putting her hand up to signal to Mrs Lionel who was locking her shop's door. 'She would. You've rung me about something else.'

'Yeah, I have. The coroner's running DNA tests on the

bones now that Dr Connelly is on the scene.' He hesitated, coughed, and started again. 'But, in the meantime, the police have been contacted by another woman claiming to be Albert Connelly's daughter.'

'Agnes had *two* daughters?' Rosemary said. 'Tabitha didn't mention a sister.'

'Well, that's it. Agnes didn't have two daughters, but Albert did.'

'Ah. And this other woman has contacted you. Why?'

'She claims that her father murdered Agnes.'

'The plot thickens.'

'Yeah. Anyway, thought you might like to know.'

'Thanks, Ronnie.'

'Bye, Rosemary.'

Mrs Lionel looked at Rosemary expectantly as she ended the call. 'Trouble?'

'Not yet. Accusations.'

'Historical deaths are messy.'

'Apparently.' Rosemary pointed down the footpath. 'Hannah's here. And Heather.'

Hannah had, for once, changed out of her jeans and lumber jacket. She wore a long, patterned dress with black boots. Heather, on the other hand, was dressed as she always did in flowing layers held loosely in the middle with a leather belt.

'Hello, dears,' said Mrs Lionel, touching Heather's arm lightly.

'Mrs Lucious Lionel,' said Heather dreamily, putting her cheek on the older woman's shoulder.

'Let's go,' said Rosemary. 'The mayoral residence awaits.' She indicated her car.

'We aren't going to Franco's?' Hannah tipped her head at the light still on in the patisserie.

'Change of plan. We're going to Mr Sparkling's new abode.'

'Ha,' said Hannah. 'If only Holly had realised that. She thinks our new mechanic is a bit of all right.'

'He's a bit of too old for her,' said Mrs Lionel severely.

Hannah shrugged. 'Not much choice in a town like Mulbury.'

Rosemary said nothing, but silently agreed with Hannah. As she climbed into the car, she glanced back at her shop. Sunny sat at the door, her orange coat catching the streetlight and making her look like she was glowing. *Who needs a human partner,* Rosemary thought as she pulled the car out on the road, *when you could have the intelligent company of a cat instead?*

THIRTEEN

Although the carload arrived on time, many of the other invited residents of Mulbury were already at the old mayoral residence. The building had been shuttered ever since its last owner departed and, even now, some windows were covered with heavy boards. The steps leading to the front door were clean, as was the welcoming patch of cracked pavers, but the knob on the vast wooden door was gone. Hannah put her ear against the boards. 'I can just hear them inside,' she said, as the door swung open with her pressure.

'Come in,' called a voice.

'We are,' said Hannah, looping her arm through her sister's and taking off down the hallway.

'I haven't been in here for a long, long time,' said Mrs Lionel quietly as Rosemary walked with her along the dimly lit hall. 'It looks like the place was stripped.'

The walls along the hallway had telltale square markings of missing paintings. Rosemary glanced into two side rooms as they passed. Each was empty, their walls cracked.

They emerged into a huge living area that was crowded with people and not much else.

'Hello,' said that voice. 'Welcome.'

Robert Sparkling stepped forward. Although Rosemary hadn't expected him to be in his mechanic's overalls, she was still taken aback to see him in a crisp, open-necked shirt and pressed trousers. His shoulders were broad, making buttons strain at his chest, but his waist was slim. He'd brushed his spice-coloured hair back, exposing his forehead, making him seem younger. 'Hello, Mrs Lionel, Rosemary.' He shook their hands in turn. 'I'm sorry,' he said to the younger women. 'I don't know you.'

'I'm Hannah. This is Heather. Our other sister, Holly, is making dinner for our father tonight so she couldn't come.'

'Oh, they could have had dinner here instead.'

'No,' said Hannah. 'If he'd come, I couldn't.'

Robert's eyes widened slightly. 'Oh. Well, it's lovely to have two of your family here.'

Hannah pushed her hair out of her eyes. 'There's a whole heap of people here. I don't know all of them.'

Rosemary scanned the crowd standing around the room, holding a variety of glasses in their hands. There were a lot of familiar people in the vast room, including Jules and Roman's extended family who were busy arranging a series of glass bottles on the crooked mantlepiece at the end of the room.

'That's what those children have found so far in the hills around Mulbury,' said Mrs Lionel, noticing Rosemary's gaze.

'No Hand of Hela yet?'

'Only the remnants of a rubbish tip.'

Rosemary nodded, looking away from the bickering teenagers. In the back corner, standing in a small arc around

Jasper, were Adelia Lochard and two men holding film equipment. Jasper held his glass high, and Adelia kept batting at it so it lowered, but it was like Jasper had it on a spring. It rose in front of his face again.

'Monday dinners are usually a quieter affair than this,' said Rosemary, accepting a glass of white wine from Robert.

'I've taken advantage of the night to have a quasi-house-warming.' Robert handed a glass to Mrs Lionel. 'I only bought the place last week and I thought I'd have to wait for settlement to move in, but no one seemed bothered when I asked to take residence immediately.'

'This house has been empty for a very long time,' said Mrs Lionel, sipping. 'You have a big job ahead of you to do it up.'

'It's like a manor,' said Hannah. 'Like one of those English homes they restore on television.'

Rosemary sipped at her wine. 'You would have the money to restore it, no doubt.'

High spots of colour lit Robert's face. 'You've remembered me.'

'It took a while. You and Dean lived on the other side of town, and we didn't mix.'

'No, we didn't.' He shook his head slightly and dropped his voice so only she could hear him. 'But I was always aware of you, even if you don't remember me.' He held her gaze with those infinitely deep, dark eyes. 'I wrote you a note in Oceanic Cerulean. I put it in your locker.'

'I didn't use my locker. Alasdair did.'

'Ah.' Robert smiled ruefully. 'Foiled by Alasdair.'

'Don't worry. You weren't the only one.' She held out her phone and enlarged the picture so that he could only see part of a sentence. 'Is this Oceanic Cerulean?'

Robert put his hand on hers to shift the screen towards

the light so he could see the photo she'd pulled up. 'That's Bower Bird Blue. Very specific in the way that it was blended. Very Australian and not at all common, even back when it was first produced. You can't get it any more.' He lowered the phone, keeping his hand on hers. 'It had quite a strong odour of phenyl, as some older inks did. What's the letter about?'

Rosemary extracted her hand and slid the phone into her pocket. She was saved from saying anything more by Hannah nudging Robert roughly. 'So,' said the younger woman, gazing around at the walls. 'Are you going to restore this place like they do on television?'

'Well,' said Robert, moving away from Rosemary and passing a full glass to Heather who politely gave it back to him. 'First I'll worry about making it sound and then I'll see what I can do to restore its former glory.' He smiled at Heather and offered the glass to Hannah. 'To tell you the truth, I don't mind if I *don't* do it up. There's a certain charm in it being old. As long as it doesn't leak.'

Rosemary noticed the faded wallpaper and the cobwebby cornices. She'd seen other houses in Mulbury restored and some had turned a perfectly liveable place into a hideous parody of the richness of the goldfields, albeit with cheap taps and split system air-conditioners. She preferred the hint of decay, the evidence that people had lived and loved and possibly died within the walls. There were stories in old houses that should never be covered up.

'Who are *they*?' Hannah pointed at Adelia and gang with her glass.

'Jasper is the subject of a documentary,' said Rosemary.

'Why?'

'His mother was a famous writer.'

'Yeah, but they're filming *Jasper* not his mother.' Hannah shook her head. 'I'm going over to see.'

'Me too,' said Heather, following her sister and letting her hand run down Robert's arm as she passed.

'You'll need to get used to those sisters,' said Mrs Lionel. 'They are very precious to Mulbury. Heather is particularly special.'

'Now that I'm living here, I'll get to know everyone, I hope.' Robert raised his glass at Kelly Flanagan, who was wiggling her fingers in his direction. She stopped when she saw Rosemary and turned abruptly away.

'Do you need a hand in the kitchen, dear?'

'No, thank you, Mrs Lionel.' Robert bent down to the older woman's ear. 'I used to be a shearers' cook. What I'm turning out will be nothing like Roman's meals. I hope that's okay.'

'Yes, dear, of course it is.' Mrs Lionel smiled up at him. 'We're here for the company first, food second. I just hope you knew that Rakisha is vegan.'

'It was the first thing she told me when I met her.'

'That's good. Well, sing out if you need a hand.'

'I will.' He glanced at Rosemary, nodded slightly, and went out along another corridor that, she surmised, led to some sort of kitchen.

It was nearly half an hour before he emerged again. The crowd had helped themselves to more wine and beer, and the noise had grown. Robert stood in the doorway, holding up a gong, and smiling. Felicity Capriccio screamed when he hit it, although she wasn't the only one, just the loudest. Several drinks were spilled at the same time.

'Take a seat,' said Robert. 'Dinner is on its way.'

The crowd at the back of the room cleared to reveal a long row of trestle tables stacked with a range of crockery that had probably been on the shelves of an op shop the day before. There were some chairs, but mainly boxes, to sit on. Rosemary saw Jasper excusing himself from Adelia and making a beeline for her. 'Rescue me,' he said frantically as they sat.

'You agreed to her request to film.'

'Yes, but I didn't know she'd follow me around day and night.' Jasper grabbed Hannah's arm as she passed and sat her on the other side of him. 'Stay there,' he hissed at her.

'What about Heather?'

'She's with Mrs Lionel. Just sit there and don't let Adelia take your place.'

Hannah grinned. 'Not fond of being in the limelight?'

Jasper grimaced. 'I thought she'd focus on Mum but then she found out about the skeleton and then that I had been sick.'

Rosemary frowned. 'Did you mention the curse to her?'

Jasper picked up the fork in front of him and twirled it around on its tines. 'I might have. It probably slipped out.'

'She thinks you're *exotic*,' said Hannah.

'Like an animal at the zoo,' said Rosemary mildly.

'You aren't helping, you two.' Jasper took a gulp of his drink and ducked his head as Adelia looked in his direction.

'What about Patti?' Hannah said. 'That woman came to Mulbury because of Patti's dresses.'

'Oh, Patti's fine.' Jasper slid down in his chair. 'She's designing costumes and Adelia seems really pleased. It doesn't seem enough, though. I swear, that woman sees opportunity in every chance meeting.'

Rosemary said nothing but she didn't agree with Jasper. Adelia saw Jasper Lu, grinning and friendly and handsome in that willowy way of tall, slender men, and he had a story behind the good looks. Several stories. Firstly, that of a mother whose son didn't know of her fame. Secondly, the coincidental discovery of someone's else's mother in his backyard. Stitch that together and what a documentary you could make.

'Speaking of mothers,' started Rosemary.

'Were we?'

Rosemary growled at herself. 'Apologies. I was thinking aloud. Ronnie rang me just before we came out. It seems that Albert Connelly had another daughter.'

'Tabitha didn't say anything,' said Hannah.

'Tabitha may not know.'

'Tricky.' Hannah shook her head. 'Puts a whole new twist on it.'

'Especially since this daughter thinks Albert killed his wife.'

'Big twist.' Hannah sat up. 'What's for dinner?'

Robert placed a large pot with a wire handle in the middle of the trestles. He lifted the lid with a mini crowbar and set it carefully on the table. 'Plates, please.'

As each person handed their plate over, he served a ladle of the pot's contents—a steaming, rich stew—and piled two or three scones on top to act as dumplings. His quantities were generous. Rosemary heard Felicity start to protest but her voice died down as she ate. Silence settled over the table until Gerry said, 'Good heavens, Robert. What have you made us? It's utterly delicious.'

'A camp cook's favourite. Beef stew made with whatever you have in the cupboard.'

'You must have a generous cupboard, dear,' said Mrs Lionel. 'I remember feeding farm hands. They eat heartily.'

'As are we,' said Kelly, in that singsong voice Rosemary had heard the other day. 'I say this is possibly the best thing I've ever tasted.'

'I doubt that,' said Robert, settling in his seat. 'But I can guarantee by the end of the night you won't need to eat for three days. Unless, of course, you're shearing. If that's the case, you'll be wanting more by daybreak.'

Rosemary glanced around the table. Roman was nodding at Jules as she explained what she thought was in the stew. Rosemary doubted it contained ingredients that Roman would normally stock and was fairly sure he would never buy. Rakisha had a separate pot that was very similar to the beef the others were eating, but it must have been suitable as she was tucking in like everyone else. Adelia and her film crew had put aside their equipment and ate like there was no tomorrow. Leif and family were doing the same, although Rosemary suspected it was how they ate every night.

Robert kept refilling plates until his ladle scraped the bottom of the pot. As he took it back to the kitchen, Jasper leaned over to Rosemary. 'Did Ronnie say who this second daughter was?'

Rosemary shook her head. 'No. Only that there was one.'

'Tabitha is coming back soon,' he said. 'We should tell her.'

'We will. It could be an awful shock.'

'Do you think the new daughter knows about the old one?'

'No idea.'

Jasper frowned. 'Families.'

'As you know, Jasper, they're complicated.'

It only seemed ten minutes since they'd had double helpings of stew when Robert emerged from the kitchen with another huge pot, this one full of a chocolate syrup pudding, with an aroma that made everyone lift their heads and sniff in wonder. He put that pot on the table and placed a large jug of cream next to it. 'Who's for dessert?'

Everyone, of course.

After their meal, the crowd subsided into a mellow, slightly groaning mob. Even Felicity's chatting took on a blurry quality, as if she was half asleep which, as Rosemary noticed, she was by the way she'd tipped in her chair. Rosemary leaned back as well, gazing at the row of bottles on the mantlepiece. She felt the youngest child's eyes on her and pointed at a particularly interesting green bottle on the end. 'What can you tell us about these?'

'We dug them up,' said Eliza. 'The metal detector told us there was gold in the ground, so we dug and found these.'

'Any gold?' asked Jasper.

'Tin cans,' said Calvin. 'Turns out our metal detector doesn't know the difference.'

'I thought it was a cheap buy,' said Leif, scratching at his stomach. 'Now I know why.'

'We might find the Hand tomorrow,' said Antonio.

'Keep digging,' said Felicity. 'It's got to be somewhere.'

An image of a gold-rush-ruined landscape filled Rosemary's head. 'These are treasures in themselves,' she said, nodding at the bottles.

'Treasures!' said Eliza.

'I like them,' said Penelope. 'They're all different shapes and colours. I've been looking them up on the internet.'

'Have you found what they were used for?'

'Milk.' The girl pointed at each one. 'Tomato sauce—you can tell by the brand name. Perfume, although I can't get the lid off. Poison, because it's written on the side.'

'See the ribs along the glass?' Marco said. 'They were put there to stop people drinking it by accident.'

'That's sensible, dear,' said Mrs Lionel. 'They didn't

have childproof tops in those days.' She squinted at the row. 'I recognise some of these, especially that milk bottle. I imagine these are all dated from the 1950s or so.'

'That's what Grum said,' said Marco. 'They didn't have garbage trucks back then so people buried their rubbish.'

'They also had less rubbish than we make today,' said Mrs Lionel. 'Well, I think they're a very interesting find.'

'We'll find more tomorrow,' said Eliza.

'Would you like to display them in my shop, dears? If we wash them well, I think they'd be quite an eye-catching collection among my products.'

'Can we, Mum?' asked Marco.

'Oh yes, how exciting!' Felicity turned to Mrs Lionel. 'Aren't they just my little mudlarkers!'

'No mud,' said Calvin. 'Only dirt.'

Felicity ruffled Calvin's hair. 'Well, *dirt larkers* doesn't have quite the same ring, does it?'

'Drop them to me on your way back to Jules' house,' said Mrs Lionel. 'I'll wash them and then you can set them up.'

The excited noise started again, with some children agreeing to the plan but some apparently not. Mrs Lionel left them to it, turning to Rosemary. 'Should we offer to wash the dishes?'

'Too late.' Rosemary indicated the kitchen door where the silhouettes of Kelly, Rakisha and Adelia could be seen with tea towels slung over their shoulders.

'Too bad.' Mrs Lionel smiled and settled back with a cup of tea.

Eventually, the children packed up their treasures, ready for Mrs Lionel to clean, and everyone made for the door. Eliza almost dropped a blue bottle but Rosemary, walking behind her, caught it deftly. She held it in her hand for a moment, studying its shape and size, before holding it out in her palm. 'Is it alright if I have a lend of this one?' she asked. 'I think I recognise it.'

'Will you give it to Mrs Lionel then so she can wash it?'

'Yes.'

Rosemary slipped the bottle in her pocket, keeping a hand on it in case it fell out. It had such a familiar shape. Where had she seen it before?

FOURTEEN

Unusually for the season Mulbury was having, it rained for two days straight. It wasn't a drought-breaking, sodden type of rain but more of a drizzly, useless sort. Mrs Lionel stepped out on Wednesday morning intending to rake the Square back to neatness after the council men's work in restoring the barricade around The Exceptional Tree, but the drizzle soaked through the scarf she'd placed around her head and left an uncomfortable drip down her neck. 'Let's leave it, Percy,' she said.

The little dog didn't appear to notice the rain but followed her happily enough back to the veranda over The Green Mulbury.

Under shelter, Mrs Lionel took a moment to study the Square. The rain made the leaves on the Tree darken, and it cast a gloomy shadow over the entire area. The new barricade was a solid vintage-green painted wood which was better than the previous one but gave the impression that the Tree was an animal in a pen. Branches hung wet and low over the top rail. 'It looks ashamed,' said Mrs Lionel to Percy, who wagged his tail at her voice. 'Very undignified.'

'What is?'

'Oh, hello, Hannah, dear. Heading to work?'

'Yeah, making sure the shed is organised before we get more deliveries.' Hannah scanned the footpath. 'Was someone here?'

'Pardon, dear?'

'You were talking to someone.'

'Was I?' Mrs Lionel was careful not to look down. 'I was lamenting the new fence around The Exceptional Tree.'

Hannah stared across the Square. 'It looks weird.'

'Weird, indeed.'

Hannah nodded to the older woman and strode off to work, pulling her hair back into a short, messy pigtail as she went.

Mrs Lionel paused for a moment before going to The Preserved Mulbury and jangling in the door. 'Rosemary?'

'In here.'

Rosemary stood behind the kitchen counter, Aunt Lilibeth's recipe book spread out before her.

'Looking for something in particular?'

'Yes.' Rosemary tapped the book. 'Every now and then, Lilibeth scribbled a note about cures and remedies, mainly related to the produce she was preserving. See?' She swivelled the book so that Mrs Lionel could read a sentence that said *Honey, lemon and ginger infusion soothes the sore throat*.

'Oh, yes. My mother used to make the same drink whenever we were sick.'

Rosemary turned the page.

'You seem to be looking for other things.'

'I am certain that I've seen some more unusual remedies in here, ones that didn't relate to lemons or apples or potatoes.'

'What did she use potatoes for?'

'Burns. Somewhere in here she says to rub a slice of raw potato on a burn.'

'Now that one I haven't heard.' Mrs Lionel watched as Rosemary flicked through more pages. 'But you're looking for something specific. Why would that be?'

Rosemary pulled out the bottle she'd borrowed from Eliza. 'I've been thinking about where I've seen this before.'

'Can I have a look?' Mrs Lionel took the bottle and turned it over in her hands. 'You know we're talking about a time when lots of things went into bottles, and the bottles themselves were generally very similar.'

'Yes.'

'Why have you taken an interest in this one?'

'I'm not sure. I thought Aunt Lilibeth may have drawn it in here.'

'She has done some lovely illustrations of jams and pickles, but why would she draw a bottle like this one?'

'Once again, I don't know. I have this feeling...' Rosemary flipped through a few more pages.

'Can't you just match it up to some picture from the computer?'

'Like you say, it's a fairly generic bottle.'

'Hmmm.' Mrs Lionel put the bottle up to her nose and sniffed delicately. 'I smell earth. Not surprising after being buried for so long.' She put the bottle back on the kitchen counter. 'Anyway, I just ran into Hannah.'

'Yes. She's gone to work.'

'How long do you think she'll stay with you?'

Rosemary looked up. 'As long as she needs.'

'I see.'

'What do you see?'

'What I see is a girl who's fighting with her father and is in danger of splitting her family.'

'What do you mean?'

Mrs Lionel pulled out a chair and sat at the dining table, her hands folded in front of her. 'What sort of stress do you think this is putting on Holly? She's the one straddling the gap between sister and father.'

'Holly is tough.'

'That's beside the point, Rosemary Exeter, and you know it.'

Rosemary sighed, closed the recipe book, and came to sit with her friend. 'It's difficult to know how to help.'

'Yes, it is.'

'You could talk to Richard. You're the closest person to that family.'

'I knew Louisa well and I watched that family grow up. Richard's motives have been unclear to me for some time.'

'I still think you're the best person to talk to him.'

'Well, dear, I don't.' Mrs Lionel straightened her back. 'I have taken care of those girls nearly their whole lives. Honestly, I don't have the energy to take on Richard as well. That's your job.'

'Why is it my job?'

'You know Richard as well as anyone.'

Rosemary leaned back in her chair, pulling her braid over one shoulder so it didn't catch. 'I will yell at him.'

'No, you won't. I forbid it.'

Rosemary raised an eyebrow.

'Go into that produce store and try to figure out what's really going on. You can help Hannah get some insight. Today.'

'You want me to talk to Richard *today*.'

'I don't *want* you to do anything.' Mrs Lionel reached out and tapped Rosemary's arm. 'I'm demanding it.'

Rosemary laughed, but Mrs Lionel frowned and she stopped. 'Right. I'll see him today.'

'Good.' Mrs Lionel shifted her chair back clumsily and stood up. 'You've got two hours until you open.'

'You want me to go now?'

'Why not?' Mrs Lionel glanced around the house. 'Everything looks in order here. What else have you got to do?'

Rosemary pursed her lips and it was Mrs Lionel's turn to laugh. 'Right,' said Rosemary. 'I'll go soon.'

'Soon?'

'Almost immediately.'

Mrs Lionel tugged her jacket straight. 'There is no time like the present but I'm sure you know that.'

There was silence behind Mrs Lionel as she left, and she hummed to herself as she left The Preserved Mulbury for her own shop. Rosemary Exeter was an intelligent woman so she would, of course, do exactly what Mrs Lionel suggested.

ROSEMARY WAITED a minute after her friend exited then stepped out to follow the pavement to the road between the old shops and the animal produce store. Mulbury Feeds consisted mainly of one gigantic tin shed but she noticed the stacks of garden straw bales piled neatly along the fence and a pile of potting mix bags on a pallet near the entrance.

Holly Hubbard emerged from the shed and stopped abruptly. 'Rosemary! You gave me a fright.'

'I can be scary.'

'No, you aren't. Not really.' Holly took her hat off and swept back some hair that was tickling her face before ramming the hat back on. 'Well, not often. Do you need something or are you just visiting?'

'I would like to speak to your father.'

'Oh.' Holly glanced inside the shed. 'He's talking to Hannah now but, as she isn't talking to him, it's a one-sided conversation. You're welcome to join the frostiness of our life.'

'Since Hannah's been staying with me, I've had some hints about it.'

Holly nodded. 'I hope she isn't a nuisance but I'm glad she's staying with you and hasn't stormed off to the city or somewhere. At least I know where she is.'

'She's not a nuisance. I hardly see her. She works hard.'

'Yeah, she does.' Holly sighed. 'She's working even harder now. Trying to prove to Dad that he isn't needed or wanted and that we do okay without him.'

'Which you do.'

'But that isn't the point.' Holly shrugged. 'He knows how hard we work and how good the business is, but he insists on mucking around with the books and reshelving stuff and generally just hanging around when customers come in. He hasn't mentioned the sale or what's going to happen next. It's strange, but he hasn't even played his guitar since he's been home.'

'Perhaps his muse stayed in Queensland.'

Holly laughed. 'Yeah, I hadn't thought of that.' The mirth fell from her face as she turned to Rosemary. 'I'm glad you're here to talk to him. There's something weird going on with Dad that I can't figure out. He's in our faces all the time and Heather's the only one who likes it. I just want to get on with things.'

Rosemary gestured at the pallets outside. 'You've introduced garden supplies.'

'Yes and no. The straw we've had for ages. The potting mix was the start of a new venture which has gone on hold since Dad's come home. I can hardly cope with the ordinary business at the moment.' She shrugged. 'Come on in. Dad's in the office.'

Rosemary studied Holly as she walked behind her. She was the smallest of the sisters and yet the oldest. She seemed particularly small today, with slumped shoulders and the hat that nearly drowned her head. She wasn't even walking at her usual brisk pace. It seemed that Mrs Lionel was correct. The family feud fallout was landing squarely on Holly.

The office was in a sectioned-off area of the shed full of the smaller needs of animal owners. Neat lines of plastic bottles and tubs lined the shelves, everything from worm drenches to nutrients for lactating horses. Heather's taxidermised birds sat on the top shelves: a magpie in flight over the dog grooming implements and an ibis standing elegantly at watch over the budgie food. Rosemary knew some thought Heather's hobby macabre, but the Hubbard sister was clearly very talented. The birds had been given a life after their death, and a few of the more unusual ones had sold for a lot of money.

'Rosemary, Rosie, Rose.' Heather wafted out from behind the shop counter and twirled over to Rosemary, giving her a brief hug before holding her hands out to her. 'Feathers,' she said lovingly, lifting them up for Rosemary to see better.

Rosemary touched the tip of a finely striped down. 'They are beautiful, Heather. Where did you get them?'

'Roman. He saved them for me.' Heather closed her fists gently and spun away.

'They're from Roman's chooks,' said Hannah, coming out from behind a shelf. She dusted her hands off. 'He's got those special ones that he likes to cook. Can't remember what they're called but their feathers are amazing. He saves them for feathery Heathery.' Hannah chuckled at her sister's nickname.

'Good on him.'

'Yeah.' Hannah put her hands on her hips. 'But I don't think you're here for the salt blocks.'

'I'd like to speak to your father.'

Hannah waved her hands in the general direction of the office. 'Be my guest. In fact, he's all yours.' She stalked off to resume her shelf-packing.

Rosemary went behind the counter and stood in the doorway of the office. Beyond the little room was another, Heather's bird room. Rosemary could hear her humming as she worked.

'Hello, Rosemary Exeter,' said a deep voice.

Rosemary stepped into the office. Holly leaned against the little sink they had in there, one hand on her father's shoulder as he sat at a tiny table. Holly patted him a couple of times. 'I'll leave you to it.' She nodded to Rosemary as she went.

'Rosemary Exeter,' Richard said again. 'I haven't seen you for a long time.'

'No one has seen you for a long time.' Rosemary pulled out a chair and sat as well. 'That's your modus operandi.'

Richard shrugged, brushing his hair back over his shoulder.

It was not the golden colour of his daughters, nor the neat length of Jasper Lu's. His hair was a dull brown fizz, too long uncut and, thought Rosemary, too long unwashed. He couldn't have resembled his trio of girls less. 'So, what do I owe the elegant and not requested presence of Mulbury's sternest woman?'

Rosemary stiffened at the jibe. 'Lovely to see you, too.'

Richard rubbed his face with an open palm. 'Sorry, Rosemary. I'm a little on edge.'

She said nothing.

After a minute, Richard stood and went for the kettle. 'Coffee? I've only had two this morning.'

'Tea, preferably,' said Rosemary when she noticed him reaching for the instant coffee.

'Can do. I get you tea and you tell me why you're here.'

Rosemary waited until he'd placed the boiling, milky tea in front of her. 'Your daughters have progressed this business beyond anything you could do. Sell it to them.'

'Whoa! Cut me down without any chance of defence!' Richard plunked into his chair, spilling his drink onto his faded jeans. He wiped his leg and sat the mug down on the table. 'How do you know I'm not going to sell them the business?'

'Everyone knows you aren't.' Rosemary sipped her tea, burning her tongue. 'Not much is secret in Mulbury.'

'Yeah, I get that. I've *lived* that.' Richard rubbed at his face again and Rosemary saw how the shadows under his eyes had darkened. Richard was at least ten years younger than her, but he seemed ancient.

'Are you alright?'

'If you mean, am I healthy then, yeah, guess so. Nothing wrong with me like Louisa had.' His face creased and Rosemary waited for the tears, but he swallowed them back. 'If you mean, is there something wrong with my head, then I say there has been for a long time.'

'I was asking about your health in general.'

'Tell you something, I don't like the cold these days. Give me Queensland's humidity any time.'

'Then sell the business to your daughters and go back.'

He looked at her sharply. 'Harsh, Rosemary. Harsh. I can't leave my girls permanently.'

'You'd still be in Australia.'

'Thanks for the reminder. Can't afford to go anywhere else.'

Rosemary sighed quietly in exasperation. 'Then sell the business to them.'

Richard sat up and slammed his fist on to the table. 'I can't!'

From Heather's bird room came a loud whimper.

'Heather...' Richard stood up and went into the room, speaking softly to his daughter until Rosemary heard her laugh quietly. He came back out and smiled sheepishly at Rosemary. 'Got to remember to be careful.'

'Heather's stronger than she looks.'

'But she's also...' Richard sat noisily again. 'She's the one who keeps me coming back.'

'Holly and Hannah look after her.'

'That's not what I mean. I know they do. Heather is the centre of the family, you know?' He put one finger out and moved it in a circle. 'We all spin around her.'

'That's a lot of pressure to put on her.'

'She doesn't know.'

'She knows a lot.'

'Well, then, she doesn't show it.' He rubbed his face for a third time. 'Anyway, why are you here telling me what to do?'

'I am trying to work out why you won't sell Mulbury Feeds to your capable daughters and let them get on with it.'

Richard put his head down and was quiet for a long time. Rosemary sipped at her tea, but it was too dreadful to drink. When he didn't say anything, she rose, tipped the tea into the sink, and started to leave.

'I'm working on it,' he said as she got to the doorway.

'On what?'

'On telling them my reason.'

It was only the despair on his face that made her hesitate. She stood, stared at him so hard that he cringed, and said, 'Hurry up then. You'll lose them all, otherwise.'

'You should understand.'

She stopped. 'What?'

'You, of all people, should know how difficult it is.'

'I should?'

Richard took his mug to the sink and dumped the rest of the coffee in. 'Yeah, you should.' He put his hands on the sink and stared into its depths. 'It's why you kept Alasdair's shoe shop for so long.'

'I didn't.'

'You did. It took you a year to sell it.' He turned his head but didn't look at her. 'What was your reason for waiting, Rosemary Exeter? Could it have been that you couldn't bear to let go your last connection to your husband?'

She waited a moment, but he'd dropped his head again as if he'd run out of words. As she walked briskly back to The Preserved Mulbury, she wished heartily that Richard Hubbard was back in Queensland, minding his own business.

FIFTEEN

The rain cleared, leaving the air damp and the ground muddy. Mrs Lionel didn't bother with the broom on Thursday morning, instead taking a rake with her across to the Square. 'It's sensible,' she said to Percy. She'd just stepped from the road when a shriek from the Square halted her.

The Exceptional Tree was washed clean from the rain and lifted its olive-green leaves to the sky. But underneath, spearing the top rail of the barricade, a leafless branch stood dark and foreboding. Rakisha was next to it, laughing excitedly.

'What on earth, Rakisha?' asked Mrs Lionel, hurrying across.

'Oh, it's so wonderful, darling.' Rakisha clapped her hands together. 'Our Tree is defiant. It's all-powerful. It's surreal!'

Surreal was the most apt word among Rakisha's rambling, thought Mrs Lionel. The Tree waved gently in a morning breeze, but the branch must have come down straight and hard. The barricade was sheared in two. She shuddered to think what they might be looking at now if there'd been a person wandering past. Then again, in the back of her mind was the thought that the Tree wouldn't have done that. 'Oh, I'm as bad as her.'

'What was that, darling?' Rakisha gave Mrs Lionel a sideways look before resuming a little jig that made her bangles rattle.

'I was wondering, dear, why you are up so early?'

'Oh, yes, it's far too early for my energy to be activated.' Rakisha whirled to face Mrs Lionel. 'I had this dream, darling. A dream that said to me to rise and be ready. Be *ready*, darling! And I'd just finished dressing when a sound like a thunderbolt drew me outside and look! The Tree!'

'I didn't hear anything.'

Rakisha jangled her bangles. 'No, darling, of course not. You must be in tune with the world to hear its noise.'

Mrs Lionel frowned. She woke each morning without an alarm clock and watched the dawn glow while noting which birds were cherishing the light. 'I am in tune, more than most.'

Rakisha shook her head. 'Not to this! This marvel of ancientness!'

Mrs Lionel went back to studying the Tree. Its broad trunk was silver, wrinkled in places with scars and gouges and insect tracks marking it at random intervals. It was home to many creatures: ants and insects along and within its bark, families of galahs in its hollows and magpies in their sticky nests along its branches. The fallen branch was dead wood, with no bark. It didn't resemble any of the Tree's living branches and, if Mrs Lionel hadn't been so tuned into the natural world of Mulbury, she might have mistaken it for a branch from another tree.

'My goodness!' said a voice. 'What a mess.'

Felicity and two of her children crossed the Square to stand next to Mrs Lionel. She had a woollen coat on that buttoned to her throat but left her legs exposed. Legs, saw Mrs Lionel, that were clothed in flannelette pyjamas decorated with sleeping sloths. The pyjama legs ended in a wrinkled mass that couldn't quite tuck into the sheepskin-lined boots Felicity wore. 'Hello, dear,' said Mrs Lionel. 'Did you hear the crash as well?'

'Crash? No, didn't hear a thing. Well, the frantic beating of my own heart was quite loud as I chased these two around.' Felicity waved a hand at Eliza and Antonio. 'They've been digging.'

The children stood stroking the dead branch and turned at their mother's comment. '*Excavating*, Mama,' said the boy.

'In my day, we called it digging because it involved a shovel, dirt and a lot of mess.' Felicity ruffled her son's hair. '*Excavating* my ar-'

'Find anything?' asked Mrs Lionel hastily. 'More bottles?'

'We found an old shoe,' said Eliza, drawing a leather sole from her jacket pocket.

'And these.' Antonio pulled two glass stoppers from a bag slung across his chest.

'Ah, yes,' said Mrs Lionel. 'I remember these. They were used before screw tops or corks.'

'What pretty things,' said Rakisha, leaning over to get a better look. 'How marvellous, darling.'

'No gold nuggets?' asked Mrs Lionel.

Antonio shook his head. 'Not yet.'

'Well, these are riches of a kind, though.' Mrs Lionel tapped the shoe sole then the stoppers. 'You're digging up history. Pardon me. *Excavating* history.'

'That's what Pops says.' Antonio put the stoppers back in his bag. 'Although we keep finding the same things.' He pulled a bottle out. 'Now we have three of these.'

'More, if we count the broken ones,' said Eliza. 'Mum says we shouldn't keep the bits of glass.'

'I'm only worried that you'll cut yourself.' Felicity reached out and patted the fallen branch. 'What's happened here?'

'Oh, it's the Tree talking to us, darling.' Rakisha flicked her grey curls back over her shoulders. 'It doesn't like the confinement.'

'The barricade, she means,' said Mrs Lionel. 'This is the second time it's been wrecked. Strangely, we've never had any branches fall from the Tree before the barricade went up.'

'It was timely, then?'

Rakisha snorted. 'It was the *cause*, darling. No one should disturb the energy lines of a living thing.'

'I see,' said Felicity, nodding slowly as if she didn't see at all. 'I remember this Tree. It's always been here, dominating the town. I used to think of it as pretty but there's something much more majestic about it.'

'It is an ancient one, darling.'

'Yes, very old, I'd say.' Felicity leaned down to her children. 'There's more history in this Tree than in any bottle you'll find. Imagine the things it has witnessed.'

'It bears many scars.' Mrs Lionel pointed to a branch above their heads. 'It only just escaped the bushfires of 1983. See how dark that branch is?'

Eliza craned her neck to look at the branch, but Antonio shook his head and held up the found bottles. 'I think these are the best.'

Mrs Lionel held her hand out for one. 'They are little

snippets of history in their own right.' She held one up. 'This one still has a substance in it. Be careful not to get it on you.'

'The lids are rusted on.' Antonio twisted the top of one. 'I can't get them off.'

'That's a sign to leave them on, then.' Mrs Lionel handed the bottle back. 'What else have you found?'

'Rusty tins, buttons, wire, rags.' Eliza grinned. 'And a skull.'

'An animal skull,' said Felicity quickly. 'Not another you-know-what.'

'Human, she means,' said Antonio. 'Not another one of those. This one had teeth like this.' He bared his teeth and thrust the top ones forward. 'Pointy, like a sabre tooth tiger but not as big.'

'Ah,' said Mrs Lionel. 'A carnivore. A rat, maybe.'

'Yep.' Antonio put the bottles back in his back. 'Mama, can we have breakfast now?'

'Darlings,' said Rakisha. 'Come and have breakfast with me.'

Felicity gave Mrs Lionel a quick look.

'Rakisha's granola is quite delicious.' Mrs Lionel lowered her voice so only Felicity could hear. 'Very edible.'

'Okay then. Breakfast at The Sweet Potato.'

Rakisha clapped her hands together and twirled once. 'Do you prefer almond milk or soy milk, darlings?' she said as she ushered Felicity, Eliza and Antonio away.

'They aren't really milks,' Mrs Lionel heard Antonio say as they reached the door of the café. 'Milk comes from mammals.' The door groaned closed behind them.

Mrs Lionel turned back to the Tree, chuckling. The Square went back to its peaceful morning stillness, broken only by little waves of leaf movement as an errant wind came past. After a few minutes, Mrs Lionel patted the fallen spear, lifted her rake, and started the task she had come to do quite a while ago. Percy jumped around the rake, pouncing at its movement until she shooed him away.

SOMEONE—NOT Mrs Lionel nor Rakisha—must have notified the council about the fallen branch. By mid-morning, when the first trickle of tourists had already entered the shops under the veranda, a council truck from Big Town pulled up and two men went to the broken barricade, shaking their heads. Rosemary watched as best she could from inside her shop but all they did was to write notes and take photos. One waggled the branch, but it was clearly caught among the splintered bits of rail and his heart wasn't in it to try any harder. Rosemary went outside to see better once the tourists had finished with her chutney, only to find Mrs Lionel already watchful on the footpath.

'I expect you've already seen this.' Rosemary tipped her head towards the Square.

'Oh, yes. Rakisha was first to notice it, though.'

'Right.' Rosemary looked at her friend. 'What do you make of it?'

'It's an old Tree. Branches are bound to fall. Darren said so.'

'Right.'

They watched for a while longer, then Rosemary said, 'I spoke to Richard.'

'Oh? And?'

'I am none the wiser.'

'Yes, you are.'

Rosemary turned to her friend. 'What do you mean by that?'

'You said *I am none the wiser* in a tone that meant you are slightly the wiser for having talked to Richard.'

'You make no sense.'

'I am, however, correct.' Mrs Lionel paused for a moment to watch the council men climb back into their trucks and leave. 'Something he said made you pause and think.'

Rosemary lifted her head slightly. 'It wasn't what he said—I don't think he knows himself what his issue is—it was the way he said it. Something is troubling him that he can't yet articulate.'

'Poor man.'

'Poor *man*? What about his *daughters*?'

'Now, you know I love those girls with all my heart, but I think sometimes they're so busy they forget that Richard is still grieving for Louisa.'

'More than them?'

Mrs Lionel frowned and crossed her arms. 'Rosemary Exeter, you know more than most that grief is complex and cosmic. He doesn't grieve more or less than the girls grieve for their mother. It's just different.'

Rosemary said nothing.

'I'm glad you spoke to him, dear.' Mrs Lionel reached out and patted Rosemary's hand. 'Perhaps your next mission is to help him understand his reluctance to sell to the girls.'

'I'm not the best person to do that.'

'Yes, you are. You have an insight into difficult decisions. And, usually, you're quite objective.' Mrs Lionel put both her hands into her apron pockets. 'Perhaps not in this case so much. Has Hannah been getting to you?'

'I hardly see Hannah. She works, comes to my place late, eats dinner, collapses into bed. She's a very hard worker.'

'Ah, that's it then.'

Rosemary turned to face her friend. 'For someone I have known since I moved here, I still find you unfathomable at times.'

'Good.' Mrs Lionel peered at her watch. 'What do you say that we get going now and meet up after close of business? That should give you a while to figure it out.'

'Right.'

'Agreed?'

'I'm walking with Jasper tonight.'

'After that, then. I'll cook you dinner. Eggplant curry.'

'Right. Thanks.'

'Lovely. I'll see you then.'

Rosemary scowled after her friend, but Mrs Lionel had walked back to her shop, greeting potential customers as they came to crowd in front of her window display. She ushered them inside, giving Rosemary a final, wicked smile.

Back inside her own shop, Rosemary continued the tasks she'd been doing when she'd noticed The Exceptional Tree. She filled the shelves with jars of marmalade that flashed gold as they caught the sun through the skylight. She put new bowls of fruit in the window display: an orange, some cumquats and the few remaining intact pomegranates. Lastly, she updated her website, adding pictures of her latest produce and emailing a winter newsletter to her devoted mailing list. Sunny watched from the doorway, tail folded elegantly around her legs, putting up with the pats and cries from tourists in the shop who always acted like they'd never seen a ginger tabby cat in a preserves shop before.

Jasper knocked at her door at two minutes after five o'clock. She was waiting for him, her puffy jacket already on. She slipped out the jangling door and stood on the pavement to pull on her gloves. 'What is it?' she asked when Jasper remained quiet.

'Nothing.' Jasper plunged his hands into his pockets and bowed his head.

She stared at him critically. 'Hardly. Are you sick?'

'No.'

'Is Snowy sick?'

Jasper shook his head. 'I swear that dog has never been better.'

'Even upside down on his couch?'

He cracked a smile. 'Especially then.' He indicated the path. 'Shall we?'

It took half a block before Jasper's woes became obvious to Rosemary. They were walking up the hill toward the cemetery when a van parked on the side of the road switched its lights on and three people jumped out. Rosemary tensed for an ambush, but Jasper tugged her sleeve to make her move. The people came out of the glare, and she saw who they were. 'Are they still following you around?'

Jasper nodded glumly, letting his long hair shadow his face. 'They're very persistent. I just get to the point of relaxing, thinking that they've gone, when suddenly they appear again. Adelia Lochard is one of the most tenacious women I've ever known.'

'They've a keen interest in you.' Rosemary glanced back at the film crew. 'You could tell them to go away.'

'But they're here for Patti, aren't they? I mean, I don't want to create any bad Mulbury blood. And they aren't really doing any harm.'

'Right. Invading your privacy, being nuisances...' Rosemary watched as the cameraman behind her tripped and nearly fell. 'Being a public danger.'

'Oh, they're mostly okay.' Jasper reached his hand out for Rosemary's. 'But I would prefer them to leave us alone.'

She squeezed his hand and let it go. 'Ignore them. They can't hear what we're saying. They're probably more interested in the recovery from your sickness.'

'Actually, they're more interested in my mother than me. Adelia wants facts but I don't have any.'

'You're lucky, then. You can't tell her much even if you want to. They'll have to do their own research.'

They walked on without mishap and after passing the cemetery, Adelia called out a solid 'Good night' and the film crew left to walk back down the hill. Jasper and Rosemary finished their constitutional without further interference and, she noted sadly, without much more conversation.

'Mrs Lionel's cooking me dinner,' she said as they arrived back under the veranda. 'Come along. She always has too much.'

'Not tonight, Rosemary, but thanks.' He stepped closer and bent to her ear, even though no other soul was within cooee. 'I'm actually having dinner with Robert.'

'Robert.'

'Yes, you know, the mechanic. He invited me. To his new house.'

'Just you?'

'You sound...incredulous?'

'No, I don't.'

'It's okay. I was, too. But he was genuine enough. Just being friendly. And, no, not in a potential boyfriend way. He wants my advice.'

'On what?'

'Old books. He has a stash.'

'Right.'

Jasper grinned, making his face relax. 'I'll tell you about it tomorrow.'

'Only if you want.'

'Oh.' Jasper reached for her hand again but let his drop without touching. 'I will. See you tomorrow.'

I'll be making sure of that, thought Rosemary as Jasper disappeared inside The Read Mulbury.

SIXTEEN

Friday dawned, frozen. Ice formed in buckets and dog water bowls and made little glaciers out of gutters. Normally, frost was followed with huge, blue days, but the clouds crept over Mulbury and trapped the cold. Rosemary put on an extra layer as she dressed and stoked the fire to an acceptable glow. Hannah ate quickly and left for Mulbury Feeds looking like someone preparing to hike up Everest. Sunny refused to budge from the bed, even as the house slowly warmed. 'You'll have to get up sooner or later,' said Rosemary. The cat tucked her tail in tighter and didn't open her eyes.

Cold weather put off tourists who still visited but made short, sharp dashes into the cafés and boarded their buses without a glance at the wares on Goldmarket Road. Rosemary settled for a quiet day, one in which she could browse old recipe books and design more labels and imagine scenes in which Jasper and Robert Sparkling ate dinner and sorted books. It was a mild shock to hear the jangle of the bell just before lunch, and to see a tall, sullen woman with neat hair tucked into the nape of her neck enter the shop wearing a long woollen trench coat in a vivid emerald green.

'Hello,' said the woman, pulling fur-trimmed gloves off, one finger at a time.

'Welcome,' said Rosemary, stepping out from her counter. 'Still cold out there?'

'Obviously.' The woman waved her hand down her coat. 'Pleasant in here.'

'Yes. Are you looking for any preserve in particular?'

'Preserve?' The woman glanced around the shop as if noticing for the first time that she was in one. 'No. I have all the condiments I need. I came in because yours was the only place I was able to enter.'

'Sometimes people close their shop to have lunch, particularly on days such as these.'

'Hmm.' The woman placed her gloves in her bag and unbuttoned her coat. 'There's a dress shop on the corner filled with cameras and lights so I assume they're filming advertising. The bookshop was dark as if it wasn't open and there was no sign that the owner was on a lunch break.'

Rosemary's eyes narrowed. Jasper didn't close his shop without letting someone know. She strained to remember whether she'd heard breakfast noises through the wall this morning, but she'd been too busy with the crackling fire to notice.

'So,' said the woman, 'that leaves you.'

'Leaves me to what?'

The woman walked over to the shelf and ran a finger along the rows of chutney. 'Tell me about this quaint little town.'

'Mulbury has a hard history,' said Rosemary, folding her arms across her chest. 'I don't think of it as *quaint*.'

'Don't you?' The woman walked over to Rosemary and

extended her hand. 'I'm Marguerite Kent. I like your no-nonsense attitude. How would you describe the place in which you live?'

Rosemary shook the cool fingers. 'Rosemary Exeter. And I would describe Mulbury as *contained*.'

'Ah. Secretive?'

'Not always.'

'Sometimes, then.' Marguerite reached into her handbag and pulled out a piece of paper. 'As with this.'

Rosemary took the proffered paper. It was a copy of a news article announcing the discovery of the skeleton in Jasper's backyard. Someone had snapped The Read Mulbury. She could see the startled face of Jasper inside the shop looking out at the camera. 'Yes. This was a secret.' She handed the article back and studied the woman's face. 'Like *you* are a secret.'

Marguerite's face was impassive. 'I sense you know who I am.'

'An educated guess. Are you Albert Connelly's second daughter?'

'I'm not absolutely sure I can claim to be his *second* daughter. He had, by my reckoning, several dalliances. I'll just say I am his daughter.'

'Is your mother still alive?'

'Oh yes. My mother, Augusta but she's known as Gus, is frail but living. She was as sharp as a tack until the last twelve months.' Marguerite shrugged. 'She used to run her aged care home in a similar way to how she ran my life, by snapping her fingers and making people jump.'

Rosemary looked for a glimmer of unhappiness on Marguerite's face, but it was motionless. Up close, she could see how the woman had applied makeup that covered any blemishes of normal skin and drawn sharp, symmetrical eyebrows onto her broad forehead. Only the slight redness of her eyes betrayed any emotion. The red made her look slightly weary and worn. 'Mothers can be tyrants.'

'Was yours?' Marguerite tipped her head curiously.

'No. But my husband's was.'

'And does he suffer now?'

'Alasdair has gone.'

'Oh.' For the first time since she'd entered the shop, Marguerite seemed uncertain. 'I'm sorry to hear that.'

Rosemary said nothing.

Marguerite straightened. 'Are you able to tell me any more than the media about this?' She waved the paper.

'There are no more public details.'

'That wasn't what I was asking.'

'There are no more public details.'

'I see. So I will have to go on assumptions. The skeleton is most likely my father's wife who disappeared in 1950. There will be an investigation because the backyard of that shop is not where she was supposed to be. There will be a lot of suspicion cast.'

'Which is why you are here.'

'Yes, that's right. Mud sticks, as you know. I would prefer it not to stick to the wrong person.'

'Which, in this case, is your mother?'

Marguerite pulled out her gloves and put them on. 'As horrible as she was a mother, she is still my mother. She did not have anything to do with this.'

'Do you have evidence of that?'

Marguerite tucked one hand into her coat pocket. 'None whatsoever. Call it the wish of a daughter.' She turned to go. 'Lovely to have met you, Rosemary Exeter.'

'Likewise.'

Rosemary watched as the woman exited, her coat

swaying gently against the top of her calves. She walked across the road towards Mullings of Mulbury and disappeared inside. Rosemary waited a moment, then hurried out of her shop to The Read Mulbury. The shop was dark, as Marguerite had said. Rosemary put her hands up to the window, shielding her eyes from the outside light, and tried to see into Jasper's kitchen, but the gloomy day prevented her from seeing anything. She tried the door. It was locked.

A laugh from the shop next door made her turn. Patti flounced through the doorway of Patricia's wearing a skater skirt broadened with layers of tulle. Behind her, a cameraman followed, stepping carefully over the front step and walking steadily to where Patti now stood in front of a rack of shirts. She unhooked one and lay it across her body to emphasise its unusual cut and the fabric which, to Rosemary, resembled a tablecloth.

'Alright then, Rosemary?' Gerry slipped quietly from the shop and sidled his way over to her, avoiding the chaos and lights of the crew.

'Have you seen Jasper this morning?'

Gerry shook his head. 'No. Not that I've been looking. This lot have been here since the crack of dawn, interrupting breakfast and rearranging the shop.'

'What are they doing?'

'Adelia wanted some shots of Patti in case she gets nominated for a fashion award connected to something or other. I can't remember what she said.' Gerry eyeballed Rosemary. 'That woman talks a language I can't understand. A mix of film school and haute couture. We're just simple Mulburians, Rosemary. That world is not ours.'

'It could be Patti's.'

Gerry looked across at his wife, who was caressing the

shirt as if it was a cat. 'Do you think? Oh, am I going to lose her?'

'No.' Rosemary watched as Patti beamed at the camera. 'Her world is here, and in her head. She's a true creator, Gerry. She won't be tempted by the trimmings of success.'

Gerry sighed. 'Thank you, thank you.' He lowered his voice. 'I get so worried sometimes that I will be left behind. I am not creative, as you well know. Patti is so much more than me.'

'Rubbish.'

'Pardon?'

Rosemary gripped Gerry's shoulder. 'Patti would never think that.' She nodded towards Gerry's wife. 'You're wanted.'

Patti beckoned to Gerry, who hurried over to her. She took his arm and held the shirt out with the other, talking earnestly, although Rosemary couldn't hear what she was saying. The cameraman lifted his head to find Adelia, who stood at the edge of the footpath. She waved her hand for him to continue filming but it was clear that Patti's attention was now on something else. She shook the shirt, Gerry nodding, and then held it up in front of them in order to study it better. Rosemary smiled as the cameraman lowered his camera in frustration. Patti was having an idea, one that she was only sharing with Gerry, and the cameras had been forgotten.

Rosemary left them to it and went back through her empty shop to emerge on the balcony that extended out across her yard. Both Mrs Lionel's and Jasper's, on first glance, were empty, but as Rosemary walked to peer over the edge, a sudden movement on Jasper's side made her turn. There he was, wrapped in a thick blanket, standing up from the outside chair he kept to sit and soak up any winter sun. She waved to catch his attention. 'What are you doing, Jasper?'

He sat down again heavily. 'Sitting.' His voice was croaky and his face as pale as it was, Rosemary noted, when he'd been at his sickest.

'You're cold.'

'Freezing.'

'Why don't you go inside?'

'Locked out.'

'Why didn't you wake me up? I've got your spare key.'

'Forgot.'

Rosemary frowned. 'What is wrong with you?'

'Cold.'

'Wait there.'

He had little choice. Rosemary hurried through her house, scooping up the set of spare keys she had for every shop under the veranda. She unlocked The Read Mulbury, pushed the heavy, sighing door open and picked her way through shelves and stacks of books and Jasper's kitchen to the back door. He stumbled in as soon as she opened it and slid into a chair.

'Better,' he said.

Rosemary felt his forehead. 'You don't have a fever.'

He shrugged and shivered. 'Feel bad. Sick.'

'Right. Where do you keep your medication?'

He pointed with a hand that still clutched the blanket.

She flicked the kettle on and went where he had indicated. His bathroom was much smaller than hers, and sparse. She hunted through the cupboard until she found paracetamol and came back. 'Have these. Then get into bed. I'll make you tea.'

He swallowed the tablets and pulled the blanket around him more tightly. 'Don't want to get into bed.'

'No choice. Come on.'

She led him into the bedroom, tugged the blanket from his shoulders, and pulled back the bed covers. There was an awkward moment as she considered helping him remove his outer layers of clothing that passed before she could blink when he slid, fully clothed, into the bed and shut his eyes. All she had to do was tuck him in. She did, feeling slightly disappointed and then cross with herself at her nonsense.

'Thanks,' he said, snuggling further under the duvet.

There was not much more she could do besides put a lemon and ginger tea on his bedside table and go back to her shop. Every hour or so she slipped away to check on him. A look at the colour of his face at regular intervals told her he was recovering, and by four o'clock, he'd drunk the cold tea. Rosemary shut shop at exactly five o'clock and found him sitting up in bed, face a better colour but with eyes shadowed. 'You need to take better care of yourself,' she said, folding her arms across her chest.

'Yes, Mum.'

'What happened?'

'I had dinner with Robert.'

'Yes. And?'

'I felt a bit odd after I came home and went outside for some fresh air.'

'Locking yourself out.'

'I didn't actually try to get back in.' He shook his head. 'I'm not sure why.'

'What did you eat at Robert's?'

'Delicious things. A vegetarian risotto. Gateau cake.'

'Drink?'

'Two beers. We weren't drunk, Rosemary.' He pushed the covers back and stood. 'Think I'd better go...' He nodded towards the bathroom.

Rosemary went to the kitchen, automatically filling the kettle. The little house was warm, heated as it was with hydronics. Jasper came back, taking off his sweater as he went. He flung it with a clunk into the laundry.

'Oops,' he said. 'Warmer in here than out there.'

'It was the coldest night of the year so far.'

'Really?' Jasper rubbed his head and pushed his hair back over his shoulder. 'I didn't notice.'

'Either you were very drunk—which you say you weren't—or very sick if you didn't notice the cold.'

'It's true, Rosemary. I didn't notice until you called out to me.'

Rosemary went to retrieve the sweater, rummaged in its pockets, and pulled out a small, clear bottle. She held it up for Jasper to see. 'Did he drug you?'

'What? No!' Jasper shook his head. 'That's a bottle that one of Felicity's kids left behind. I'm going to return it. Honestly, the things that go around in your head.'

'I'm checking. We don't know him or his habits.'

'He knows you, he says.'

Rosemary sat at the table and put the bottle in front of her. She shook her head. 'He went to school with Alasdair and me, but I didn't have anything to do with him. He was in the wrong group.' She shrugged. 'Or perhaps we were in the wrong group.'

'What do you mean?'

'He was in a group that I didn't belong to. Us and them. You know how it was at school.'

'I was home schooled until I was fifteen. I was so stunned at being at school at all that I don't remember anyone except my siblings.'

'I didn't know you were home schooled.'

'Ah, Rosemary.' Jasper tapped the table and grinned mischievously. 'You don't know everything about me.'

'And you, Jasper Lu, know hardly anything about me.'

'You know, when I say that about me, I'm sort of joking. But when you say that about you, you definitely aren't.'

Rosemary said nothing.

'Anyway, I'm sure it was nothing to do with Robert.' Jasper leaned back in his chair. 'It was a good night besides nearly freezing to death. He's got an interesting collection of very fine old books and he's going to do great things with that house. It'll take him years.'

'He's settled into Mulbury.'

'I'd say so. The business is going okay and he's drawing up renovation plans. You'll know all about it soon.'

'Why?'

'He's having a working bee in a couple of weeks. I volunteered us.'

'Thanks for checking with me.'

Jasper grinned again. 'My pleasure.' He stood up and went to the fridge. 'Will you stay for dinner? There's left-over pasta here.'

Rosemary shook her head, standing as well. 'No. Hannah is still at my place, and I left in a bit of a hurry to look after you.'

'Well, thank you. How did you know where I was?'

'I had a visit from Marguerite, who was trying to contact you.'

Jasper turned, slamming the fridge door. 'The other daughter? What did she say?'

'She's trying to keep her mother from being a suspect. No doubt she'll be back to see you.'

'What did you think of her?'

'She's very lean.'

'What does that mean?'

'Just what it says. You'll have to wait and make a judgement for yourself.'

'Isn't Tabitha visiting tomorrow as well? Maybe we'd better get Ronnie here to witness the convergence of sisters.'

'I'll call him.' Rosemary pushed her chair in. 'Get a good night's sleep, Jasper. Make up for last night.'

'I will.' He stepped forward, hesitated, then gave her a brief kiss on the cheek. 'Thank you. You've saved me once again.'

'Don't be ridiculous.' Rosemary patted his arm and made her way through the bookshop and out the door before he could see how hot her face had become.

SEVENTEEN

Rosemary was finishing her breakfast with Sunny perched on the back of the couch when the lock turned and the shop door jangled open. 'Mum? It's us.'

Ronnie had jumped at the chance to see Tabitha and Marguerite, and it was all Rosemary could do to stop him coming directly to Mulbury when she'd called last night. As it was, she could see from the slightly rumpled look on Honey Blossom's face that he'd been chomping at the bit to get here as quickly as possible and had probably hauled his wife out of bed. 'Just in time for warm bread,' Rosemary said, stepping over to give her daughter a hug.

'Getting harder, isn't it?' asked Honey ruefully, rubbing at her abdomen. 'Wait until I'm out here.' She extended her hand another thirty centimetres away.

'You won't get that big.' Rosemary took the cake tin she offered. 'Still baking?'

'Can't seem to stop.' Honey wandered over to the kitchen bench and sniffed deeply at the wholemeal loaf on its board. 'Trying out a heap of birthday cake shapes just to be sure.' She grinned at her mother. 'And the tennis club wanted round cupcakes decorated with their logo for a fundraiser. Ever made an entirely round cupcake, and not one that's just round on the top?'

'Only accidentally.'

'Right, eh? Ronnie had to eat a fair few failures.'

'Which didn't worry me.' Ronnie hung his satchel on the back of a chair and reached over to scratch Sunny under the chin. 'They didn't taste like failures to me. Cuddles liked them, too.'

Honey stared at him. 'You gave the dog *cake*? You know he's on a diet.'

'Oh.' Ronnie's face mottled. 'Only crumbs. He was hungry.'

'He always *looks* hungry, but he isn't.' Honey picked up a knife. 'I am, though. We left home without eating anything.'

'Have as many slices as you want,' said Rosemary, placing two plates next to the bread. 'Lemon butter for that?'

'You bet.'

They sat to eat, Rosemary taking the loaf crust as second breakfast. Ronnie jiggled in his seat, taking off every now and then to peer out the shop window in case the Connelly sisters appeared. He was coming back through the doorway to the house when Hannah stepped from the spare bedroom. Ronnie slammed into her, and Hannah shrieked.

'Sorry!' said Ronnie. 'Sorry, sorry!'

'Whoa, Ronnie, you scared the living daylights out of me.' Hannah saw Honey at the table and gave her a little wave. 'I thought I heard you come in.' She glanced at her phone. 'I am so late. But I am so tired.' She yawned widely.

'You need a day off, Han,' said Honey. 'No one can work seven days a week for ever.'

'You think? Isn't that normal? Your mum does.'

'I know.' Honey gave Rosemary a hard look. 'But she won't be able to when Tallulah arrives.'

'Honey,' said Ronnie. 'We'll be able to look after Tallulah between us.'

'I know that,' said Honey, lightly touching Rosemary's arm. 'Mum won't be able to resist visiting, that's all.'

'That could be the case,' said Rosemary.

'Nice,' said Hannah, yawning again. 'I'd better get going.'

'What about breakfast?' asked Ronnie. 'You can't do all that hard work without breakfast.'

'I can eat with Holly and Heather.' Hannah pulled on her hardy outdoors coat. 'Dad doesn't get up until late, so I don't have to face him over the kitchen table.'

'You still not talking to him?' Honey asked.

Hannah shook her head. 'What's there to say? Holly does all the talking. I just work.' She pulled her spiky blonde hair back into a rough knot and nodded to Rosemary. 'See you later.'

Honey shook her head slowly and ate another bit of toast without saying anything more. Ronnie did one more pass of the windows than sat down beside her. 'Maybe they aren't coming?'

'Ronnie, it's barely eight o'clock in the morning.' Honey poured more tea. 'Be patient.'

'What is it that you're particularly interested in, Ronnie?' asked Rosemary, pushing the milk jug in Honey's direction. 'These two women are not suspects, are they?'

'No, no, they were way too young when Agnes Connelly died. Tabitha was living in Mulbury, but I can't see any record that tells me where this other one was. What did you say her name was?'

'Marguerite. And, according to her, there may be more children. Albert Connelly got around, apparently.'

'She said that?' Ronnie picked up a butter knife and twirled it on his palm. 'I haven't found a trace of any others, but it could be true. Do you think we have a range of suspects if Mr Connelly had a suite of lovers?'

'I don't know.'

'I don't think so,' said Honey. 'If another woman was in the picture, I reckon there'd be more Tabithas and Marguerites snooping about. If it is poor Agnes Jasper found in his hole, then this Albert must be the main suspect. It was his backyard.'

'Uncle Geoffrey always said that the main suspect is usually the one suspect.'

'Meaning?'

'The murderer is nearly always the obvious person. In this case, Albert.' Ronnie scraped his chair back noisily and went to stare out the shop window again.

'I swear,' said Honey in a low voice to Rosemary, 'if he keeps doing that, I'm driving back to Big Town and leaving him with you.'

'I'll find him something to do.'

'If you could, Mum.' Honey leaned back in her chair and sighed contentedly. 'I'll keep Sunny company.'

Rosemary smiled and walked over to join Ronnie at the window. 'Mrs Lionel needs help with her window display, Ronnie. You could do that and watch at the same time.'

Ronnie frowned thoughtfully. 'Yes, yes, I could do that. Will I go next door now?'

'Why not? Mrs Lionel will have been up for hours.'

'Back soon, Honey,' Ronnie called to Honey as he jangled out of the door.

'Mrs Lionel didn't really need any help, did she?' Honey said as Rosemary came back in.

'She needs help every day,' said Rosemary, picking Sunny up and letting the cat rub her head on her chin. 'She just doesn't want to ask. Ronnie already helps her a lot.'

'He enjoys coming to Mulbury. He enjoys Mrs Lionel's shop. I don't think it would take much to make him stop being a private investigator.'

'He isn't liking it?'

'Oh, he likes the mysterious dead body jobs. Not the photographing of wives and husbands who hate each other. And the insurance work nearly drives him insane.' Honey shrugged. 'I think he'd be very happy to stop altogether.' She rubbed her stomach. 'But not yet. We need to think how we're going to manage when Tallulah is born.'

Rosemary watched her daughter's face closely. 'Why?'

'We both work for ourselves, Mum. You know how hard that can be.' Honey leaned forward to hold Rosemary's arm. 'If we don't work, we don't get paid.'

'Ronnie will continue his work.'

'Yes, but I'll have some time off and you know I earn much more than him. He's still starting out as a PI. At least I've been running my drama classes for years now.'

'Honey, it'll be okay.'

'Easy for you to say.'

'I wouldn't let you starve.'

'I know that, Mum. It's the mortgage and the bills...'

Rosemary put her hand on Honey's and patted it several times. 'It will be alright.'

Honey tipped her head on one side. 'Somehow, you always make me feel better even though saying *it'll be alright* doesn't automatically make it so.'

Rosemary sat down, Sunny still in her arms. 'It's because I'm always right.'

Honey laughed, a deep chuckle that made Rosemary smile. 'Yeah, you usually are.'

They sat quietly for a while, Rosemary enjoying the warmth of the cat against her chest and the sight of her daughter at her table. Honey had hair the colour of polished boots, much more like her father's than the deep brown of her mother's. She had Alasdair's green eyes, too. Sometimes it caught Rosemary by surprise, a glance or gesture from Honey that made her see Alasdair from the good times, before whatever it was that got to him. Mrs Lionel knew she had occasional thoughts like that and had asked whether it made Rosemary sad. It didn't. It was more like reliving a happy memory from a long time ago.

'Mum, you're staring at me.'

'Not staring. Looking.'

'Hmph. Same thing. Anyway.' Honey held out her phone to show Rosemary a photo. 'This is how my round cupcakes turned out.'

Rosemary was about to compliment her on perfect renditions of tennis balls when Ronnie jangled furiously back through the door.

'Are they here?' called Honey.

Ronnie appeared at the house doorway, strawberry blond hair awry. 'Who?'

'The two women you've been waiting for all morning.'

'Oh. No.' He beckoned to Rosemary. 'You'd better come. It's Rakisha.'

Rosemary set Sunny carefully down. 'What's she done this time?'

'Oh, it's more what she's *doing*.'

'Have they come to fix the barricade?'

'They're trying.'

Rosemary and Honey followed Ronnie outside into the weak sunshine. The Square was almost empty, it being too early for tourists. But a large workman's truck and trailer took up quite a bit of space next to The Exceptional Tree, as did a broad length of hessian. As they crossed the road, Rosemary could hear Rakisha's high-pitched voice. 'Oh, no you don't, darlings. Not today.'

'Oh boy,' said Honey as they went around the truck. 'What is she doing?'

Rakisha had bound a length of hessian around her waist and then twisted it through the branch that had speared the barricade. The end of the branch appeared above her head, making her look like a totem pole, while its leafy twigs seemed to add volume to her already voluminous hair. Two council workers stood in front of her, hands on hips. 'We're just here to fix this, lady,' said one, a tall woman wearing a pointy beanie. 'Then we'll be on our way.'

'We'll be quick,' said the other, a much smaller man with earmuffs. 'We don't like working Saturdays so you can guarantee a speedy resolution.'

'Resolution?' Rakisha tossed her hair back, making something rattle. Chains, Rosemary realised, as she spied the loops threaded in and out of the railings and ending up through the hessian at Rakisha's waist. 'Attempting to put boundaries on this magnificent Tree isn't a resolution, darlings. It's sacrilege.'

The short worker looked at the other. 'It's just a barricade.'

'It's a limitation.' Rakisha noticed Rosemary. 'Tell them, Rosemary, darling. Tell them the Tree does not like being interfered with.'

'The barricade has been broken twice,' said Rosemary.

'We know,' said the taller worker. 'It's becoming an expensive project.'

'Then leave it, darlings.' Rakisha rattled her chains again. 'Leave it as it was.'

'We can't,' said the short one. 'It's been reported as a dangerous tree. We have to do something and putting up a little rail isn't too bad.'

'It wasn't dangerous, darlings, until the rails went up. Was it, Rosemary?'

'I've never seen a broken branch until the barricade went up.'

'Ah,' said the tall worker. 'It does drop branches, then.'

'Only because the Tree is concerned.' Rakisha wiped a tear from her cheek. 'It has never experienced being locked in.'

The short worker's eyes widened as if he was experiencing some concern himself, but the taller one put a hand on his arm. 'Listen, Mrs...?'

'I am not partnered,' Rakisha said haughtily. 'My name is Rakisha.'

The woman smiled. 'That's a splendid name. I'm sorry to have offended you.'

Rakisha let her shoulders drop. 'No matter, darling. You have it correct now.'

'My name is Anne, which is nothing as exotic as yours.' Anne laughed. 'Well, Rakisha, I was going to say that we should talk about this...' she waved at the broken railing '... challenge we have in front of us. The council will want the Tree to have some sort of barricade for the safety of those who want to see it. I can understand that you think it might be too much, after all this time, and that people won't be able to stand at the trunk and look up into this network of branches.' Both workers stared upwards, the pale sunlight dappling their faces, but Rakisha stared steadily at them.

'What are you suggesting, darling?'

Anne dropped her gaze back to Rakisha. 'A compromise. Something to suggest to the council team that suits both purposes. A safety barrier that isn't threatening to the ...' She gestured at the Tree.

'Ambience, darling. It shouldn't threaten the *ambience*.'

'Okay, yes. That's what I was thinking.' Anne glanced at her colleague. 'Maybe we could have a cup of tea and talk about it.'

'I have tea,' said Rakisha, dipping her head towards The Sweet Potato. 'Earth-friendly coffee, as well.'

'Do we have time for this?' hissed the short worker loudly.

'Yeah, Dave, we do.' Anne put her hands in her jacket pocket. 'What do you think, Rakisha? It's cold standing here doing nothing. You must be freezing.'

Rakisha looked at Rosemary, who gave her a nod. 'If you insist, darling. We will talk but it may not come to anything.'

'It'll be a start, eh, to talk? You never know. I've worked many a thing out over a cup of tea. I reckon I could do even better with earth-friendly coffee.'

Rosemary studied Anne's face but couldn't see a trace of irony. Neither could Rakisha, apparently, because she pulled a key from a bag tied around her waist and undid the lock on the chains, letting the metal drop heavily to the ground. Dave unwrapped the rest of it, looping it together, while Anne undid the hessian where it was tangled around the rails. The three of them walked towards Rakisha's café.

'That's the power of suggestion,' said Ronnie.

'Or the power of listening,' said Honey. 'I get the feeling that not many people listen to Rakisha, do they, Mum?'

'Not enough.'

'Let's see if they reach a compromise.' Ronnie shrugged. 'Well, I'm going back to Mrs Lionel's until the Connellys arrive.'

'You won't have to wait long,' said Rosemary.

'Are they here?'

Rosemary pointed to a car pulling up outside The Read Mulbury. 'Here's Dr Tabitha now.'

EIGHTEEN

Tabitha Connelly had not had a good morning. The drive from the city had taken much longer than she'd thought. There'd been a car accident on the freeway and, although she was glad to see the occupants of the two vehicles involved arguing noisily in the middle of the road clearly uninjured, the resulting police and fire truck involvement had blocked the road for ages. She'd been hoping to arrive in Mulbury before the little town had fully awoken so she could explore alone and unchallenged. Now, late and without breakfast, she parked in the street alongside Gold-market Square in full view of a young man with ragged strawberry blond hair who seemed very excited to see her.

'Dr Connelly?' asked the young man as she stepped out of the car.

'Yes,' she said. 'Who are you, then?'

'Ronnie Edwards.' He stuck out his hand and she shook it briefly.

'How do you know my name?'

Ronnie tilted his head to one side. 'You said you'd be back to visit.'

'Not to you, I didn't.'

'No. You were speaking to Rosemary and Mrs Lionel. She's my mother-in-law.'

'Mrs Lionel?'

The young man's face flushed a violent shade of patchy crimson. 'Rosemary.'

As if hearing her name, Rosemary Exeter came over to where they stood. 'Hello, Tabitha. A cold morning. Would you like a tea or coffee?'

'That would be lovely, thank you.' Tabitha shivered. 'It wasn't even this cold when I left the city this morning.'

'Clean air and a town well above sea level.' Rosemary indicated her shop. 'Come inside.'

Clean air should smell like nothing, thought Tabitha, *but Mulbury is full of fragrance.* She followed the tall woman into her shop, getting a whiff of nutmeggy perfume. The shop, with its range of neat preserves and the polished chestnut-brown colour of the floorboards, smelled of cane sugar and balsamic vinegar. There was the striking ginger cat sitting in the doorway to the living quarters looking intently at Tabitha, as if she'd been waiting as well. Tabitha breathed in the warm sunshine of her coat as she bent to stroke her.

'Oh,' she said, looking between the young man and Rosemary as they entered the kitchen area. 'I'm interrupting something. Or are you a welcoming committee?'

'Welcome,' said a young woman sitting at the table. She grinned. 'Not so much a welcoming committee, it's just that this little town looks forward to visitors.' She extended her hand. 'Honey Blossom.'

'Tabitha Connelly.' The kitchen was alive with the freshness of baked bread. 'Do you work here?'

The young woman chuckled, and Tabitha felt her cheeks redden. 'No,' said Honey, 'I work for myself.'

Tabitha patted her cheeks. 'I'm so sorry if I've said something wrong.' She let her hands drop. 'This place. This town. It gets under your skin, doesn't it?'

'Oh, yeah,' said Honey, looking up at Rosemary. 'It got under Mum's skin a long time ago. Isn't that right, Mum?'

Tabitha watched the pair as they exchanged warm glances. *So that's what it's like,* she thought sadly, *to have a mother who is alive and loving.* She looked away and sighed. Visiting Mulbury had seemed like a good idea at the time, a chance for resolution about a lost mother. *I wonder if instead I'm stirring memories long put to bed?*

ROSEMARY WATCHED the play of emotions across Tabitha's face as she made more tea. She sat the pot heavily on the table. 'I understand...' she said to Tabitha during the next break in the conversation, '...you've come to talk to Jasper again.'

Tabitha leaned forward on the table. 'Yes, I've been thinking. Was there anything else in the... area he dug up besides, well, Mum?'

'It was the police who excavated the hole in its entirety. If there *was* anything else, they would have it.'

'Yes, I suppose you're right. But Jasper has been living in that house for years now. I wondered whether he'd ever found things in the backyard. Perhaps he was planting a tree or some vegetables and dug a clue up, but it was so long ago he's forgotten.'

'Jasper hasn't planted anything in that backyard since he moved in.'

'But he must have occasionally tidied it up. Pulled a few weeds out, that sort of thing.'

'Yes.'

'Well, I think it's worth asking if he's found anything.'

'It wouldn't hurt,' said Ronnie. 'I hadn't thought of that.'

'If he knew of something obvious,' said Honey. 'Surely he would have said something.'

'Something obvious, probably.' Tabitha chewed her bottom lip. 'But would something obvious be so obvious without finding a skeleton in your backyard?'

'True,' said Ronnie. 'Jasper might have forgotten about things he found when he first took over the shop from Mr Arthur. How long ago was that, Rosemary?'

'Mr Arthur shut the shop about three years ago. Jasper reopened it soon after.'

'He had to clear it out,' said Honey, pouring tea. 'I remember. It was full of leftover books and boxes of stuff that Mr Arthur just walked away from. But Mr Arthur cleared the shop when he bought it, didn't he?'

'He got rid of the printing press.' Rosemary passed the bread board to Tabitha. 'I assume he got rid of everything. He wasn't known for his sentimentality or his patience.'

'He tried to change the door.' Honey leaned forward and tapped her finger on the table. 'I really remember that day! It was too heavy, and he couldn't undo the hinges. I thought he was going to bring out a sledgehammer and knock it out.'

'Why would he want to change the door?' asked Tabitha.

'He hated old things.' Honey shook her head. 'He came to a beautiful little place like Mulbury and tried to turn it into a shopping mall bookshop. Needless to say, it failed.'

'Lucky.' Tabitha spread lemon butter onto a slice of bread. 'That door smells so rich.'

'The door smells?' Ronnie put his elbow on the table and his chin in his hand. 'I've never sniffed it.'

'Oh.' Tabitha shrugged. 'Sorry. It must be my research coming to the fore. Suddenly I remember how things smelled when I was a little girl. And the smells remind me of things.' She laughed. 'Your door smells of burnt sugar, and the lemon butter reminds me of this shop when it sold sweets. Lemon sherbets! Oh, I haven't had one of those for so long!'

Honey swivelled in her chair to look at her mother. 'Now there's a thought, Mum. You could make sweets to sell in your shop.'

'I have thought about quince paste toffees when I over-cook the paste.'

'Perfect! And you had so many lemons.'

'I don't think lemon sherbets have a lot of real lemon in them.'

'Hmmm....' Honey frowned. 'Maybe not. Still. You could expand your range with sweets.'

Ronnie grinned. 'Always thinking like an entrepreneur, aren't you, Honey?'

'Yes, I am.' Honey smiled at Tabitha. 'Sorry. We got off track.'

'Oh, no, that's fine. It's nice to hear...' Tabitha waved her hand. 'Family banter.'

'You don't have children?' asked Honey softly.

'No. I'm a single lady.' Tabitha laughed briefly. 'Not that it usually worries me but with this discovery I can't help thinking of my mother and how life would have been with her.'

'You had your father.'

'Oh yes. And he was a lovely, lovely man.' She shook her head. 'I cannot believe he had anything to do with her death.'

Rosemary said nothing. Tabitha's grief was coming off her in waves. Even Sunny crept silently back to her bed near the fire and curled up with her tail over her eyes as if it was too much. 'Well,' Rosemary said. 'How about we go and see Jasper before the shops open?'

'How about Honey and I stay here?' asked Ronnie, glancing out the window again. 'We can open the shop when it's time and you won't have to hurry.'

'Yes,' said Honey. 'And I'll get a chance to look through Aunt Lilibeth's book. That is, if I'm allowed.' She grinned.

'Honey, what a ridiculous notion.' Rosemary stood, leaned over the kitchen bench to retrieve the precious heirloom, and handed it to her daughter. 'But take it with you and I'll chase you to the ends of the earth.'

'You'd only have to go to Big Town, but don't worry. I'm looking for cake recipes.' Honey pulled out her phone. 'I promise not to tear out the pages.'

Rosemary shook her head once and put her hand out to shepherd Tabitha. 'Shall we?'

The women left through the jangling front door, which Rosemary tried unsuccessfully to sniff without Tabitha noticing. The Square remained empty except for the council truck, the splintered barricade and the unapologetic Exceptional Tree. The Sweet Potato's windows were lit with the glow of sandalwood candles and Rosemary imagined the council workers trapped inside with the heavy scent in their nostrils and the interesting taste of earth-friendly coffee in their mouths. She shook her head and steered Tabitha towards The Read Mulbury. The heavy door was shut. She knocked, resisting the impulse to sniff the solid wood.

Jasper appeared a moment later, smiling when he saw who it was. The door sighed open. 'Hello,' he said. 'Welcome back, Dr Connelly.'

'Tabitha, please.' Tabitha smiled. 'I only use my title to try and get better seats on an aeroplane.'

'Oh,' said Jasper, stepping back and waving them through. 'Does it work?'

'Not yet. In fact, last time I think I was downgraded.' Tabitha paused to run her hand down a display of short story anthologies. 'You have such a wonderful selection here.'

'I base it on my own interests,' said Jasper, letting Rosemary go first.

'Regency romance dominates,' said Rosemary to Tabitha as she walked towards the kitchen, giving Snowy a pat along the way.

'Regency romance?' Tabitha nodded thoughtfully. 'I prefer romances of the paranormal kind.'

'Really?' asked Jasper. 'I don't mind a shapeshifter or two. Particularly in Victorian times.'

As Rosemary thought it would, the conversation about romance genres went on for fifteen minutes before there was break enough for her to say, 'Jasper, Tabitha wonders whether you would have any artefacts from the shop as it was when Mr Arthur sold it to you?'

Jasper took a second to focus on her, no doubt, Rosemary thought, because he was still thinking of Miss Middleton possibly dallying with a werewolf or two. 'Artefacts?'

'Items. Things. Stuff.' Rosemary pointed to the tops of

the kitchen cupboards. 'Anything you might have put away or saved. Tabitha would be keen to see it.'

'Oh.' Jasper scratched his chin. 'The police asked me whether I'd found anything else, but I thought they meant in the ground like I found...' He looked at Tabitha. 'Well, they wanted to know what else was in the backyard.'

'And you said you'd found nothing.'

'That's right. I mean, not to say that there isn't anything out there, but I've never found anything.' He laughed. 'Maybe I should get Felicity's tribe to dig it over.'

'They like digging?' asked Tabitha.

'They're trying to find gold nuggets.'

'Not gold nuggets,' said Rosemary. 'A gold nugget. The Hand of Hela. Local legend.'

'No luck?'

'None whatsoever.'

'They like digging up bottles.' Jasper stood and retrieved the bottle that he'd taken from Robert's. 'Well, they may not like digging up bottles but that's what they're finding.'

'May I?' Tabitha held out her hand for the bottle and brought it close to her face. 'There's so much plastic these days that it's a treat to see real glass.'

'Do you recognise what it's for?' asked Rosemary.

'No. There's still liquid in it or it's got full of water from being in the ground. Does the lid come off?'

'Yes,' said Jasper. 'Easily. I spilt it on myself at Robert's and tried to wipe it off.' He put his fingertips to his mouth. 'It might have flicked onto my face as well.'

Rosemary eyed Jasper. 'You didn't say that before.'

He grimaced. 'You didn't ask. Why? Is it important?'

Before Rosemary could answer, Tabitha had the top off the bottle and had raised it to her nose. She yelped and plunged the top back on.

Jasper sat up in alarm. 'What is it?'

'That smell.' Tabitha pulled a handkerchief from her sleeve and wiped hard at her nose. 'I recognise it.'

'What is it?'

'Hang on...' She put both hands over her face and sat quietly. Jasper gave Rosemary a worried look, but she raised a warning finger. 'That smell... reminds me of...' Tabitha was still for another minute. 'Ah.' She put her hands down. 'Got it.'

'What is it?'

'Well, I don't know for sure. But there's a sense memory attached.' She lifted the bottle up again and jiggled it, making the remaining liquid splash around in its depths. 'Something to do with rats.'

'Rats?' Jasper rolled his shoulders uncomfortably. 'I hate rats.'

'Do you think it's a rodenticide?' asked Rosemary.

Tabitha frowned. 'A poison to kill rats? Ah. That could be it. I remember something about a mouse plague. *Rat* plague. They were in the shop. They ate the paper.' She straightened suddenly. 'They made a nest in the paper! I remember that.'

Jasper pointed at the bottle. 'So that's rat poison?'

'Possibly.' Tabitha wrinkled her nose. 'Smells a bit like... I don't know, actually. Only that it's familiar. Although something doesn't add up...' She stared at the bottle and shook her head.

Rosemary took the bottle from Tabitha and placed it in the laundry. 'Could be anything.' She washed her hands. 'No wonder you got sick, Jasper. You probably ingested poison.'

'I'm better now.'

'Still.' Rosemary indicated the sink. 'Clean up.'

The others followed suit, washing their hands separately. Tabitha splashed water on her face. When she came back to the table, she sat slowly and folded her arms over her chest. 'Maybe tell the children not to go digging any more.'

'Or to be very careful with the liquid in those bottles.'

They sat quietly for a minute. Jasper sighed. 'My curse rises again.'

'What curse?' asked Tabitha.

'Jasper has an imaginary family curse.'

'It's not imaginary.' Jasper pointed at the laundry. 'I was the only one to get an effect from the contents of that bottle.'

Rosemary scowled. 'Bad luck, not a curse.'

Jasper shook his head. 'You're saying it's not a curse, just that I'm an idiot?'

'You don't seem like an idiot to me,' said Tabitha. 'I'm the one that took the lid off and sniffed.'

'We'd better tell Felicity.'

'I'll ring Jules,' said Rosemary.

Jasper sighed. 'In the meantime, I'll hunt around in the cellar to see if I packed away anything that could give us a clue from Mr Arthur's bookshop. That's the only place I would have stored things he'd left.'

'Thank you,' said Tabitha. 'I appreciate it.'

A knock on the door made Jasper stand up. 'I'd better open shop.'

'Do you need to go?' asked Tabitha to Rosemary as Jasper wound his way to the front door.

'No. Honey and Ronnie can handle The Preserved Mulbury for now.'

Tabitha's phone rang. As she rummaged in her pocket to fetch it, Rosemary went into the lounge room to give the woman some privacy. She sat down on the couch with

Snowy, a welcome move for the dog who licked her hand happily.

Just as a pair of deep voices moved closer inside, Tabitha gave a throttled shout. Rosemary stood. Robert and Jasper appeared in the loungeroom. Tabitha came to the doorway, the sound of her crashing chair behind her. 'Rosemary!' she said, and then seemed to strangle on her words.

Jasper rushed forward. 'What is it, Tabitha?'

Tabitha clutched at her throat and shook her head, but as Jasper tried to steer her to a chair, she pushed him away. 'No,' she said hoarsely, 'I'm okay. No, I'm not. I am but I'm not.'

Jasper stepped closer to her in concern. 'Who was on the phone?'

'The police.' Tabitha stared across at Rosemary, her face twisted. 'The DNA result came back. The skeleton is not my mother.'

NINETEEN

There was silence for about ten seconds, then Snowy snorted loudly in his sleep. This made Robert look down at the ancient dog, Jasper take a step forward, and Rosemary move to Tabitha who looked like she was on the verge of collapsing. She helped the stunned woman back to a kitchen chair. 'They didn't say anything else?'

Tabitha shook her head. 'Nothing else,' she croaked. 'I don't suppose they could.'

'Then who was it in my backyard?' Jasper shook his head. 'This is bizarre.'

'Was there anyone else reported missing during that time?' asked Robert, moving into the kitchen to gaze out to the yard. 'Or maybe even before the printery was established?'

'Ronnie said they were able to determine the approximate age of the skeleton and how long it had been buried.' Rosemary put a hand on Tabitha's shoulder. 'The timing of Agnes Connelly's disappearance is commensurate with that.'

'Then maybe she did jump down a mineshaft.' Tabitha

sniffed back some tears. 'Somehow, that makes me feel worse.'

'Worse than someone murdering her?' asked Jasper.

Tabitha's brow wrinkled. 'I don't want to believe that she would leave me unless she had no choice.'

'Oh.' Jasper ran a hand across his face. 'Of course.'

Robert turned a sympathetic face towards Tabitha. Rosemary saw him notice the bottle on the table and take a step towards it. 'There it is. I said to Jules this morning that her kids had left five bottles behind, and I could only find four. I'd forgotten Jasper had this one.' He reached out to take it.

Tabitha jumped. 'Careful!'

Robert jerked his hand back. 'What is it?'

'There's poison in the bottle.'

'After all this time?'

'We think it made Jasper sick.' Tabitha shook her head. 'He was very lucky.'

'I had no idea.' Robert shook his head. 'Are you okay?'

'I am now.' Jasper tilted his head towards Rosemary. 'Someone took care of me.'

The way the two men turned their attention to Rosemary made her lift her chin. 'As if I could've left you on the balcony to freeze.'

'Still,' said Jasper, 'it was-'

Whatever it was, it stayed unheard. The door of the shop heaved open and several voices talking together drowned him out. Jasper's shoulders slumped. 'Adelia,' he muttered. 'I thought she'd finished with me.'

'Jasper! Jasper Lu!' Adelia's slim form presented at the doorway to the house. 'We need more shots with your mother's books. I have just discovered she won the Nebula three times. Such an extraordinary achievement. Perhaps you can do a little exposé of the winning books?' Adelia waved her hand around at *exposé* as if critiquing your mother's books was as easy as walking. Her hand stopped mid-flight, though, when she saw Robert.

Rosemary looked swiftly at the mechanic. His face was impassive.

'I recognise you.' Adelia walked through the lounge, startling at Snowy on the couch, but keeping her eyes on the tall man in his leather jacket. 'Robert Sparkling, Esquire.'

'Not Esquire. But, yes, I am Robert Sparkling.' Robert put his hands into his jacket pockets. 'Have we met?'

'We have now.' Adelia glanced behind her, beckoning the film crew through with a quick flick of her fingers. 'How intriguing that you are in this little town. Mind you, it's full of surprises. Billionaires, fashion designers, sons of cult literary figures, and skeletons. Quite the place to be for a film-maker.' She stepped around the couch and faced the kitchen, leaving enough room for the cameraman.

'Do you mind?' asked Jasper. 'This is my house.'

'In which you said you didn't mind if we filmed you *at large* in true documentary style.'

'You don't have permission to film *us*,' said Rosemary.

'No, that's true.' Adelia waved her hand again and the cameraman shifted his lens away from Rosemary. 'We'll cut those bits.'

Robert was next to Jasper, making it a seemingly difficult task to not include at least parts of Robert in any shot. He noticed and took a few steps sideways. The cameraman widened his focus.

'So, Robert Sparkling, what's your story?'

'Nothing you need to know.'

'Moved here?'

Robert shifted his weight from one foot to the next. 'I'm the local mechanic.'

Adelia put a hand tinged with red-hot nails over her mouth but couldn't stop the guffaw from escaping. 'You work as a *mechanic*? You *work*?'

'Yes, I *work*.' Robert's voice was hard. 'Of course.'

'Of course, of course.' Adelia let her hand drop. 'And what have you bought in this little town? How many properties?'

'The garage was for sale. I'm a mechanic so there's no guessing what I did.'

'Yes, you're a mechanic. Yes, yes.' Adelia's mouth twisted the word mechanic around like it tasted salty. 'And a home? You plan to live here?'

'I bought a house.'

Rosemary saw Jasper twitch and glared at him. Although she agreed that the mayoral residence was a notch above what most people think would be a house, she didn't want to give Adelia any more fodder.

'Lovely, lovely. Anything else? There would have to be more purchases than that. You could buy the whole town if you wanted.'

Robert's lips were a firm, thin line.

Adelia switched to Jasper. 'And you're friends with one of the wealthiest men in Australia?'

Jasper's twitch was in danger of becoming a tic. Rosemary moved around the table so she partly blocked the cameraman's wide angle. 'We were in the middle of a private conversation when you came in. You could respect that.'

Adelia smiled. 'My apologies for the disruption, of course, but I'm delighted that this little town is so full of wonder! I imagine that the place is teeming with back stories that I'd love to bring out into the light.' She stared at Rosemary. 'Perhaps you have one?'

Jasper moved to block Rosemary from Adelia. 'I can hear someone at the door. Would you excuse me?' He glared at the cameraman who followed Jasper back through the lounge and into the shop. Adelia hesitated, gave Robert Sparkling a little wave, and left.

'Goodness,' said Tabitha, fanning herself with the Regency romance that Jasper had left on the table. 'She's a force of her own.'

'Yes.' Rosemary looked at Robert. 'A billionaire?'

Robert shrugged, the high spots of colour appearing again on his cheeks. 'My father was an entrepreneur and he passed his wealth on. You don't remember him?'

'No. If I didn't remember you, I would hardly remember your father.'

'I couldn't help but remember *you*. You were the year above. You had long, dark hair. You were clever.' He shrugged again. 'I admired you.'

'How sweet is that,' said Tabitha, propping her chin in her hand and gazing at Robert. 'After all those years, you still remember your first crush.'

Robert laughed shortly. 'Crush? I suppose so.'

'Lots of water under that bridge,' said Rosemary.

'Not much has changed. There's something about you, Rosemary Exeter.' He twitched his shoulders. 'I mean, you still have long, dark hair and you're still clever.'

Rosemary took the end of her braid and held it out. The silver strip that ran from her right temple made it through to the tips. Hardly dark, she thought, but felt disinclined to point it out.

'Gosh,' said Tabitha, 'it sounds like you still have that crush.'

Rosemary kept her eyes on Tabitha, feeling the air in the little kitchen thicken. Voices saved the moment again. The film mob reappeared, lenses trained on Jasper, who had walked in with a severe-looking woman in an emerald coat.

Rosemary stood. 'Marguerite.'

The woman entered the kitchen. 'Rosemary Exeter.' Her gaze travelled to Tabitha and stopped. 'Ah.'

'Ah?' Tabitha looked across the faces in the room. '*Ah?*'

Footsteps hurried through the shop and Ronnie appeared in Jasper's lounge. 'Sorry, can I come in?'

Jasper raised his hand. 'Hi, Ronnie. Do you need Rosemary?'

'No. Well, yes. Maybe. Rosemary?'

'Here, Ronnie.'

Ronnie got as far as the couch and stopped. 'Oh, I see you. And I see...well, I was just coming to tell you...but I see you know.' He straightened. 'Hello. I'm Ronnie Edwards. I'm not sure that I've been introduced to everyone.'

'Ronnie is my son-in-law,' said Rosemary. 'And a private investigator.'

'You don't say?' Adelia beckoned her crew closer. 'Investigating what?'

'Oh.' Ronnie's face mottled and he glanced at Tabitha. 'I can't say.'

'Agnes Connelly's skeleton?' Adelia grinned. 'How marvellous.'

'The skeleton is not my mother,' said Tabitha loudly. 'I've just found out.'

'I beg your pardon?' Marguerite bent a little to stare at Tabitha. 'You *are* Tabitha Connelly?'

'Yes.' Tabitha frowned. 'And who are you?'

But Ronnie had recovered enough to blurt out. 'It's not Agnes Connelly? How do you know?'

Rosemary gave a little shake of her head, but it was too late.

'My DNA didn't match.' Tabitha hiccupped. 'My mother is still missing.'

'If the skeleton isn't your mother,' said Marguerite slowly. 'Then who is it?'

Tabitha slammed the novel down. 'Who *are* you? Why do you know me when I don't know you?' She sniffed suddenly. 'Wait. What are you wearing?'

Marguerite put a hand on the lapel of her jacket. 'A coat.'

'I can see that!' Tabitha sniffed again. 'Whose coat?'

'My coat, obviously.'

Tabitha shook her head. 'Before it was yours. Whose coat was it?'

Marguerite's smooth forehead creased. 'It has always been my coat.'

Tabitha shook her head and put her hand on her head. 'No...oh, I can't quite get it.'

Marguerite looked at Rosemary then gazed at the ceiling. 'She's not what I was expecting.'

Silence fell until Tabitha took her hand away and stared up at the tall stranger. 'You haven't answered my question.'

'No. I'm wondering whether I should.'

'Why wouldn't you?'

Marguerite sighed and glanced around at the crowd of people. 'I don't suppose I could sit down?'

Jasper jumped into action. He took Marguerite's coat as she peeled it off to reveal a perfectly tailored lilac pantsuit and pulled out a chair for her to sit down. He nodded at Ronnie and then towards the kettle. Ronnie took a moment but finally got it and went to make tea. Marguerite settled down, her back to Adelia. 'I will tell you once any excess people in the room are gone.'

'That means you,' said Robert firmly, ushering Adelia from the doorway. 'And me. Time for us to go.'

'Are you going back to work?' asked Adelia, moving backwards and smiling coquettishly at him. 'Perhaps we could walk with you.'

'Walk wherever you like in public.' Robert lifted his hand to Jasper. 'Later.'

Jasper mouthed a thank you to Robert as the mechanic kept the film crew moving out the door. 'I am so sorry for that,' he said, helping Ronnie with the teapot. 'They aren't in town for much longer and I think if I talked about the Nebulas, they would leave much sooner.'

'They're like bees in a honey pot,' said Tabitha. 'Now.' She folded her hands in front of her on the table and stared at Marguerite.

'You have no idea?'

'Of whom you are? None whatsoever.'

'There's no other way of softening this.' Marguerite matched Tabitha's hand posture. 'I am your half-sister.'

Tabitha kept her gaze on the woman in front of her, but Rosemary saw the plethora of emotions run across her face. Amazement then disbelief, followed by denial then surprise, and lastly sadness. 'I have a sister?'

'Possibly more than one.'

'How do you come to that conclusion?'

'Your father—our father—enjoyed a dalliance or two, so I've been told.'

'By whom?'

'My mother.'

'Oh.' Tabitha rubbed her thumbs together. 'And she's still alive?'

'Oh, my word, yes.'

'Aren't you lucky.'

Marguerite let her head tip slightly. 'Is that all you have to say?'

'Oh, no.' Tabitha leaned back and shook her head. 'Once I process this, I'll have a lot to say. Just not right now.'

Jasper served tea, placing the remaining Florentines in the middle of the table where they stayed untouched. Tabitha sipped noisily while Marguerite held her cup without drinking. Finally, Ronnie broke the quiet, pulling back a chair noisily and plonking himself down. 'Sorry, sorry,' he said, appearing not to notice Rosemary's stern *stop it Ronnie* look. 'But if the skeleton is not your mother, Dr Connelly, or your mother, Ms Connelly, then who on earth is it?'

TWENTY

Despite many cups of tea, the rest of Franco's biscuits, and a batch of scones that Rosemary whipped up while the others were talking, the answer to that question remained elusive. Ronnie told the sisters what he knew, pulling the photograph of the suicide note up on his phone to show them. Jasper disappeared into his cellar to rummage among his boxes for items he may have forgotten about. Rosemary went back to check on Honey, who was sitting happily at the shop counter leafing through Aunt Lilibeth's book.

'Not much happening today,' she said, as Rosemary jangled back through the door. 'I've read this book from cover to cover, including the warnings.'

'Warnings?'

'Yeah, you know.' Honey held the book up. 'See? Right at the bottom. She's written *Warning! Do not use these bottles for preserves* and drawn a picture.'

Rosemary plucked the book from her daughter.

'What is it, Mum?'

'I knew I'd seen that bottle somewhere. Lilibeth's drawn it in here. She's even shaded it blue.'

'What bottle?'

'One that Eliza loaned me. I've given it to Mrs Lionel to wash.'

'Why would Lilibeth warn about using it?'

'It'll be an early poison bottle before they marked it as such.'

'Poison!' Honey stole the book back. 'Lucky you haven't used any, then.' She glanced slyly at her mother. 'Or have you?'

'Certainly not.'

Honey chuckled. 'I sold the rest of your marmalade. The ones in the *nice* bottles. Any more in stock?'

'I'll get some.' Rosemary went into her own cellar to retrieve more jars of the golden preserve, pausing a moment to run her gaze over the shelves. Everything stored in there was neat and accounted for. She compared it to Jasper's mess of collapsed cardboard boxes. There was a strong possibility of finding something from the past at the back of Jasper's cellar. The real issue was locating it among the paperbacks.

'Is Ronnie okay in there?' Honey stood to help her mother restock the shelves.

'Yes.'

'I imagine he has those sisters bailed up.'

'He's asking a lot of questions.'

'Is he finding out anything useful?'

'We've found out that the skeleton is not Tabitha's mother.'

'Really? Who is it?'

'No one has any idea.'

'No hints from the sisters?'

Rosemary shook her head. 'None. They were too young to remember anything from the time the skeleton was buried. Tabitha has vague, warm thoughts of her mother, and much stronger happy ones of her father. Marguerite remembers nothing of her father, and the way she talks about her mother is guarded.'

'Guarded?'

'Let's say it's not oozing happiness.'

'I see.' Honey put the last jar on the shelf and ran her hand across her abdomen. 'I'm going to make sure this baby knows happiness.'

'Of course, you are.' Rosemary put her arm around her daughter's shoulders. 'There's no way you wouldn't.'

Honey smiled and put her head momentarily on Rosemary's shoulder, but a crash outside made them both look out the shop window. 'What was that?'

The council truck in the Square was moving back towards the road, dragging the fallen branch of The Exceptional Tree behind it. It stopped as its nose hit the curb, leaving the branch stretched out behind it. Jumping up and down next to the branch, purple skirts bouncing, was Rakisha. Even inside the shop, Rosemary could hear her laughing.

'Does that mean they've come to some sort of arrangement that Rakisha is happy with?' asked Honey, turning to her mother.

'Best we go and see.'

They left the shop at the same time as Mrs Lionel came out of hers, tugging her coat over her shoulders. 'Any idea what's going on, dear?' she said, coming up beside Honey.

'None whatsoever,' said Honey, giving the older woman a quick hug. 'But Rakisha is happy.'

'That could be for a number of reasons,' said Mrs Lionel quietly as they crossed the road. 'Some of them less than desirable.'

By the time they got to Rakisha, Anne and Dave were out of the truck. They stood next to the dancing Rakisha, gazing thoughtfully at the large branch. 'You think this is going to work?' asked Dave.

'It's possible.' Anne rested her hand on Rakisha's shoulder. 'Tell us again what we're doing.'

'Oh, darlings, it's a divine idea! And you're sure can get the other one back?'

'Yep,' said Dave. 'I know exactly where it is.'

'Wonderful, wonderful!' Rakisha caught sight of Rosemary, Honey and Mrs Lionel. 'Oh, darlings, we've had the most wonderful idea!'

'What about, Rakisha?' asked Mrs Lionel.

'The nasty, horrible barricade, darling.' Rakisha stepped up and over the branch, nearly coming to grief as her skirt caught on the end, but righting herself in time. She looped her arm through Mrs Lionel's. 'We are going to give these gifts back to the Tree!'

'What gifts?' asked Honey.

'The branches, darling girl.' Rakisha waved her bangles at the dead limb in front of her. 'We're going to use these gifts from the Tree to create an *entanglement*.'

Honey turned to Rosemary. 'A what?'

Rosemary shrugged.

'An *entanglement*, darling.' Rakisha let Mrs Lionel go and wove her hands in and out of each other. 'We'll use the twigs and leaves and wood from the branches to create an artistic entanglement of the Tree's form and place it under the Tree as a way of appeasing its discontent.'

Honey craned her neck to see the council workers. 'And you understand what she's saying?'

Anne grinned. 'We've come up with a plan that suits all parties.' She held up her phone. 'I have verbal approval. We have to fix the current barricade, but it may not have to stay there if we can produce a more artistic version.'

'It's going to be so charming, darlings!'

Mrs Lionel touched Rakisha's sleeve. 'Do you know someone who will be able to help with its construction?'

'Not construction, darling Mrs Lionel! *Creation*. It's going to be an earth-friendly creation that extends the reach of the Tree while satisfying the vile orders of our local council.' She grinned at Anne and Dave. 'And we have before us two dissidents of that vileness prepared to wreak havoc on bureaucrats who wouldn't know an entanglement from a thornbush!'

The moment of silence that followed indicated to Rosemary that most who had heard Rakisha's speech were still tackling its meaning, but eventually Anne raised her phone again and said, 'We've got verbal approval. And we should be able to get our gardening team to help.'

'That's all worked out well, then,' said Mrs Lionel.

'Fingers crossed,' said Anne, glancing at Rakisha. 'And on that note, we'll do a temporary fix on the barricade and head back to Big Town.'

The little crowd watched as Dave unhitched the branch and reversed the truck back to the barricade. Rosemary indicated the shops across the road. 'I'll go and check how things are at Jasper's. Are you still happy keeping shop, Honey?'

'Yes, very happy.' Honey pointed to the garage. 'I saw the film crew come out of the bookshop. They followed that new man for a bit but I think he told them to go away. They piled into their van and headed for Big Town.'

'Adelia Lochard has her fingers in many pies.'

'What does that mean?'

'She knows a lot.'

'I imagine she makes it her business to know as much as she can,' said Mrs Lionel. 'I'd better go. Come on, Honey. A new bunch are here.'

Rosemary waved them goodbye as a tourist bus pulled up in Goldmarket Road, exhaling a chattering bunch of older people. She followed a small group of them back to The Read Mulbury and helped a particularly frail gentleman with the heavy door.

Inside, Jasper was already showing a woman his collection of real-life crime stories. He stepped aside to whisper to Rosemary as she passed. 'I found a box of old things. I just can't get to it. The box is stuck behind some comics.' He grimaced. 'It's a bit messy down there.'

Rosemary had to stop herself from agreeing wholeheartedly. 'Do you know what's in the box?'

He shook his head. 'I've never looked. I'd forgotten it was even there. Dirty, dusty things left over from Mr Arthur.'

'It's a wonder he hadn't thrown them out.'

'Yes, it is.' Jasper smiled at the woman as she gathered several books in her arms. 'He hated old things so much. But the box was crammed in the corner so he probably didn't see it there.'

'How are the others in there?' She tipped her head towards his living quarters.

'I don't know. Excuse me for a moment.' Jasper turned back to his customer.

The kitchen was quiet when Rosemary entered. Ronnie was writing in his notebook. Tabitha watched him intently, but Marguerite sat stony-faced in her chair, hands in her lap, staring through the window. She turned to Rosemary. 'We are no further along with this investigation since you left.'

'It has reached a stalemate?'

'Apparently so.'

Ronnie finished writing and sat back. 'That's so interesting, Dr Connelly. I'd never thought to use sense memory in my work.'

'It's not foolproof, Ronnie,' said Tabitha. 'But it's surprisingly useful. And my research showed that the sense of smell is the single strongest of all, but not stronger than all senses coming together.'

'Well.' Marguerite pushed her chair back and stood. 'I need the smell of fresh air after the revelations of the morning.' She reached for her coat and Rosemary saw Tabitha's nose twitch. 'Perhaps you'd like to meet up for afternoon tea, Tabitha? We probably should get to know each other better.'

'That would be lovely, Marguerite.'

'Three o'clock at...' She sought out Rosemary. 'Where would be best?'

'Three o'clock on a Saturday leaves you with little choice but either The Sweet Potato or Mullings of Mulbury.'

'Go with Mullings,' said Ronnie. 'Rosemary won't recommend it but I do.'

'Mullings it is.' Marguerite put her hand out to Tabitha, who shook it. 'Until then.'

'I just can't place it...' said Tabitha softly as Marguerite made her way out of the shop. 'I'm so close...'

'What can't you place?' asked Ronnie.

'Oh...nothing.' Tabitha stood as well. 'I'm going to get some air as well.' She shrugged. 'Despite spending time here, I've done little else than worry about that skeleton. Now that I'm back to square one with finding my mother, I can do some exploring.' She smiled briefly. 'Take my mind off things.'

Or, thought Rosemary as Tabitha left, *focus on what other memories Mulbury has for you.*

———

RONNIE AND HONEY left for Big Town shortly after, leaving Rosemary with an unexpected rush of tourists who'd been stranded when their bus broke down just outside of town. The long walk had made some very hungry, so the cafés and Franco's Patisserie were busy. From her vantage point in the shop, Rosemary watched as Tabitha and Marguerite had to eat their afternoon tea on a bench in the Square rather than in the cosy confines of Kelly Flanagan's shop. They sat a little distance apart from each other. Although physically quite opposites, Rosemary smiled at the way they mirrored each other's gestures, Tabitha raising her left hand to eat as Marguerite raised her right. They sat there gesturing compatibly until the day cooled. Marguerite pulled her coat more closely around her as she stood to leave and, once again, Rosemary saw Tabitha lift her head as if noticing a particular fragrance. They shook hands and departed, Marguerite towards Big Town and Tabitha in the direction of a local bed and breakfast.

Rosemary made a gorgonzola macaroni for dinner and had it on the table when Hannah let herself in through the shop. The young woman sighed heavily as she sat, stroking Sunny's back with one hand, and rubbing her own head vigorously with the other. 'Rosemary, I owe you so many favours for putting up with me. Feeding me. Letting me sleep in your spare room. Putting up with my grumps. I promise I'll make it up to you.'

'Slip me a bag of chicken feed and we'll call it quits.'

'Done.' Hannah breathed in the steam rising from the pasta dish. 'This smells heavenly, like something Mum used to make. I could eat the lot.' She stared at Rosemary with wide eyes. 'But I won't. There'll be plenty for you.'

Rosemary chuckled and passed a bowl of broccoli over to Hannah. She watched her eat for a moment, then leaned towards her. 'Hannah, do you remember how your mother smelled?'

Hannah didn't seem to think the question odd. 'Oh, yeah. Of course. Like fresh hay and toffee.' She shrugged and ate another mouthful. 'I don't know why as I can't remember her making or even eating toffee. She was more of a savoury type. But toffee it is.' She smiled suddenly. 'We kept her favourite sweater. Do you know, Rosemary, sometimes we take it out of its box and smell it? Is that weird?'

'No.'

Hannah sighed. 'I don't think it is, either.' She closed her eyes. 'After all these years, you'd think it would have lost its scent. Maybe it has and we're imagining it.' She opened her eyes and ate a few mouthfuls more. 'Doesn't matter. It doesn't take much to trigger our imaginations when it comes to Mum.'

'You miss her.'

'Of course.' For a split second, Hannah's fork wobbled. 'But we don't want her to be here if she was still sick. If you know what I mean.'

'I do.'

'Hmmm.' Hannah peered across at the pasta dish. 'Do you mind if I have some more?'

Hannah was usually quiet company in the evenings. The moment she sat on the couch, even with Sunny scooped in her arms, she fell asleep, a strand of hair rising and falling gently on her cheek as she breathed in and out. Rosemary watched her over the top of her reading spectacles, but she didn't stir, not even when Sunny extricated herself enough to pad at the young woman's stomach before settling down again into the warmth of her arms. 'You look quite at home there,' Rosemary said.

Sunny lifted her head. *I make myself at home wherever I like,* she seemed to say.

Rosemary slipped her glasses off and inspected her cosy loungeroom. Orange light flickered from the fire, creating dancing shadows on the warm walls. She sniffed. There was the faint odour of lemons, the sweet tang of cooked sugar, and a brief, sharp whiff of baked gorgonzola. All very present but also tinged with the memory of a larger-than-life Aunt who spent her days humming in her kitchen.

Perhaps Tabitha is correct. Smell is the strongest sense memory of all.

TWENTY-ONE

A horrified squeal drew Rosemary out of her shop the next morning and into the bitter cold of another frost. Felicity Capriccio stood on the path with her family, all dressed in warm coats, gloves and hats. The children had their city-clean shoes on, and Leif a pair of brown Oxfords that reminded Rosemary of Ronnie's Uncle Geoffrey. Mrs Lionel was in the doorway of her shop clutching a box that rattled as she went to take Felicity's arm. 'It's alright, dear,' she was saying. 'I've checked all these ones and they're perfectly fine.'

'Poison!' said Antonio. 'We nearly died!'

'No, you didn't, dear.' Mrs Lionel gave the boy a firm look. 'The only bottle that we realised was potentially dangerous was left at Mr Sparkling's. Jasper had a bit of bad luck, but all is well now. There's a lesson to be learned here, though, isn't there?'

'Yes,' said Eliza grimly. 'We need to buy a better metal detector.'

Mrs Lionel frowned but before she could say anything,

Felicity spotted Rosemary. 'Oh, Rosemary, we've come to say goodbye. Goodbye!'

'Goodbye!' chorused the younger children, while Calvin raised his hand politely.

'You're going back to Sydney.'

'Yes, our little holiday has finished.' Felicity put her arms around Penelope and kissed the top of her head distractedly. 'The Hand of Hela remains a mystery, but we had a lovely time with Grum and Pops, didn't we, kids?'

'Pops is the best cook ever,' said Marco as his family cheered.

'Yes.' Felicity sighed. 'You lot have to get used to me cooking again.'

'And me,' said Leif. 'I do the weekends.'

'True,' Felicity reached over Penelope to shake Rosemary's hand. 'We'll see you again. We aren't leaving it as long to return to Mulbury again.'

'Roman and Jules would really appreciate that,' said Mrs Lionel, finally getting Leif to take the box of bottles. 'They find it hard to get away as the restaurant is doing so well.'

'My parents are very clever businesspeople.' Felicity waved her hands at the shops under the veranda. 'But then again, this town seems full of clever businesspeople.'

'Yes, it is,' said Mrs Lionel. 'Here come some shining examples of that now.'

Hannah, Holly and Heather were walking across the road from Mulbury Feeds. Hannah's face was bright red, Holly's was pale, but Heather's was rosily healthy. They stopped just short of the family. Heather was singing softly.

Felicity gave the sisters a little wave and clapped her hands on her two boys' shoulders. 'Come on then, lovelies.

We're off.' She steered them over to Goldmarket Square, the children shouting, 'Bye! Bye!' as they went.

'The noise level in Mulbury will go down a notch,' said Rosemary, coming to stand next to Mrs Lionel.

'Hmmmm.' The older woman had her eyes on the sisters. 'What's going on here?'

Another few seconds passed before Holly came up to Mrs Lionel. She threw her arms around her and buried her face in Mrs Lionel's scarf. 'Holly, what is it?'

'She's had enough.' Hannah moved to her older sister and put a hand on her back. 'She's leaving.'

Although the last two words were whispered, Heather stopped singing. 'Leaving? Leaving?'

'Good one, Han.' Holly stood straight, wiping her eyes with the back of one hand while beckoning Heather over with the other. 'That was subtle.'

'Sorry, but it's true. Heather needs to know sooner or later.'

Mrs Lionel took Heather's hand. 'Let's go inside and talk about this.' She beckoned to Rosemary. 'You, too.'

The frog croaked long and loudly as they trooped inside, Heather holding Mrs Lionel's hand with both of hers and walking sideways because of it. Her long, golden curls hung almost to her waist and needed a wash, Rosemary thought. It was unusual to see Heather so unkempt as her sisters took such good care of her. Rosemary frowned as she shut the door firmly, silencing the frog mid-croak.

Mrs Lionel manoeuvred Heather on to her couch and made a funny clicking gesture at the ground that only Rosemary seemed to notice. Holly sat beside her sister with her hands in her lap, staring at the coffee table like she'd never seen it before. Hannah paced to the window and back, turned, and did it again. Mrs Lionel looked at Rosemary and shook her head slightly.

'What's happened?' asked Rosemary, perching on an armchair.

'Dad sold the business,' said Holly softly.

'Right. We knew he was going to but what else has happened?'

Holly lifted her head. Her eyes were shadowed. 'Isn't that enough?'

'Yes, but it's not new news.' Rosemary glanced at Hannah. 'Something happened today.'

'The last straw happened today.' Hannah stopped pacing and rubbed both her hands through her short hair which, Rosemary noted, could also do with a wash as it was streaked with dirt. 'You remember that we were branching out into garden supplies?'

'Yes.'

'Well, I'd forgotten that we'd had a big order of potting mix and compost and other stuff. All in bags, ready to sell to the gardeners of Mulbury. The delivery was delayed. We knew it would take months. Today it turned up.' She put her hands on her hips. 'Dad had a hissy fit. Said it was a waste of money, that the new owner hadn't been consulted. That the stuff would have to be returned. That we should be running down stock ready for the takeover this week.' Hannah stamped her foot. 'This week! *Tomorrow!* He sold the place and it's going to the new owner tomorrow!'

Her shouts died down, leaving the lounge room feeling hollow. Rosemary felt a spark of rage in her chest, and she breathed deeply to quell it. 'You still don't know who bought the business.'

'He won't tell us!'

'Why on earth not, dears?' Mrs Lionel put a hand to her head. 'I don't understand.'

'Neither do we.'

'He's a coward,' said Holly. 'It's as simple as that.'

Hannah let her arms drop to her side. 'Yes,' she said sadly. 'Our father is a shell of a man.'

'Oh, Hannah.' Mrs Lionel sighed. 'Some people don't cope well after a significant loss. Your father is one of those. He can't help it.'

'Maybe not,' said Hannah. 'But this takes the cake.' She sent a desperate glance at Holly. 'He's driving our sister away.'

'Do you all have to leave?' asked Rosemary. 'The new owner has their own staff?'

'Oh, no, didn't I tell you?' Hannah shook her head violently. 'We're part of the handover deal. We keep running the business and get wages for doing it. Dad tells us we'll *be better off* and *have more money* and *get more free time*. He completely missed the point of all our hard work. Mulbury Feeds is our business! *Ours!*'

'Used to be.' Holly chewed her lip. 'Anyway, that's it. I'm out of here.'

'Holly,' said Heather. 'Holly, Holly, Hol.'

'I know.' Holly patted Heather's hand. 'I can't think straight and I need some time away.'

'This is ridiculous.' Rosemary straightened her back. 'He has to tell you who now owns the business. There'll be employment contracts to sign. This can't be hidden.'

'He says we'll know tomorrow. The new owner is arriving at eight o'clock in the morning.'

'I'll be gone before then,' said Holly.

Hannah gripped the top of the couch. 'No, Holly, please. Wait with us. Please.'

'I just don't know that I can, Hannah.' Holly covered her face with both hands. 'I was already not coping with him and you carrying on. I don't think I can handle this.'

Hannah shot a pleading look at Mrs Lionel, who walked around to sit next to Holly.

'Listen, dear,' the older woman said. 'We can't possibly understand the stress this has put on you, but it's not time to make big decisions.' She put a gentle hand on Holly's back and rubbed it. 'I'm going to suggest that instead of leaving, you come and stay with me for a while and help me out with the shop. These days, I do need a bit of a hand. Ronnie Edwards helps me make my soap and I could do with some more when I make...' She glanced at Rosemary.

'Tinctures,' mouthed Rosemary.

'...tinctures. I bought very large bottles of vinegar which are becoming very heavy to handle. Would you do that for me, dear?'

Holly opened her fingers to peer at Mrs Lionel. 'I know what you're doing.'

'And what would that be, dear?'

Holly's hands left her face. 'You're being your usual wonderful self and throwing a lifeline to me.'

'No lifeline, dear. I truly do need a hand.'

Holly's lips curved momentarily. 'Sure. And we owe you so much, I'll give you a hand. Tinctures? I don't even know what they are.'

'Stuff made from other stuff in very large bottles,' said Hannah, grinning.

'That's correct,' said Mrs Lionel. 'Very heavy, large bottles.'

'And what about Heather?' Hannah ruffled her youngest sister's hair. 'Where is she going to stay if I'm at

Rosemary's and Holly's at Mrs Lionel's? We could draw straws.'

Heather batted Hannah's hand away. 'Dad,' she said.

'What about him?'

'I'm staying with Dad.'

'Heather, we're angry with him. You can't stay there.'

'*You're* angry with him.'

'You are, too.' Hannah tilted her head. 'Aren't you?'

Heather twisted a strand of her hair around her fingers. 'No. He's Dad.'

'But you have to come with one of us!'

Heather shook her head. 'Dad,' she said firmly.

Hannah threw up her hands. 'He's twisted her mind.'

'Now Hannah,' said Mrs Lionel. 'That isn't fair. Maybe Heather understands your father better than you?'

Hannah blushed. 'I'm sorry, Heather. Your mind isn't twisted. But, honestly, how can you stand him?'

'Dad,' said Heather again.

'He's our dad,' said Holly. 'That's what she means.'

'I get it,' said Hannah. 'Doesn't make me any less mad with him.'

'Well,' said Mrs Lionel, getting up stiffly. 'That's settled. Holly, you can have the spare room as long as you want.'

Holly stood as well. 'I'm going to get a few things now in case I change my mind. I'll be straight back.'

'I'll put some soup on for lunch.' Mrs Lionel held her hand out to Heather. 'Come on, dear. You can help me cut up the pumpkin.' She eyeballed Hannah. 'So can you.'

'I'll leave you to it,' said Rosemary.

'Oh, wait!' Mrs Lionel swooped on something that was on the kitchen bench. 'Here's that little blue bottle you gave me to clean. Wasn't it Eliza's? Could you see whether they're still there, dear?' She handed the bottle to Rosemary.

It was too late. Rosemary left the sisters and their guardian angel to their various devices to scan Goldmarket Road and the Square, but the rowdy family had gone. She slipped the bottle into her jacket pocket and went back to her shop. Sunny sat in the windowsill and gave her mistress a baleful look as the door jangled. 'What is it, Sunny?'

'It's me,' said a voice from the house, and Jasper Lu appeared, brushing his long hair over his shoulder.

'I was next door.'

'I know.' Jasper shrugged. 'Sorry, I came to show you something and then I heard shouting through the wall of Mrs Lionel's place. Hannah?'

'Yes.' Rosemary went to the firebox and rubbed her hands together in front of it to warm them. 'She was upset.'

'So I heard. Everything alright now?'

'No. Stable for now. The new owner takes over Mulbury Feeds tomorrow.'

'I see.' Jasper's troubled face cleared as he shook his head. 'Well, I was coming to show you what I'd found.' He pointed to a box on the kitchen table. 'I finally got it out of the cellar.'

Rosemary went to the table. 'What's in it?'

'Bits and pieces. Not very useful. They're pretty dirty.'

'And you put it on my table without cleaning it?'

'Oh.' Jasper's face warmed. 'I didn't think.'

'No.' Rosemary lifted the dusty lid from the box and put it carefully on the floor. 'What rubbish got left behind?'

'Not all of it is rubbish. See?' He pulled out a few items. 'A few old household things, a bundle of receipts from book deliveries, and a couple of bits I thought Dr Connelly might like because I reckon they're from the printery.' He sat a stumpy pot on the table. 'I think this is an ink well.' Some metal items clattered on the wooden top. 'A few letters and some pieces from the press. Not much use by themselves.'

Rosemary ran her fingers through the letters and marvelled at how they would have been set by hand into the press, ready for inking. 'A lost art,' she said.

'Pretty much.' Jasper reached out for the ink well. 'This is rather beautiful, though.'

The pot was a deep, burnished charcoal colour with a smaller, stubby top. Jasper picked it up and unscrewed the lid to reveal a glass bottle stained dark with old ink. Wrapped around the glass to stop it moving was a thick pad of blotting paper. He pried it out to reveal splotches of deep blue soaked in the layers. Rosemary held out her hand and he gave her the paper.

'Looks like a portable ink pot,' she said. 'The paper would capture any spills, but the lid holds the ink bottle in place.' She ran a finger down the outside of the pot. 'Bake-lite. They used it a lot in the first half of the twentieth century.'

'It's quite old.' Jasper handed the pot to her and she fitted the paper back inside. 'I wonder if Tabitha remembers it?'

As Rosemary raised the pot to screw the lid back on, she caught the faded scent of long forgotten writing, and gave Jasper a hard look. 'You know, she just might.'

TWENTY-TWO

Tabitha and Marguerite did not appear in Mulbury on Sunday, although Rosemary glimpsed Tabitha's car driving down the road towards Big Town. She hoped one sister was going to visit the other in an act of kinship but it was difficult to imagine strong relationships between them yet.

'Oh, you never know,' said Jasper when Rosemary confided her thoughts over a cup of strong afternoon tea. 'I discovered I had half-sisters when I was in my fifties.'

'You already knew your sisters. You'd been brought up with them.'

Jasper shrugged. 'Yes, but they went from being my full sisters to my half-sisters. It changes things. At least, for a while.'

'Are you okay with that now?'

'I think so. It helped me reconcile my strained relationship with Helena. We're half-siblings, not full ones, so no wonder we didn't get on.'

'But it doesn't explain how well you get on with Iris.'

He took a long, loud sip of tea. 'So, you're saying that I

was never destined to get on with Helena, regardless of heritage?'

'Yes.'

He gave her a crooked smile. 'I'm not sure whether to thank you for that or not.'

Rosemary poured more tea. They were sitting at Rosemary's kitchen table, Sunny curled up on the windowsill watching them. Jasper had come in for a quick chat but the day was slow and he'd stayed. He was good, quiet company, sitting with lanky ease in his chair and playing with the edge of the tea cosy. *It would be easy to spend more time with him.* She glanced at Sunny, who gave her a warning look. *But it's also nice to have solitude.*

Hannah's entrance disturbed her thoughts. She'd pushed through the shop door, walked slowly inside to wave at Rosemary and Jasper, and plonked herself on the couch. Instead of falling asleep, though, she sat stiffly among the cushions, staring at the firebox.

'Everything okay, Hannah?' asked Jasper, leaning towards her.

'No. Yes. I'm fine.'

'You aren't working.'

'It's Sunday, Rosemary.'

'You always work Sundays.'

Hannah sighed. 'Yeah, I know. But today I just don't feel like it.'

Jasper threw Rosemary a startled look. He left the kitchen table and went to sit in a chair near Hannah. 'You sick, Hannah?'

'No. Yes. I don't know.' Hannah scratched at her head. 'I haven't been sick for years. Maybe I've forgotten what it feels like.' She strained her neck to look at Rosemary. 'What do you think?'

'You aren't sick. You are melancholy.'

'Crumbs. That sounds worse than being sick.'

Jasper chuckled. 'I think what Rosemary means is that it's okay to take a day off now and then to think about the bigger picture.'

Hannah pulled a cushion to her chest and hugged it. 'That's my problem. I can't see a picture beyond tomorrow. It's like looking through a foggy window.'

Rosemary stood. 'Time to stop thinking altogether for a while. Tea, Hannah?'

'Yeah, thanks.' She leaned forward to where the dusty box now sat on the coffee table. 'Did the kids leave more stuff behind?'

'That's Jasper's,' said Rosemary, bringing a fresh cup and the teapot over.

'You a mudlarker as well?'

Jasper shook his head. 'I think I've been put off digging holes for life.'

'So where did you get this?'

'It was in my cellar.'

Hannah riffled through the box, pulled out the ink pot to put on the table, then sat back. 'Not very interesting.'

The door of the shop jangled open suddenly.

'Where is he?' called a high-pitched voice. 'Jasper Lu? You are not in your shop.'

'It's Adelia,' whispered Jasper. He tried to shrink into the chair, but the director appeared at the doorway.

'There you are. Come on.' Adelia curled a long, sharp fingernail at him.

'Where?'

'In with your books.' Adelia glanced at the overlarge watch on her slender wrist. 'Today's our last day in your little town and we haven't talked about your mother's Nebulas.'

'Your last day?' Jasper sat up a little. 'Then you're going?'

'Well, my friend, I have other things to do.' Adelia tapped her finger against her cheek. 'I have drained more than enough from Mulbury but you know I may be back. I hear they have no idea who your skeleton is.'

'They may never know,' said Rosemary.

'Mmmm...' Adelia didn't bother looking at Rosemary. 'Come on, Jasper. Hurry.'

Jasper pulled himself up. 'One last shoot,' he muttered at Hannah as he followed Adelia out the door.

'What I don't get...' said Hannah, settling back on the couch, '...is why he let her film him in the first place. He could have said no.'

'He thinks this is a way to find out who his father is.'

'Oh. How would that work?'

'Once the film is made, it will highlight his mother's books and the fact that she had a secret lover.'

'And he's hoping that will make someone come out of the woodwork and tell him who it is?'

'Yes.'

Hannah sighed. 'Well, good luck to him. Fathers aren't always worth the trouble.'

Rosemary opened the fire and poked it to make it glow. 'It'll turn out alright, Hannah.'

'What will?'

Rosemary sat back on her heels and closed the fire's door. 'Your current predicament.'

'What makes you so sure?'

'Because things are never as bad as you imagine.

Because sometimes the fork in the road leads to a better place.'

Hannah linked her hands together over the cushion. 'Are you saying that out of experience?'

'Yes.'

The younger woman chewed her lip. 'Can I ask you, Rosemary, about what happened?'

Rosemary turned so that she was sitting on the floor with her legs stretched out in front of her and her arms behind propping her up. 'You mean, with Alasdair.'

Hannah shrugged, then blushed. 'Sorry. I'm being nosey.'

'Yes, you are.'

Hannah wriggled. 'Sorry.'

Rosemary smiled. 'Being nosey is okay in the circumstances.' She tipped her head back to look at the ceiling for a moment. 'Alasdair has been gone for more than five years. In that time, I've built this business up to be comfortably profitable. It supports me, with enough left over for Honey if she needs it.'

Hannah nodded, vigorously at first, then more slowly. 'That's great.'

'But that's not what you meant when you said you wanted to know what happened.'

'Well, no. I was thinking more of that fork in the road. The one that made you stay with your business. After...you know...after...'

'After I found out that Alasdair was still alive?'

'Yeah, that fork.'

Rosemary let her chin drop to her chest. 'A sharp fork, that one.' She lifted her head up. 'But it made me determined to be independent. I had been hemming and hah-ing about this shop. Not after that. Full steam ahead.'

'So, you mean that it wasn't until you knew he'd left you and wasn't coming back that you started the business?'

'No. The business was already going, but not by much. I turned it into this.' She lifted one hand to take in the warm house, the golden glow of the shop, and the yard with its contented chickens.

'But I've put so much work into Mulbury Feeds!'

'You all have.' Rosemary leaned forward and crossed her legs. 'And that's good, Hannah, because it proves you have good business heads. But your fork is whether you continue as you are or build something that's yours.'

Hannah nodded slowly again, playing with the tassels of the cushion. 'That's why you don't like him.'

'Don't like who?'

'Dad.'

Rosemary thought for a moment. 'It's not a matter of whether I like him. It's how he's treated what you have done for him.'

'I think I know why he's sold the business to someone else.'

'Yes?'

Hannah was quiet for a long time. 'We've done something he could never do. He feels like a failure.'

'He said that?'

'No. He hasn't said anything. That's what I figured out.'

'You could be wrong.'

'Yeah, could be. I don't know. It feels better to have some kind of reason.'

'Maybe you'll find out tomorrow.'

Hannah sighed again. 'Maybe.'

She was quiet after that. Rosemary got up from the floor and went back to the shop to serve a couple of tourists who were intent on stocking up on tomato relish. Hannah was still on the couch when she went back into the house, the ink pot in her hands. Rosemary fed a purring Sunny, tidied up the kitchen, and shut the shop. Still Hannah sat.

It was so unusual to see the normally effervescent Hannah unmoving that Rosemary felt unnerved. She slipped out the door to see Mrs Lionel, but The Green Mulbury was vibrant with effort and it was all Mrs Lionel could do but acknowledge her presence with a tip of her head as Holly and Heather prepared herbs and spices right across the kitchen bench. Jazz music played too loudly for Rosemary to talk so she raised a hand to her friend and went back out the door. The Read Mulbury was closed, as was Patricia's, although she glimpsed Patti, Gerry and Jasper huddled around the little kitchen table, no doubt drinking a toast to the back of Adelia Lochard.

She crossed the road to The Exceptional Tree. It stood in silhouette against the star-studded evening, its leaves moving slightly to the occasional breeze. The broken barricade had been nailed together with a lump of hardwood, and there was no sign of any earth-friendly entanglement. Yet.

'Lovely night.'

Robert's voice startled Rosemary out of her reverie. 'Robert. Night walking?'

He came to stand beside her, his hands plunged into his jacket pockets. 'I often do. As do you and Jasper.'

'We do evening walks. It just so happens that at this time of the year they become night walks.'

'Twice a week.'

She turned to him. 'Are you spying on us?'

He pulled one hand out and held it up in protest. 'No! No, really. I suspect the whole town knows about your walks.'

'Meaning?'

'No meaning. Just pointing out that the town is small and full of observant people.'

She looked back at the trunk of the Tree. 'Yes. It is.'

He studied the Tree. 'Spectacular, isn't it?'

'Exceptional.'

He smiled, his teeth light against the evening haze. 'Are you walking tonight?'

'No.'

'Fresh air, then?'

She shifted so that she could lean her back against the barricade. 'Why do I feel I'm getting interrogated?'

He rubbed his head and shrugged ruefully. 'I'm sorry. I was just finishing up at the garage and I saw you come out. We haven't had much of a chance to talk by ourselves. This town has been full of excitement from the moment I arrived.'

'You caused some of it.'

'Only by being new.'

'Is it working out? The garage? Your new abode?'

'All good. The garage is ticking along. The house will take a lot of work but I'm going to see what I can do myself.'

'Is there a need for you to do that?'

'What do you mean?'

'I imagine that you could afford to pay tradespeople.'

He dropped his gaze to the Square. 'You know I could. I choose not to.'

'I understand that.'

He lifted his head and nodded towards The Preserved Mulbury. 'Going well?'

'Yes.'

'All your own work?'

'Yes.'

'Did Alasdair...?'

'He had nothing to do with my shop.'

'I'm sorry it turned out like it did.'

She looked at him sharply. 'How do you know how it turned out?'

'Oh, I must have heard.'

'Clearly, but from who?'

'Now, let me think... no, I can't remember.'

In the dimness, she couldn't see whether his face changed colour, although she studied it in silence for a long moment.

Finally, he stepped back and indicated the edge of the Square. 'Would you like to come back to my place for a pre-dinner drink?'

'No.'

'Oh.' He rubbed his head again.

She smiled. 'I have Hannah to cook dinner for.'

His shoulders dropped and he smiled back. 'I see.'

'Would you like to join us?'

He shuffled his feet and stared over her shoulder. 'Hannah Hubbard?'

'Yes.'

'And the other girls?'

'No. Hannah's staying with me for now.' She crossed her arms and rubbed them, feeling the chill seep through her sweater. 'Is there a problem?'

'No, no.' He zipped his jacket up, making it sit snugly against his hips.

'But not dinner tonight.'

'Not tonight. But thanks, anyway.'

She started back towards the warmth of her house. 'I see.'

'What do you see, Rosemary Exeter?'

She glanced back but the light had faded and Robert was in shadow. 'I think you know. Goodbye until the morning.'

'The morning?'

'The morning. See you then.' She didn't look back and he didn't say anything else, but he didn't have to. The morning would bring out Robert Sparkling's best-kept secret.

TWENTY-THREE

As Rosemary knew it would, the morning started with a bang. Hannah was up hours before dawn, trying to sneak around the slumbering household and failing miserably when she tripped on Sunny's bed near the fire and fell into a lamp. The lamp knocked against the window and then clattered its way down the wall while Hannah swore, tripped again, and knocked a pile of books from the table next to the lamp. Rosemary stayed in her bed, Sunny curled at her feet, until the noise subsided. She slipped her dressing gown on as she went out to the lounge room and found Hannah lying on the floor with the lamp and three books on top of her.

'Couldn't sleep any more?' Rosemary stooped to lift a heavy gardening tome from Hannah's stomach.

'Couldn't sleep at all, more like it.' Hannah sat up, catching the rest of the books in her arms and letting Rosemary grab the lamp. 'Sorry if I woke you.'

'Almost time to get up anyhow.' Rosemary extended her hand to Hannah and helped her up.

'I didn't squash the cat, did I?'

'Sunny sleeps on my bed in the winter.'

'Lucky.' Hannah set the books down near Jasper's box. 'Coffee?'

'Tea, thank you. Too early for coffee.'

'I'll make it, for once.'

'Right.'

Rosemary left Hannah in the kitchen and went to get ready for the day. Monday dinner was at The Preserved Mulbury that night, and she had a slow-cooked casserole to prepare before the day got out of hand. Which she fully expected to happen.

Within the hour, the radios in the dwellings on either side of Rosemary's house hummed through the walls. Mrs Lionel's was slightly louder than usual and played contemporary rock—Holly and Heather were up as well. Jasper's remained a whispering shadow, his usual news program a background to the clattering of his frypan on the stove. Hannah stopped for a moment, listening. 'I didn't realise you could hear so much from the others.'

'I don't notice it any more. Only if I *can't* hear it.'

'That would make you worry about Mrs Lionel.'

'Jasper is more of a worry.' She told Hannah about the night the bookshop owner almost froze.

'Poisoned?'

'Perhaps.'

'Just by sniffing the bottle?'

'More likely he accidentally ingested some.'

Hannah shook her head. 'He really does have a curse on him, doesn't he?'

'No.'

'You don't believe it?' Hannah shook her head. 'Don't you think the string of bad luck he's had is more than coincidental?'

'No.'

Hannah smiled. 'It takes a lot to convince you of anything out of the ordinary.'

'Yes.'

Hannah served tea and they sat in companionable quiet to eat toast. Rosemary wasn't fooled by Hannah's silence. The younger woman's knee jerked up and down, making the table wobble and Sunny stalk away in disgust. They sat until the sun rose over the misty morning, then Hannah jumped up. 'Time to go.'

'What time is the new owner arriving?'

'Eight o'clock.' Hannah picked her coat off the rack near the door. 'I'm going to get myself ready.'

'In what way?'

'You said it last night. This is a fork in the road for me.' She slipped her coat on and turned to Rosemary, a fierce glint in her blue eyes. 'I either stay and work for the new person, or I start my own business.'

'With Holly?'

Hannah's shoulders slumped. 'Holly wants to leave Mulbury. I'm not doing that.' She stood straight. 'Why should I let my father's stupid actions drive me away from the town I love?' She shook her head. 'No, I'm staying here.'

Rosemary nodded. 'Good luck.'

Hannah gave her a quick grin. 'Luck has nothing to do with it from now on.' She bent to stroke Sunny quickly and left through the jangling door.

Rosemary waited a moment. From next door, the frog croaked repeatedly, and she imagined the slender shape of Holly joining her sister and marching as one to the business that their father had sold out under them.

Her phone rang as she contemplated the scene ahead. 'Honey,' she said into it. 'How are you?'

'Right as rain, as you know.' There was a slight creaking sound as Honey shifted around in her chair. 'Just got to get in the right position. There. Are you good, Mum?'

'Yes.'

'I thought I'd let you know that Ronnie is on his way to Mulbury.'

'Why?'

'Well, my cakes have taken over the dining table so he's got nowhere to work. That's one reason. The other is that Marguerite wants to meet him there this morning. With Tabitha. It's all very clandestine.'

'Where are they meeting?'

'That's the other thing. They're coming to your place in about...' Honey paused '... an hour.'

'Right.'

'That's okay, isn't it? I told them you wouldn't mind.'

'Sounds serious.'

'But you don't.'

'What don't I?'

'Sound serious!' Honey's seat creaked again. 'You know far more than I think, don't you?'

'Do I?'

'Mum!'

Rosemary grinned to herself. 'Perhaps I do. We'll see in about an hour.'

'Perhaps I should be there as well.'

'You're welcome anytime, as you know.'

'Thanks, but this cake business has taken hold.' More creaking. 'I have five frogs in front of me, as well as an open book, a kewpie doll, and twelve lacy pink cupcakes.'

'Why would anyone want five frog cakes?'

'I have no idea. I just take the orders and smile. They're pretty cute, if I say so myself.'

'Put them on your website.'

'Already done.'

Rosemary used her phone to scroll to Honey's page. 'They look great. Are they on lily pads?'

'Edible lily pads made from icing.'

'Delicious.'

Honey chuckled. 'Took me longer than the cakes.'

Rosemary studied the way the lily pads curled upwards to cup the frogs. 'I can imagine.'

'Okay, got to go now. I've got a very special cake to make for today.'

'Have fun with that.'

'Oh, I will. Mum?'

'Yes?'

'What are *you* making now?'

'Precisely nothing.'

'That's not true. I can smell...'

'What can you smell, Honey?'

'Rich red wine casserole.'

Rosemary turned her head, but the ingredients were still in the fridge. 'How did you know I was making that?'

'It's your turn for Monday dinner, isn't it? And last time you made a lentil bake. So, this time you'll do your casserole.'

'Am I that predictable?'

'Only to me. Bye, Mum. Love you.'

'Love you, too.'

Rosemary shook her head as she finished the call. *Next Monday dinner,* she thought, *I'm doing a new recipe.*

The spare hour she had before her visitors went quickly. Casserole prepared, she did her Monday administrative tasks and checked that the shelves were heavily stocked. The dead of winter was a tricky time once copious amounts of marmalade had been made, and part of her looked forward to supplies of spring produce. The other part was glad of the respite.

Rosemary had just placed the last lemon conserve in the window display when Mrs Lionel appeared. She tapped frantically at the window. 'He's here,' she said through the glass.

'Who?'

'The new owner.'

Rosemary stepped outside. 'How do you know?'

'I've been watching.' Mrs Lionel frowned. 'Although there's no car.'

'But you're sure it's the new owner.'

'Oh, yes. Look.'

Rosemary followed Mrs Lionel's pointing finger to the large shed at Mulbury Feeds. The three sisters stood in a row in the doorway, facing in. They had their arms crossed. Richard must have been near them as every now and then his arm appeared, as if he was gesturing wildly as he explained something. 'They don't look pleased,' said Rosemary.

'They don't look anything, dear.' Mrs Lionel moved forward a few paces. 'Do you think they need us?'

It was a moot point, for Heather turned at that moment, spotted Mrs Lionel, and held her arms out. Mrs Lionel hurried towards her, Rosemary at her heels.

Richard turned as the women appeared. 'Mrs Lionel. Rosemary. We're in the middle of something. Can I help you?'

Heather was snuggled in Mrs Lionel's arms. The part of her face that Rosemary could see was tight with worry.

'Rosemary,' said Hannah, but couldn't seem to get any

more words out. Instead, she waved a finger at a figure inside the shed.

'Hello, Robert,' said Rosemary.

'We meet in the morning, as you said.' Robert smiled.

'You kept this secret.'

Robert shook his head. 'This wasn't my secret to tell.'

'It's not actually a secret.' Richard shuffled his feet and seemed to find it difficult to look at his daughters. 'It's a business deal.'

'One that I can see you haven't discussed with key people involved.' Robert was finding it hard to look at Richard as well. 'Why would that be?'

'I thought it would be better coming from you.'

Robert sighed and shook his head. 'I'm sorry this has come as a shock to you,' he said to the sisters. 'I made the offer in good faith. Your father was keen to sell, and I took the opportunity to support Mulbury.'

'You didn't know that we wanted to buy it from him?' Hannah shook her head vigorously. 'How could you not know?'

'I've only been here a few weeks, Hannah.' Robert dropped his voice. 'I'm sorry.'

'Well, too late for that now.' Hannah's eyes were bright with tears. 'And he offered us up as workers for you.'

'Again, I thought he had discussed this with you.'

'He *told* us. Not the same at all.'

Robert nodded once and sighed. 'Could you really have afforded to buy the business outright?'

'We would have found a way, wouldn't we, Holly?'

Holly didn't answer straight away. Rosemary noted the shadows under her eyes and the paleness of her face. 'The bank would have loaned us the money against the equity of the business.'

'At what cost?' Robert's voice was gentle, but Rosemary saw how Holly flinched. 'I'm not sure you have any savings or other assets beside what you've built here.'

Hannah put her hands on her hips. 'Well, that's just it, isn't it? We've spent most of our waking moments in this shed, building it up so that it supported all three of us instead of doing the other things we trained for.' She glared at her father. 'All *four* of us. Everything we made went back into it. We had a five-year and a ten-year plan, all carefully thought through. Not that it made any difference to *him*.' She sent a disgusted look to her father.

Silence fell. Richard looked like he was about to be sick. Instead of sinking to the ground, as Rosemary thought he might, he pulled himself upright and looked Hannah squarely in the eye. 'I know you think I've done the wrong thing.'

'Now there's an understatement!'

'But I have my reason.'

'Dad.' Holly's voice was weary. 'Just tell us. Please. We'll understand, I promise.'

Richard stiffened. 'Your mother's Will,' he said quietly.

Holly crossed her arms. 'What about it?'

'She owned Mulbury Feeds. She left it to me in her Will with one caveat.'

'Which was...?'

He inhaled deeply and let the air out slowly. 'When I sold, it had to be out of the family.'

Hannah snorted. 'Why would she say that?'

Richard threw his hands up. 'Because, Hannah, she had no idea how brilliant you would be at building the business up! You were kids when she died. She wanted the business sold immediately so that you girls could have the money and do what you wanted with it. I couldn't do it, I just couldn't.

And never in a million years would she have thought you wanted to stay in Mulbury and sell hay all your lives!'

The echoes of his voice died down, leaving the three girls in front of him with similar shocked expressions. Eventually Holly said, 'Why didn't you tell us, Dad?'

He let his shoulders drop. 'Because I didn't want you to feel bad about your mother.'

Holly shook her head. 'As if we'd do that.' She walked over to her father and put her arms around him. 'You are a silly man.'

Richard's arms crept over his daughter's back. 'You know, your mother used to say that.'

'I must have remembered.'

Robert Sparkling coughed, making Holly step back and look at him. 'I think we have a way forward here.'

Hannah cocked her head. 'You do?'

'Well, you have some money from the sale.'

'Yeah,' said Hannah. 'I'd almost forgotten that.'

Robert smiled. 'We need to have a long talk. All of us. Together.'

Heather pulled herself out of Mrs Lionel's arms and went to her father. Mrs Lionel stepped back to Rosemary and whispered, 'Time for us to go?'

Rosemary glanced back at Goldmarket Road where Marguerite had just stepped out of her car. 'Definitely,' she said. 'I feel another drama coming on.'

TWENTY-FOUR

Marguerite wore her emerald coat. It swept down to just below her knees, a style favoured by those from the 1940s, Rosemary noted. Marguerite didn't notice the women walking back from the produce store and made her way to Jasper Lu's bookshop, which was not yet open. Rosemary turned to Mrs Lionel. 'Second breakfast at Jasper's rather than mine?'

'What a lovely idea.'

'He's going to have an unexpectedly big turnout for an event he doesn't know is happening.'

Two more cars had parked alongside the Goldmarket Road shops. Tabitha Connelly had a little trouble opening her car door against the slope of the road, so Ronnie came over from his car and helped her. She smiled up at him, her head level with his chest. He caught sight of Rosemary and waved.

'We're headed to Jasper's,' said Rosemary. 'Why don't you join us?'

Marguerite watched as the troupe came near and shook her head. 'The shop isn't open yet.'

Rosemary nodded once in acknowledgement and bent to tap roughly on the window near the door. She could see Jasper's shadow in his kitchen. It paused, swivelled to see who was knocking, and walked rapidly through the shop to the door.

'Early-morning visitors,' said Rosemary as he opened it.

Jasper pulled back momentarily but caught himself and swept his arm down in a gesture of welcome. 'Please, come in.' He stood back as Marguerite, Tabitha, Ronnie and Mrs Lionel walked in, but stopped Rosemary as she tried to do the same. 'Has something happened?' he whispered.

'It's about to.' Rosemary patted his arm. 'Do you have plenty of eggs?'

'No. I've used the ones you gave me yesterday.'

'Bread?'

'Yes, got a couple of loaves from Franco.'

'Okay. Put the kettle on and I'll be back.'

Jasper's sigh echoed around the shop as he did what he was told. Rosemary smiled to herself as she went back to her home. He didn't always know what was going on, but Jasper had learned to play along. *He is too trusting. That's what gets him into difficulties, like being followed around by a film crew for days on end.*

Sunny greeted her with a short meow from her place on the windowsill, and Rosemary tickled her under the chin before collecting eggs from the fridge. 'I'll be back later,' she said to the cat.

Sunny licked the length of one foreleg. *Obviously,* she seemed to say.

Rosemary chuckled. As she went to leave, she paused, swept the ink pot from where Hannah had left it on the coffee table to put in her pocket, and went back to Jasper's.

At first, she thought the crowd had left and there was no

one there but Snowy on his couch and Jasper in his little kitchen space. But there everyone was, seated at the table waiting, while Jasper made too much noise clattering cups and teapots and a coffee plunger in front of them. He gave her a wild look as she entered. She set the eggs down. 'Scrambled okay for everyone?'

'Yes, please,' said Ronnie too quickly, his face the canvas for an abstract painting in shades of red.

'Thank you,' said Marguerite, her hands clasped in front of her on the table and her face grim.

'Lovely, Rosemary.' Tabitha had her chin up and didn't look at Rosemary.

Mrs Lionel just rolled her eyes at her.

'Scrambled it is.' Rosemary set about her task, waiting for conversation to resume but, after a few minutes of silence, it was clear that the conversation had never started. She waited until she'd placed heaped plates in front of everyone. When only Ronnie picked up his fork and started shovelling eggs, she sat down and put her hands around a mug of tea. 'Okay. Who's going to start?'

'Oh,' said Ronnie, a piece of egg falling from his mouth. 'I've already started.'

'Not the eggs, Ronnie. Continue on with that.' Rosemary tapped the table near his plate. 'Would you like to go first, Marguerite?'

'First?'

'At telling us what news you have.'

Marguerite nodded slowly, her perfectly made-up features immobile. She blinked and stared at Ronnie. 'You may already know.'

He stopped scraping his plate. 'I don't know anything that I didn't know before.'

'Clearly.' Marguerite dabbed at her mouth even though

she hadn't eaten anything. 'When Tabitha's DNA did not match the bones, the scientists broadened their search. My DNA was already in a genealogy databank so they requested my permission to check it against their find.' She touched her mouth again then let the serviette drop. 'The results came through. The DNA matches that of the skeleton.'

Tabitha jumped, making the whole table move sideways. 'Matches? What do you mean, *matches*?'

'What I mean is they've determined a link between me and the skeleton.' A shiver passed across Marguerite's face and was gone. 'They believe the skeleton is *my* mother.'

No one spoke until Marguerite, her impassive face suddenly red, shrugged off her coat to leave it hanging over the back of the chair, the length of it embracing Tabitha's arm before settling. 'That coat,' said Tabitha, her eyes closed. 'It feels like...'

'Didn't you hear what I just said?' Marguerite leaned over and jabbed Tabitha's arm to make her open her eyes. 'The skeleton is *my* mother, not yours.'

Tabitha shook her head. 'That doesn't make sense. You still have your mother. I don't have mine.'

'I have a person that I've called Mother all my life.' Marguerite leaned back. 'She wasn't much of a mother, but she is my only one.'

'Rosemary,' said Ronnie urgently. 'None of this is making sense.'

'Does this help?' Rosemary lifted the ink pot from her pocket and placed it on the table.

'Oh.' Tabitha stretched out her hand and carefully took up the pot. She ran her fingers along the top and twisted the lid suddenly to expose the glass bottle and its wad of blotting paper. She thrust it under her nose and inhaled. 'Dad's ink pot.'

Rosemary frowned. 'Are you sure?'

'Oh yes, definitely.' Tabitha stroked the warm, brown surface. 'A slight trace of phenol, which is in the ink. A distinctly tarry odour. Dad kept this in a drawer even though it was a travelling ink well. I used to play with it when I was very little, putting little dobs of ink on paper to see what happened. He was so upset when he realised it was gone. He thought someone had taken it. No, not taken. He used the word *hidden*.' Tabitha blinked rapidly. 'Where was it?'

'I found it among some bits and pieces left behind by Mr Arthur,' said Jasper, leaning back in his chair. 'Looks like they didn't belong to him, more attached to the old printery which had been closed for about ten years before he bought it.'

'Yes, I remember we sold all the printing tools to the new owners. Dad took up a job as a typesetter at a publisher's where they already had their own business. Oh.' She ran her fingers over it again. 'If only he knew it hadn't been lost for good. He was quite sad about it, mentioned it many times over the years as if its disappearance meant a lot to him.' She put her finger in the glass bottle and a piece of dried ink flaked off. 'Bower Bird Blue.'

'The same colour as the suicide note,' said Rosemary.

Tabitha's mouth turned down. 'Dad always had his ink pot hidden in a drawer of his rolled-top desk. You had to have known it was there to use it.'

'The note was in Agnes's hand.' Ronnie turned to his satchel and pulled the copy out. 'Experts analysed it. She would have known where the ink pot was kept.'

'The note was written in Agnes's clear and strong handwriting,' said Rosemary. 'Despite the fact she had been sick.'

Tabitha shook her head. 'She *had* been sick?'

'The official accounts recorded that she had been suffering what the doctors called hysteria, meaning a mystery condition possibly related to her recent miscarriage. She might have recovered.'

'Poor thing,' said Mrs Lionel quietly. 'She must have suffered greatly.'

Ronnie flicked through his papers. 'But there was a bit of sickness around Mulbury in those years. All women. Sounds horrible: nausea, diarrhoea, stomach pains. Isn't that what they reported Agnes had?'

'A Mulbury sickness, then,' said Jasper. 'I hope it's gone now.'

'It is,' said Rosemary. 'It wasn't confined to Mulbury. It happened all over Australia.'

'Do you mean what I think, dear?' asked Mrs Lionel. 'Poisoning?'

'Poisoning!' Tabitha clutched at the ink pot. 'In Mulbury?'

Rosemary pulled the blue bottle out of her jacket pocket where it had been a hard lump since she'd put it there. 'Is this familiar?'

Tabitha set the ink pot down and reached for the clean bottle. Quiet fell as she held it in both hands and felt its edges. She closed her eyes for a moment before looking directly at Rosemary. 'This bottle. Where did you find it?'

'The children dug it up.'

'From Jasper's backyard?'

'No. It was found among the other bottles.'

'Why do you think it could have been in my backyard?' asked Jasper.

'Well, you see...' Tabitha held the little bottle so that the kitchen light made it glow a pale aqua. 'Mum had one just like this in her apron pocket. I pulled it out once when I was sitting in her lap. She was so very cross and snatched it back. But I remember how it felt, the smoothness of the glass. And the colour... it's quite beautiful, isn't it?' She chewed her lip. 'Are you telling me it contained poison?'

'Most likely.'

'My mother carried around a bottle of poison in her apron pocket?'

'Poison was a common enough household product in that era,' said Rosemary. 'Felicity's children showed us that with their collection of bottles. Poisons were used as insecticides and rodenticides, but also to treat common ailments such as ringworm. The health authorities of the time didn't know that some caused severe side effects.'

'Such as nausea, vomiting and diarrhoea?' asked Marguerite.

'Depending on the poison and how much had been taken. Arsenic, cyanide, strychnine, thallium. They could all be lethal. In that era, there were a spate of murders and suicides that were put down to common chemicals that could be found in any household's cupboards. Commonly used with not such common outcomes.'

'What are you suggesting, Rosemary?' Tabitha's eyes were wide. 'That my mother was sick because she was poisoned?'

Rosemary said nothing.

'And the other women around Mulbury had been poisoned, too?'

Rosemary kept quiet.

'But my mother was not the one found dead in Jasper's backyard.'

'No.'

'But she was sick... Wait.' Tabitha held up the bottle. 'You think my *mother* poisoned those women? And then jumped into a mine shaft?'

'The former is a possibility. The latter is something I doubt.'

'You *don't* think my mother is in a mine shaft somewhere? Then where is she?'

Rosemary studied the pale woman in front of her. 'I suspect your mother, Agnes Connelly, is still very much alive.'

Tabitha's mouth dropped open and her hands clenched white around the bottle. Her grip was so hard that Rosemary wondered if the glass would shatter in her grasp.

'I don't understand.' Marguerite's face had lost some of its stiffness, but it was still ashen. 'How do you know that?'

Rosemary tilted her head to the back of Marguerite's coat. 'Your coat. Or should I say, your *mother's* coat.'

'What about it?'

'Tabitha, you know the answer to this.'

Tabitha blinked at Marguerite, her eyes glistening. 'This coat is *my* mother's. I recognised it, didn't I, from our first meeting? Its look, its smell.' She reached out and ran her fingers down the arm of the coat. 'The feel of it.'

'You're wrong,' said Marguerite. 'I wear the coat now but it's been in a wardrobe for decades. This coat is *my* mother's.'

Shocked silence fell. Snowy gave a dreamy woof from the couch.

'You're saying, Rosemary...' said Tabitha slowly, '...that the woman Marguerite calls mother, Gus, is actually my mother, Agnes.'

'Yes.'

Marguerite shook her head, making her neat hair untuck from her neck. 'That makes no sense at all.'

'Maybe it does,' said Ronnie, pushing his empty plate aside and laying out his papers in front of him. 'From what we're piecing together, it's a theory.'

Marguerite scowled. 'But why would my mother—the woman I call my mother—have raised me and not Tabitha?'

'It's a very good question, dear.' Mrs Lionel spoke softly. 'I can't imagine a woman giving up her child for another.'

'Perhaps,' said Rosemary, 'Ronnie could summarise what he knows.'

'Would you like me to read what will go in my report?'

'Please.'

Ronnie cleared his throat and tapped his finger on the pages as he spoke. 'Agnes Connelly was reported missing in 1950 by Albert Connelly, who produced a suicide note written in Agnes's hand. The police conducted a small investigation but, with suicide being a shameful end back in those days, they made a quick conclusion that Agnes had taken her own life.'

Tabitha put her hand over her mouth. Ronnie glanced at her in concern but she nodded for him to keep going.

'It seems that there was more to the story as well. Albert Connelly's lover had a child out of wedlock. Another taboo outcome for the era. And it's possible, but never proven, that he had more than one lover in the district.'

'That's what my mother implied.' Marguerite's brow creased. 'I mean, that's what the woman I called mother implied. She spoke about my father with vitriol and I was never allowed to see him. Of course, I did what I was told and never met him at all.'

'The sickness that was reported.' Ronnie rustled his papers. 'All women. Could it be that they'd been poisoned because someone was jealous of them? Someone who wanted to get rid of the competition?'

'Agnes Connelly,' said Jasper. 'She was the one married to Albert.'

'My mother!' said Tabitha. 'But I remember her as very loving...'

'My mother,' said Marguerite, lips pursed, 'was not a loving person. Not to me. She would have certainly been capable of doing something nasty. You, Tabitha, were too young to remember much about how she really was.'

Tabitha shook her head. 'But Agnes was sick as well. You found that report, Ronnie. Why would she be sick if she'd been the poisoner?'

'She may have done it on purpose, dear,' said Mrs Lionel. 'It would have been very suspicious if she was the only one who was *not* sick out of your father's... indiscretions. And maybe she did have thoughts about harming herself. After all, she'd just had a miscarriage.'

'All this doesn't explain why Marguerite's biological mother ended up in your backyard, Jasper,' said Ronnie.

'It's perhaps getting closer to the truth, though,' said Jasper, glancing out the window to his desolate backyard.

'Perhaps,' said Rosemary, 'Agnes Connelly went too far with her attempt to punish Albert by poisoning his lovers, and Marguerite's mother died.'

'Or,' said Marguerite, 'Agnes found out about me and wanted revenge.'

Ronnie put both hands to his head and raked his hair up distractedly. 'Albert finds out that Agnes poisoned the mother of his other child and buries the body.' He dropped his hands, leaving his hair sticking up in a messy Mohawk. 'It still doesn't make sense. It was *Agnes* that went missing. We have her suicide note.'

'We have a note in Agnes's hand,' said Rosemary. 'A steady hand, with writing that is strong and clear, and written in Bower Bird Blue ink. By the time she wrote that note, Agnes was well again.'

Ronnie shook her head. 'But Albert reported her missing...'

'Yes.' Rosemary turned to Mrs Lionel. 'What would be the ultimate punishment for a woman with a child, especially with Agnes's recent tragic loss?'

'To lose the remaining child,' said Mrs Lionel immediately.

'Correct.'

Tabitha gasped. 'He punished my mother by taking me away from her?'

'Albert Connelly may not have wanted it known that he was a philanderer, and his wife murdering a lover would certainly make that clear. He wanted to punish Agnes.'

'Oh no,' said Marguerite. 'You don't mean that he sent Agnes away with *me*, leaving Tabitha with *him*?'

'The ultimate punishment,' said Ronnie, shakily. 'To lose your own child by being cast out by your husband. It would explain why she wasn't very motherly to you, Marguerite.'

Marguerite dabbed at her eye with a corner of a serviette and sat up straight. 'Yes. It would.'

'Oh.' Tabitha pushed back her chair, and swept to Marguerite, folding her arms around her and pushing her cheek against her sharp-faced sister. 'I'm so sorry, so sorry.'

'It's not your fault,' choked Marguerite. 'It was nothing to do with us. We were just children.'

'But what about Marguerite's mother? She must have been reported missing as well?' Ronnie put the aside the report, no longer able to glean anything useful from it.

'Unless Agnes took on Augusta's identity. What did she call herself, Marguerite?'

'She was always Mrs Augusta Kent to others, although everyone knew there was no Mr Kent.' Marguerite sighed.

'Of course,' said Rosemary, 'we have no proof about any of this.'

'Not unless Gus, *Agnes*, confesses,' said Jasper.

'Well, that's up to Uncle Geoffrey,' said Ronnie. 'I can only put our thoughts to him.'

'It doesn't seem right,' said Tabitha, pulling back a little to allow Marguerite to breathe. 'An old lady being questioned for murder.'

'Age doesn't excuse her from it,' said Marguerite. 'Although she's a withered lady now, her memory and cognitive power gone. And with it, the bile she had in her.'

'Well,' said Ronnie. 'Nothing has been proven yet. She may have had nothing to do with it.'

But the heavy silence around the room did not agree with him.

TWENTY-FIVE

Rosemary expected Marguerite to leave Mulbury immediately, followed closely by Tabitha, and was surprised when the two united sisters chose to linger on. After the frank discussion closed, they stood as a pair, thanked Jasper, and wandered out into the Square where the soft winter sun was at least bright for now. Rosemary saw them pause under The Exceptional Tree to watch Rakisha dragging long, woven twigs across from the fallen branch and lay them out in a criss-cross pattern on the dirt of the Square.

'What is she doing now?' asked Jasper as he came up beside Rosemary, who was looking out through his window display.

'Constructing a Rakisha barricade.'

'What is a Rakisha barricade?'

'Something that only Rakisha could construct. It will please her and maybe even the Tree.'

He smiled at her, head tilted to one side. 'Please the *Tree*? Did I hear Rosemary Exeter say that?'

'You did, but did I mean it?'

'You rarely say things that you don't mean.'

'Correct. See you at dinner tonight?'

'Yes, of course.' He grinned back as he walked away. 'Couldn't stop me.'

Ronnie and Mrs Lionel joined her, and they walked back to The Preserved Mulbury where Ronnie sat at her table to start typing his report. Mrs Lionel patted Rosemary's sleeve and nodded towards the two Connelly sisters who were seated on a park bench to watch Rakisha. 'Do you think they'll be okay, dear?'

'They don't have a choice. If they find reason to bond out of this tragedy, then it will be one positive thing to come out of a great deal of grief.'

'And how do you think our other sisters are going?'

Rosemary glanced at Mulbury Feeds, but the only action she could see was a truck backing in with a load of lucerne hay. 'Robert may throw them a lifeline.'

Mrs Lionel rearranged her cardigan so that it fitted more snugly across her shoulders. 'I hope so. See you later, dear.'

Ronnie was hard at it when Rosemary entered the shop. She left him to being watched with narrowed eyes by Sunny, who was clearly finding the pounding of the computer keyboard distracting. Rosemary stayed in the shop until lunchtime, answering questions about ratios of sugar to fruit when the tourists wandered in. As the last of them jangled out the door, Roman jangled in, his eyes on her row of lemon marmalade.

'Rosemary,' he said, taking two jars down. 'It is so very quiet at our place now that the children have gone.' He fished in his pocket for cash. 'I am finding myself inventing new recipes to keep myself occupied. So, the marmalade. What would your good Aunt say about mixing it in ganache?'

'She would not have heard of ganache, but she would approve any inventive use. Waste not, want not was a particular favourite saying of hers.'

Roman's moustaches stretched to almost touch his ears as he smiled. 'So, I will invent.' He twirled a bottle in his hand. 'The children did not find the Hand of Hela.'

'No, but they were very useful in other ways.'

'They said they'd bring the bottles back for the historical display at the Gala in spring.'

'They'll make quite a display.'

Roman tapped his fingers on the top of the marmalade jar and gave her a dashing grin. 'We will see you tonight, Jules and me. We look very much forward to it.' He raised the jar over his head as he walked away. 'Marmalade ganache for all!'

When Roman left, Rosemary flicked the *Back in 5 pickly minutes* sign over and went to make lunch. Ronnie sat with his hands behind his head and his eyes closed, looking exhausted. She tiptoed into the kitchen, but he heard her and sat up. 'Finished and emailed! Uncle Geoffrey has it now.'

'Yes. Are you okay?'

'Yep, yep. That one was complicated, wasn't it? It makes cases like insurance fraud seem easy.'

'But boring.'

He rubbed at his head, making a patch of red hair stick out. 'You're right. Easy is boring.' He stood and stretched. 'I don't know what level of detail Uncle Geoffrey wanted so I put in everything.'

'Right. How many pages was it?'

'Twenty-seven. Do you think that was too much?'

Rosemary said nothing as she finished making sandwiches. She glanced at the kitchen clock, calculating how much time it would take for an experienced policeman to read the report, decide on an action, and then act. She gave him three hours.

It was three hours and twenty-five minutes before Ronnie came bursting back into The Preserved Mulbury from where he'd been helping Mrs Lionel in The Green Mulbury. 'Uncle Geoffrey's coming to Mulbury! He wants to talk to Tabitha and Marguerite, and I told him they were still here.'

'I invited them to dinner.'

'Oh, great, that's great.' Ronnie paused, picking at some soap flakes on his palm. 'I'm coming as well, so I think.'

'Yes. I called Honey.' She studied him. 'Although Honey said she was already on her way. Which is fine, but you two don't usually come to Monday night dinners.'

'Oh,' said Ronnie, his face a swirl of colour. 'We thought that we'd come along. Tonight. Things happening, you know.'

'I'll invite Geoffrey as well. He said he'd like to come to Mulbury for something other than police business.'

'Wow, that's perfect.' Ronnie grinned. 'Anything I can do?'

'Go back and help Mrs Lionel.'

'Okay, yes, good idea.' He ventured out the door, the bell jangling softly.

Extra guests meant more food, so Rosemary added more vegetables to the slow cooking casserole and put a pot of pumpkin soup on for entrée. She shut the shop a few minutes early and lugged a trestle table out of the cellar to add to the existing seating. Sunny helped by winding herself around Rosemary's legs until her mistress picked her up to tickle her chin. 'Lots of people here tonight, Sunny. You might want to make yourself scarce.'

Sunny stretched her head up to rub Rosemary's chin. *And miss all the fun?* She seemed to purr. *Not likely.*

Not surprisingly, most of the guests came right at six-thirty. Rosemary let them in the door, standing back as Mrs Lionel led the way, followed by Gerry and Patti, Rakisha, the Hubbard sisters, and Jules and Roman. Richard hovered at the door until Rosemary brought him in with a sharp jerk of her head, and Kelly sailed in afterwards without looking at her. A few steps behind, being polite, thought Rosemary, was Robert Sparkling, his old but very expensive leather jacket zipped up tight against the cold. He took her arm and gave her a quick kiss on the cheek. 'Always wanted to do that,' he said in her ear before following Kelly.

Jasper stepped in last, a frown on his face indicating that he had seen Robert's actions.

'No Franco?' asked Rosemary, ignoring the look he gave her.

'Too busy with his choux, so he said.'

'The life of a pastry chef is not a social one.'

'So it seems.'

Rosemary touched his arm. 'Would you go and serve drinks? Ronnie and Honey have just pulled up.'

Jasper's face lost its frown as his eyes widened. 'Honey and Ronnie...? No, I think you'd better serve drinks.'

'You can do it.'

'No, no. You're the host.' He gave her a little push. 'Go on. Be hospitable. I'll wait for them.'

'Jasper.'

'Rosemary.' He grinned at her. 'Beat it. I've got it here.'

Reluctantly, and with a puzzled glance back at which he responded with frantic *get out of here* gestures, she left him to be the butler and went to serve her guests. They'd clearly had no problems making themselves at home, as they had spread out across the lounge room chatting amiably, and already had glasses of wine in their hands. Sunny sat on her windowsill, watching.

'Smells great,' said Hannah, coming up to her and thrusting a small package tied with twine in her hand.

'What's this?'

'I wanted to say thank you for letting me stay at your place.' Hannah pushed wayward strands of hair off her face. 'I'm moving back home tonight.'

'I'm pleased for you.'

'Thanks.' Hannah looked across to Holly who was talking to Mrs Lionel. 'Robert is working with us on a business plan.'

'What sort of plan?'

Hannah grinned. 'Well, you see, Mum said the business couldn't be sold to family, but the business doesn't belong to family now. She didn't say we couldn't buy it back.'

'That's the plan?'

'Something like it. We've yet to work out the details.' She nudged Rosemary and pointed at the package. 'Open it.'

Rosemary undid the crudely wrapped present and let the paper fall away. 'It's a mouse.'

'Yep! A windup toy for Sunny.' Hannah plucked the fluffy grey form from Rosemary's hand. 'See?' She wound a key on its back and put it on the floor. The toy scuttled away amongst the guests, making Kelly scream and jump sideways.

'I can see that it will have good use.'

Hannah grinned. 'I'll show it to Sunny.'

Although Rosemary really wanted to see the disdainful look on Sunny's face when presented with a pretend mouse, more people walked in behind her. Ronnie and Honey were hand in hand, looking particularly pleased with themselves. Jasper was ushering in Marguerite and Tabitha, with Geoffrey the police officer behind them.

'Welcome,' said Rosemary to them all.

Geoffrey shook her hand. 'Ronnie's done another fine job,' he said. 'A very detailed report. Unfortunately, full of conjecture.'

'With a hint of vast probability.'

The older man crossed his arms. 'I can only go on facts, Rosemary, as you know. But I've made a few enquiries, casual ones, not for the record.'

'Right. Such as?'

'Gus Connelly is not fit to be interviewed, let alone stand for trial. She is too frail and somewhat cognitively impaired.'

'I suspected that.'

'We have, in all likelihood, identified the skeletal remains which at least puts that part to rest. Her name was Augusta Marguerite Kent.'

'Ah. Her daughter will be pleased to hear that middle name.'

'She was. Unfortunately, we will not be able to determine the cause of death. If it was poison, the traces have long gone. Poison was a common enough homicidal weapon back then but wasn't understood well.'

'Harder to use poison these days.'

'Yes and no. We're more aware of it than they were seventy years ago.' Geoffrey rubbed at his face. 'One thing we did do, though, was to veto Adelia Lochard's documentary on the investigation.'

'She was filming Jasper's involvement.'

'Yes, and she had quite a bit of other footage. Unfortunately for her, this is still an active investigation, and she can't do anything with any of it until we've studied it all.'

'Jasper will be disappointed.'

'Why?'

'He thinks it would bring out information about his missing father.'

Geoffrey sighed. 'I don't understand these things because I've always known who my mother and father were, but there's something to be said for letting sleeping dogs lie.'

'Right.'

The old policeman looked sideways at Rosemary and smiled. 'Spoken like a thinking-about-retiring copper, eh?'

'Yes.'

He shook his head. 'I don't think I'll be able to change now even when I do retire.' He lifted his head and saw Mrs Lionel. 'I'd better go and pay my respects to my old friend.'

'Right.'

As Geoffrey walked over to Mrs Lionel, Tabitha and Marguerite came up to Rosemary. 'I imagine you've caught up on the news,' said Marguerite, holding her glass delicately by the stem. 'Augusta *Marguerite*.' She swirled her wine.

'Yes.' Rosemary handed something to Tabitha.

'Dad's ink well.'

'It's yours now.'

Tabitha held the brown pot to her cheek before slipping it into her coat pocket with a teary smile at Rosemary. 'Goodness, what a time it's been.' She took a gulp of her drink, and used the back of her other hand to dab at her face. 'I certainly didn't expect all this to happen when I returned to Mulbury.'

'We would never have met if it hadn't,' said Marguerite, looking down at her sister.

'No. Odd, isn't it?' Tabitha smiled up at her. 'You know, you have a particularly lovely fragrance about you, sort of spicy.'

Marguerite raised a perfect eyebrow, but Rosemary saw her eyes crease in a hidden smile. 'Now *that* is odd.'

'What will you do now?' asked Rosemary.

'Now that we've found each other?' Tabitha's smile dropped. 'I need to see my mother. Agnes. Something about attempting closure.'

Marguerite put a firm hand on Tabitha's shoulder. 'I need to see her, too. Not to ask her anything, but to try and let all that nastiness go. What happened back then was a lifetime ago. We need to move forward, not backward. I think we can do that.'

'Yes.' Tabitha reached up to put a hand on her sister's. 'We can, even if it takes a while. We can do it together.' She straightened. 'Are there more drinks anywhere, Rosemary?'

'That way.' Rosemary pointed to the kitchen bench. 'Help yourself.'

The drinks were certainly going down quickly and the chatter was cheerful. Eventually, Rosemary got everyone seated at the tables. The soup and casserole went down quickly, and conversation started to fade as full stomachs took their effect. Honey cleared the plates away, frowning at Rosemary as she rose to help. 'I'm not useless, Mum. Not yet.'

'I didn't say you were,' said Rosemary, but her words were lost in the after-dinner mutterings.

Mrs Lionel leaned over. 'Lovely, dear. You have excelled yourself once again.'

'Thank you.'

Mrs Lionel sat back. 'And now, another secret is revealed.'

'Mulbury's had enough secrets lately.'

'Oh, this one's rather nice.'

The lights dimmed. Rosemary saw Ronnie standing, grinning at the switch. He looked over at the shop entrance where Honey was walking in slowly, holding out a platter. She moved to the table, and people parted enough for her to place a cake in the centre, a cake that was an exact replica of Sunny the ginger tabby, with a long row of orange candles flowing down its back.

'Happy birthday, Mum.'

Rosemary sat up straight. 'You remembered.'

'Why wouldn't I, Mum?'

'No reason, except recent multiple distractions.'

'We all knew,' said Roman, stroking his moustaches with a finger. 'We were keeping dad.'

'Mum's the word.' Jules rolled her eyes. 'We were keeping quiet about it.'

Honey held out a knife. 'There you are, Mum.'

Rosemary hesitated. 'I'm not sure I can do it.'

'Why ever not?'

Rosemary shifted so that Honey could see Sunny sitting on the windowsill. The look on the cat's face said it all.

'I know,' said Hannah, pushing her chair back. 'I'll distract her with the mouse.'

Rosemary couldn't watch. As she plunged the knife into the evenly textured cake, she imagined Sunny stalking from the room with her nose in the air. *No more dinner parties that include mice,* the cat would be saying. *In fact, no more dinner parties ever, ever again.*

ACKNOWLEDGMENTS

A Pretty Pickle owes much of its detail to the mudlarker of Sheepwash Creek who uncovered so many treasures during lockdown. Thanks, Mel.

Thanks also to my editorial team and ARC readers who help me see what I should be seeing but just can't.

All remaining errors are entirely my own.

Mulbury Mysteries

#1: A Sticky Situation

Mulbury is a quiet place where visitors wander happily around Goldmarket Square. When the body of an old man is found under The Exceptional Tree, everyone assumes that he died peacefully. Everyone, that is, except Rosemary Exeter.

A small-town mystery with quirky residents and an unimpressed cat.

Novella: One Christmas Pickle

Christmas time in Mulbury, Australia. Plum puddings, roast turkey and blistering hot days. Who overcooked the fire brigade's fund-raising Santa? With the team of fire-fighting volunteers stuck in Mulbury until their truck is fixed, and almost certainly one of them a murderer, Rosemary hides the one clue she has while searching for others.

A Mulbury Mystery Christmas novella with punch... and brandy sauce.

Other books by Juno Harvey

Because I Know it's True

Since the car accident that altered her family's lives, Grace Worthington has always been a loner. Now, with her father's death, she is truly alone. When she reads about Alexander

Cameron's search for his missing sister, she sees an answer for both their problems. She has no family: he has no sister. Grace follows Alexander back to Scotland, and becomes involved in the biggest act of her life.

ABOUT THE AUTHOR

Juno Harvey lives in Victoria, Australia, with her family.
She makes jam on the weekends and works in a university
during the week.

Want to join Juno's Reader's Team?
Go to www.junoharvey.com and receive a free story!

https://www.junoharvey.com/

Books of light...and shade.